Elements

Air over a Dragon's Scales

Katie Fraser

· 1 ·

The world loves pirates, but book pirates are not the friend of the Indie Author.

Please minimise the scourge of book pirates by ensuring the version of this book that you are reading has been purchased or is lent through a legitimate eBook lending service.

Thank you

First published as 'Through the Fig Tree', May 2016.

This rewrite first published November 2024
Copyright © 2024 Katie Fraser
Cover Art © 2024 Matt J Pike
All rights reserved.
Print ISBN-13: 978-0-6480590-6-6

Dedication

For Russell, who told me I needed to rewrite this book many years ago.

Thanks and acknowledgements
Rewrite

I first published this book in 2016 and, over time, I came to accept that it needed to be rewritten. Largely because I have learnt so much more about story craft and spelling and grammar in that time.

Note that I said accept, because I spent a lot of stubborn time with my heels dug right in, refusing to change anything. I have bene on such a journey of personal growth over the last eight years and am no so much more than I was in 2016, so this work can now become so much more than it was.

If you read the first version of this book, when it was published as *Through the Fig Tree*, and are now re-reading it, I hope that you agree it is now a better, stronger, tighter story.

If this is your first read, enjoy.

Either way, thank you for picking up my book, readers make the author's world go round.

Map

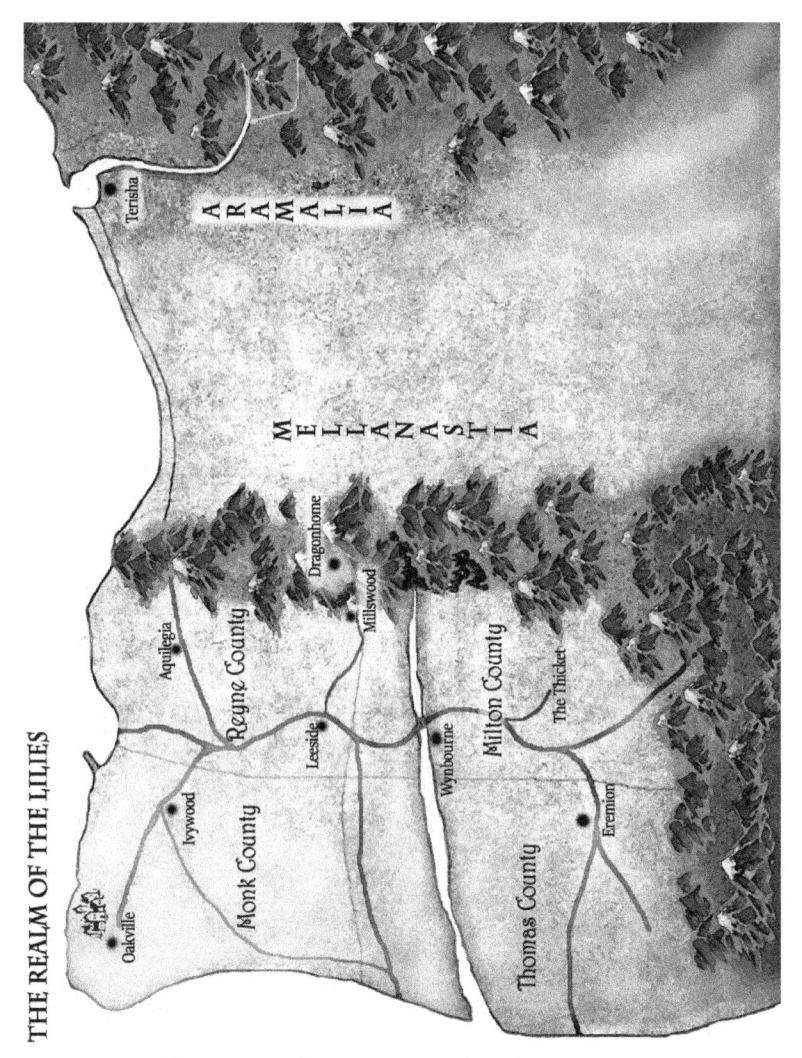

THE REALM OF THE LILIES

ARAMALIA

Terisha

MELLANASTIA

Dragonhome
Millswood

Aquilegia

Reyne County

Leeside
Wynbourne

Milton County
The Thicket

Ivywood

Monk County

Oakville

Thomas County
Eremion

Map made using inkarnate.com by Chris Lowe

Chapter One
VIOLET

"Daniel!" Violet cried out.

He didn't turn back.

She thumped her hand on the arm of the park bench, then shook the pain out. In hindsight, hitting cast iron was never a good idea.

The lush tropical plants and hundred year old trees seemed to mock her unhappiness as she watched the man she loved walk away from her.

For his part, he walked stiffly, his back straighter than she'd ever noticed, his steps slow, heavy and deliberate.

But he didn't look back or divert from his path towards a huge Moreton Bay fig tree. He walked between two thick roots that rose almost to his hips at the trunk. She expected him to turn then, or climb the roots and skirt around the base of the tree, instead there was a swift flash of light and he disappeared.

She waited, watching, her heart accelerating to a rapid tattoo in her chest. Certain he must have simply bent down between the roots, she rose and stretched up onto her toes, but only saw an empty space at the base of the tree.

"Daniel?" She called, rising from the bench. She hurried towards the tree, muttering a curse when she tripped on an outlying root and nearly fell.

The tree must have been relatively young as it was only about a metre around, not like some of the older ones in the park. She examined all the gaps between the giant roots, half expecting to find an Alice hole to fall down. She stopped on at the spot where Daniel had disappeared her second lap and examined the tree from the ground up.

Two tall roots formed a nook that was lined with a layer of twigs, leaves and litter, which showed no signs of disturbance. She advanced cautiously, avoiding a partially buried, broken beer bottle and a plastic bag holding a small puddle of water and dirt. She ventured in cautiously and paused when she noticed something glittering at the point where the two roots met the trunk, where something shiny nestled in the leaf litter. She knelt down for a closer look and froze when she realised what it was.

A silver locket with an emerald on the front.

"That rat bastard," she muttered, then put on a whiny, voice in a poor imitation of him. "Green for your eyes and silver for my heart... You'll be forever in my heart."

Ugh, I was so dumb! No man talks like that in real life.

Because he'd only given her the necklace, and a promise that wasn't quite forever but was definitely 'maybe a few months', two weeks ago. *Two weeks!* God, she had such bad luck with men. There were the liars, the attempted gaslighters (she'd learnt how to spot them early), the cheaters and the sloths.

"Violet, I'm sorry. I have to return to my parents," Daniel had said, his voice flat, just before disappearing. "I have heard that my father is facing some trouble and my family need me."

"Can't I come with you?" She'd asked.

"No, that would be impossible, what would you do?" he'd replied. "You have your work here, and your friends, it would turn your life upside down."

"I'm pretty sure there are nursing jobs everywhere in the world," she pointed out.

"Violet, we come from two different worlds."

She'd grunted, momentarily too annoyed to even form words. *Money. That was other thing.* Daniel was a snob.

"Whatever," she finally managed to say. Then she unclasped her necklace and thrust it at him. He'd tried to coax her to take it back, but she was not interested.

And now, the cold green stone gave off a betraying sparkle in the dappled sunlight under the tree.

Bitterly, she thought back to his comment about it being like his heart. *Twisted like the design or cold like the silver?*

She took a deep breath and her gaze wandered up, as she moved to spy the sky between the branches overhead. However, when her eyes reached the height of her belly, she caught sight of a strange pattern.

At the point where the two roots she stood between reached the tree, a raised row of bark extended up the trunk, converging just above her head. At the height of her belly button was a round, raised gnarl, with three concentric circles around it. She bent down to look more closely at the gnarl, slowly reaching out her index finger.

The centre of the protruding gnarl was smooth and warm, and she was startled by a distinct click when she applied pressure on the spot.

A slight glow appeared on the right-hand side of the bark frame. She blinked.

"Okay, that's weird. Maybe a form of post-traumatic shock from watching my boyfriend disappear?" She said to herself.

Violet moved her hand towards the edge of the frame and pushed. The bark moved slowly inwards, opening a larger gap between it and the trunk. She straightened slowly as the trunk-door swung open.

As she moved back, the shimmer of her necklace caught her eye from the bed of leaf litter. *In hindsight*, she thought, *there might be a little more to Daniel than he told me.* She scooped the necklace up and studied the design. Fine lines of silver whirled around and framed the emerald held in the middle.

She moved her gaze from the necklace to the door, considering her options.

"I mean, that man definitely lied to me," she said to the locket. "But if I was about to disappear into a tree, I probably wouldn't do too much explaining in advance either."

She thought back on the times she'd met him.

The first time he'd come into her ED at work after tripping on an escalator. *Who even did that?*

Then there was the broken ankle from a treadmill.

And the dislocated shoulder, when he'd fallen off a BMX bike at a BMX race track.

She'd put it down to some kind of early mid-life crisis, and maybe it was. He'd finally asked her out after the BMX incident and he'd taken her to some pretty swanky places too. *Which is why I automatically thought he was talking about money when he mentioned 'different worlds'.*

She'd read enough fantasy novels to know this could get weird. *Didn't I even see a Barbie movie like this once?*

"Screw it."

Violet tossed the coiled necklace in the air, caught it and shoved it deep in her pocket.

"Let's see what this weird-ass tree has to offer."

Her uncertainty resolved, she straightened, placed her right hand against the door and pushed.

Chapter Two
VIOLET

The door opened into a large round room, despite the impossibilities provided by the size of the tree trunk. The room was dome-shaped with cream-coloured walls, a packed dirt floor and two doors directly opposite each other, one behind and the other before her.

She turned and noticed that the door she had come through had closed, but it looked exactly the same from in here as did on the outside, the three-ring pattern still visible on the textured bark of the fig tree. She walked across to the other door, her heartrate kicking up a couple of beats per minute with each step.

The door ahead of her had smooth purple-grey bark, like a plane or gum tree, over a creamy-pinkish trunk. The middle of this door held a lump of bark, like the trunk was growing over a spot where a branch had been removed. She ran a hand over the smooth trunk, then instinctively pressed a finger to the centre of the lump, where the bark had not quite grown over yet. There was a click similar to the one she had heard before and the door swung towards her.

After opening the door fully, she stepped towards the doorway, but before she could step out of the bigger-on-the-inside tree space, her way was blocked by two crossed spears. She stopped short.

A short man in royal blue livery stepped out from beside

the doorway and stood at attention.

"Who seeks entry to the Realm of the Lilies?" he asked.

"Umm..." she began, "I guess I do?"

"And you are... ?" the man asked, a hint of exasperation in his tone.

"Violet Truman."

"State your reason for travelling to our realm, Violet Truman."

"I'm looking for someone?"

The guard gave her an annoyed look, so she continued.

"My boyfriend, Daniel? I saw him come through here not long ago."

"Ha! Really? Daniel, Prince of the Realm, is your boyfriend?"

She stepped back, shocked.

"Well," Violet said, "I didn't know he was the Prince, but yes, he's my boyfriend. Or at least he was... it's complicated." She rubbed her forehead, to stave off what felt like an incoming freight-train of a headache.

When the guard still looked sceptical, Violet reached into her pocket and pulled out the necklace Daniel had given her. She held it by the chain, with the pendant dangling out from her fist. The breeze made the necklace twirl a little as it hung there, causing the emerald to send off myriad sparkles from its facets.

"Will this help convince you?" she asked.

The sight of the pendant caused the guard to catch his breath. In turn, the two guards from either side of the door turned, poking their heads around the doorframe without letting their crossed spears waver.

"Sir, isn't that the necklace the prince had made?" the first guard asked.

"By the monks at Oakville?" the captain mused, having regained his composure. "Well, it certainly sounds like the descriptions that the rumour mongers were giving out."

The captain waved his hand and the two guards stepped away from the door.

"My lady, my name is Henry Keith and I am the captain of this post," he said, waving Violet forwards. "Please forgive me for my impertinence, it is very rare for someone to find the doorway and even rarer for someone to know where they have come."

"Don't worry," Violet said. "I assure you that I did not know where I was coming to, or that I knew a prince."

A look of light confusion crossed Captain Keith's face, but he shook it off.

Maybe that question was above his pay grade.

"Lady Violet, please step through. May I arrange for you to be escorted to Wynbourne Manor where you will surely find the Prince? He only passed through here a short time ago, but he left swiftly, as we always have transport ready for him. He did not mention that you would be coming through..."

"No, he was not expecting me to join him here," Violet said, then placated the worry that immediately appeared on the man's face. "Don't worry, I'm sure he will be glad to see me."

"I'm very glad to hear that. I have to choose who can come through and who must be denied entry. I would hate to have to make a decision that might jeopardise my position by annoying our future king."

Violet gave him a soft smile, took a deep breath and stepped through the door. She paused to examine her surroundings.

The tree she had stepped out of was tall and maple-like, with the same purple-pink trunk she had seen on the door and deep green leaves. She was standing near the edge of a thicket of similar trees, on a small rise of land. The thicket was on a slightly rolling plain, surrounded by a crop of something that looked like wheat, and a couple of ponds and a few more thickets dotted around the area. To the left was a long, low building with smoke trickling slowly from two tall chimneys. The spears leaning against the wall indicated that the building was a barracks for the soldiers posted there.

Violet was charmed by the countryside and the brilliantly fresh air being brought to her on a light breeze. She heard chirruping bird calls and saw butterflies fluttering at wildflowers.

While Violet admired the view, she barely noticed Captain Henry walking towards the barracks, calling out orders as he went. The barracks quickly became a hive of activity as soldiers in varying levels of dress started bustling about.

Violet watched on as three soldiers in full uniform came to stand before their captain, spears in hands and swords in scabbards. Four more soldiers, who were not wearing tabards over their white, loose-fitting shirts ran around to the left hand side of the building and disappeared. An additional five soldiers, who were missing their shirts altogether, came from the other end of the building. This group of men were red-faced, covered in sweat and carried wooden swords in their hands. The leader of these, a well-built, brown-haired man came and stood at attention in front of the captain.

"Lieutenant Markham," the Captain began. "This young lady, Violet Truman, has just ventured through into our realm. She is a friend of the prince. I would like you to escort her to Wynbourne."

"Yes, sir," said Markham. "Certainly, sir."

As Markham walked away, the captain turned to the three uniformed soldiers in front of him and asked them to relieve those in the thicket.

The three soldiers started up the rise, towards the spot where Violet still stood, watching the men spring into action. She turned towards the building when she heard a whinny and an easily recognisable clip-clop sound.

The four white-shirted soldiers had returned, leading two horses. Violet was immediately concerned by this sight, fearing she knew exactly how she would be travelling to the castle. The captain came back up the slope towards her.

"My lady, your horse is ready and Markham will be with you momentarily to escort you to meet Prince Daniel."

"There may be a problem with that," Violet said, raising a finger. "I have never ridden a horse."

"Don't worry," Captain Keith comforted. "We have a very placid mount for you, and Markham will take good care of you."

He led her across the yard to where the two horses stood.

"Her name is Star, you can pat her if you like."

Violet walked slowly up to the horse, one of the only things she had ever heard about horses was that it is bad to walk behind them if they don't know you are there, so she made sure she kept in Star's line of sight.

"Well aren't you a beautiful girl," Violet said. She admired the horse's glossy black coat and slowly reached out a hand to rub her nose.

Star let out a soft whinny as Markham walked out of the barracks dressed in full soldier regalia, complete with helmet. Ever observant, he turned to his captain and suggested they find some more appropriate clothing for 'the lady.'

"We have heard stories from the prince about your world, my lady," Markham said when he saw the indignant look on Violet's face. "However, here, it is rare for a woman to expose her arms and it would be difficult for you to ride in those trousers."

The captain nodded in agreement and asked someone to find some clothing that would fit her. Violet reflected that it probably would be difficult to ride in tight jeans and that she would surely get sunburnt if she went riding across the unknown countryside in her sleeveless T-shirt.

A few minutes later, the soldier returned with a pile of clothing and some sturdy-looking boots.

"Please follow me," he said.

He led her into the barracks and opened a door to a small room for her.

"There is a bag there for you to place your clothing in. The boots were the smallest I could find, they may not fit but they will be less noticeable than your own shoes."

Big assumption that I have small feet there, let's see how that goes down.

She had to agree on the change though, black thongs and hot pink toenails probably would catch a few eyes. He turned and closed the door behind him, saying he would wait for her. Violet studied the room. She spied a few bits of hay poking through the mud-covered walls and but the wooden boards on the floor were smooth. The neatly folded clothes had been placed on a bench, and a bed—a simple piece of canvas stretched over a wooden frame—sat in the corner.

Violet sighed and slouched down onto the bed, releasing some of the tension she had felt building since she'd arrived in this place, barely five minutes earlier. She had no idea if what was happening to her was even possible, so she didn't even try to wonder *how* it might be possible. Instead, she simply leant over and unfolded the clothing.

She found a pair of brown loose-fitting trousers with a drawstring waist, a cream-coloured cotton shirt with a lace-up neck and a pair of soft woollen socks.

She pulled the shirt straight on over her own top. If they had thought her toes would be distracting, she didn't want to know what they would think of the purple lace bra that would be perfectly visible if she wore the shirt alone.

She left the lacing of the collar undone, leaving the shirt

to billow over her chest and belly. She stood and kicked off her thongs, then took off her jeans. She picked up the trousers and sniffed them hesitantly. They smelled clean, with the light scent of lavender drifting off them. Satisfied, she pulled them on. When she felt the prickling on her legs, she was glad that she had selected sensible underwear rather than the little lace ones that matched her bra. Being men's trousers, they only just accommodated her behind, but fit her legs fairly well, although they were a little long. She tucked a little bit of the shirt hem into the waistband of her pants before pulling the drawstring tight and dropping the rest of the shirt to cover the top of the pants.

She unrolled the socks which, thankfully, had the same lavender scent as the trousers. They felt fairly soft, which was a bonus, and she rolled them on, hiding her outlandish pink nail polish. She looked at the boots, they did look very well made, as well as well-worn, the leather was very soft and they looked like they would fit her.

She pulled on the left boot with little difficulty, it settled about halfway up her calf. She had left the extra length of pant leg under her foot, thinking it would provide a little extra support, but it bunched up under her arch, so she tugged on it until it sat behind her heel. She gave her right foot the same treatment and stood, stretching out her legs. The soles were fairly soft, flexed easily when she stood on her toes and were easier to walk in than she thought they would be, although they were a touch tight around the toes. *But, since I'll be riding, that shouldn't be an issue.*

She turned to the last item in her pile, a canvas bag, and began to shove her belongings inside. She heard a jingling when she picked up her jeans. She reached into a pocket and pulled out her necklace, remembering that she had shoved it back in there after the captain had acknowledged that she knew the Prince. She looked at it for a moment, in wonder. *A prince had this beautiful piece made for me.* She studied it for a moment, before putting it around her neck. *I may as well wear this if it gets me a little quick respect.*

As usual, the pendant settled into the nook in her throat and she sighed as she thought of the first time she had worn it and what they had said to each other as he put it on her. Her feelings for him were muddied. He had shown so much love and affection for her, yet he had left her completely with little more than goodbye. He had obviously left a few gaping holes when talking about himself as well. She shrugged, *I'll be asking him about it soon enough.*

She picked up her bag and walked to the door, straightening her shirt as she walked. She pushed the door open and was surprised to see Markham waiting for her.

"Much better," he said, nodding.

His eyes lingered on her throat for a moment and she stared at him defiantly, waiting for the seemingly overbearing man to pass judgement, but he simply led the way out.

The horses were still being held in the middle of the yard and some supplies had now been added to a pile nearby. Violet noticed a few nose bags for the horses and some water flasks. There were a couple of bulky bags behind the saddles too, but she did not try to work out what was in them. Markham turned and asked if she was ready.

"As ready as I will ever be," she replied.

He sensed her nervousness and gave her a smile, it was the first she had seen from him and it made him look much younger than the grim mask he had worn earlier.

"No need to worry, my lady," Markham said. "It is a smooth and easy ride to Wynbourne Manor from here, and it will not take us very long to get there."

She walked over to the soldier holding Star and waited for him to help her mount. Someone approached with a stool for her, but she was momentarily distracted by Markham hoisting himself onto his horse and into the saddle with ease. She snorted and muttered, "Show off."

The soldier started instructing her, raising flutters in her stomach.

"Place your right foot on the step and your left foot in the stirrup," he said. "Then left hand on the saddle horn, right hand on the back of the saddle. Now you only need to hoist yourself a little higher, so use your left arm to lift your body up and bring your right arm forwards as you put your right leg over."

She followed his instructions as he gave them and was surprised when she was actually able to haul herself up. She managed fairly well, but nearly ended up sitting on her right hand and then sat fairly heavily in the saddle, spooking the horse a little.

Star paced a little before the soldier on the reins calmed her. Then the soldier calmed Violet, too, as she was a little spooked by Star's movements.

The captain came over when horse and rider were both settled.

"It has been a pleasure to meet you, Lady Violet," he called up to her. "I wish you a safe and pleasant journey and hope you find the Royal Family in good health."

"Thank you, Captain," Violet said. "I appreciate all of the help you have given me."

With that, Markham saluted his captain and they prepared to move off.

Chapter Three
VIOLET

Violet accepted Star's reins from her helper.

"She will need little guidance and will probably just follow the other horse, but if you need to, just pull the reins on one side or the other to get her to turn and pull back gently to get her to slow down or stop. Make sure you are gentle though. She is a well behaved horse and will not need manhandling. To get her to start moving, simply tap your heels, gently, against her belly."

Violet nodded her understanding and tried to commit the instructions to memory.

He continued his instructions. "The main thing to remember while riding, especially for a beginner, is to relax. If you tense up your muscles while you are in the saddle, you won't be able to move for days."

Violet immediately tried to relax her muscles, consciously suppressing her apprehension about being on a horse. She looked up and noticed Markham watching her. He raised his eyebrows questioningly and waved an arm up the road. She nodded her readiness to leave.

Following the instructions, Violet gently pressed her heels against the horse's flanks and Star moved off. Markham followed her lead and they drew abreast of each other as they started towards the road.

"Oh, but remember to stay tall," called the other soldier.

Relax, but stay tall. Thanks for that sage advice.

Violet studied the surrounding countryside. It felt like

spring. The air smelled fresh and clean, and she saw the bright green new growth of bulbs by the roadside. The sun was out, and it was warm in the sunshine.

The road was hard packed earth with trees on the left and paddocks to the right, edged with a hip-high, stone wall. Violet felt the walls were built more to stop animals wandering in or out than to deter trespassers. Wildflowers grew in the protection of the wall and Violet smiled at their dainty beauty.

They rode in silence, and Violet noticed that Markham seemed alert and vigilant, surveying the countryside with more than her casual glances. After a time, his cautious air made Violet nervous and she asked if he was expecting any trouble.

"I'm not expecting trouble. I simply feel it is always better to be ready for it. The people of this realm are currently facing difficult times, and I would not risk trouble for myself by allowing any harm to come to you."

Violet nodded her understanding, but still felt a little insecure, the mention of 'difficult times' reminded her that Daniel had spoken of trouble for his father too.

"What sort of difficulties?" Violet asked.

"I'm sorry, but if the Prince has not told you, I do not think I should," Markham said.

Violet sat silently for a few minutes, wondering how she could at least make some use of the travel time. Then she realised a point that Markham had missed.

"Prince Daniel told me nothing of this realm at all. So, why would he have told me of the trouble?" When Markham still looked speculative, she tried another angle. "Could you at least tell me some of your history?"

He shook his head. "Just because we will be riding for some time, does not mean we have time for an info dump, Lady Violet."

She humphed at him and passed her judgement

internally, *Yep, I was right, pretentious ass.*

"Fine. Will you at least tell me where we are?"

"We are in Milton County, the south-eastern portion of the Realm of the Lilies. Wynbourne Manor is located on the western border of this county and is about half a day's ride from the thicket where you entered this world. The royal family spend the four cycles of spring in Wynbourne."

"Four cycles?" she asked and bit her lip as Markham sighed.

He explained. "Please, I think it would be wise for us to stop chattering now, it is my duty to protect you and I do not feel as though I can carry out that duty when trying to teach you what our children learn at their mother's knees."

Thus, Markham cemented Violet's opinion of him.

Violet turned her eyes back to the scenery. They were currently riding along a ridge and she could just make out the misty blur of mountains on the horizon to her. They seemed to reach high into the sky, but were much too far for her to make out any features.

She suppressed the urge to ask about them.

Extending from the feet of the mountains was a green band of land, dotted with thickets and cottages. Around the cottages she saw women in long skirts chasing goats away from laundry and chickens away from kitchen gardens. In one yard she saw a few young girls skipping rope and their laughter carried to her on the breeze. She smiled at their boisterous fun, and then laughed as she spied the group of young lads who were hiding behind the wood store and obviously plotting something with the buckets of water by their knees.

Violet began to become aware of the saddle beneath her and started to wonder if they would take a break, or would ride straight on to the manor. She had been in the saddle for nearly two hours and needed to stretch her legs—and massage her... seat. The merry tinkling of a stream sounded ahead and Markham led them off the road into a clearing bounded by the stream.

Violet spied a stump to use as a mounting post and tried to guide Star up to it. Markham leapt from his mount and reached for Star's reins. Violet obediently handed them over and sat patiently as Markham led them to the post.

"Now, to dismount, take both feet out of the stirrups, then lean forwards in the saddle as you flick your right leg back around. Reach your left foot for the block as you lower yourself off," Markham instructed.

Violet tried to commit the instructions to memory and then to follow them. Unsuccessfully. She caught only the edge of the block with her left foot and slid rather inelegantly out of the saddle, landing quite heavily on her right foot as she planted it solidly on the block to stop herself from falling.

"Not bad for your first time. I'm sure you understand that I could not assist you while I was holding the horse steady," Markham told her.

Violet barely refrained from rolling her eyes at him and gave him a wry smile instead. *Of course he couldn't.* She thought as she arched her back to stretch out the aches before lifting her heels on the mounting post in turn to stretch out her sore leg muscles. She pulled her shoulders towards each other to ease the strain in them and rolled them in circles to loosen her muscles.

"How long are we stopping?" Violet asked.

"Long enough to let the horses drink and rest a little. Take this," he said, handing her a beaten tin cup. "Fill it from the stream, but don't drink too quickly."

Violet accepted the cup from him and strolled to the stream. It wasn't very deep, and the water was as clear as any she had ever seen come from a tap at home. She perched on a couple of rocks on the banks and filled the cup in the icy water. The tin cup quickly cooled from the water and she relished the chill it gave her fingers. She asked Markham if all waterways were as clear as this one.

"This stream is fed by the melt water from a glacier directly to the east of us. There is a much larger river which is the main outlet from the glacier, but this stream was created to divert some of the water along the roadways so it can be used by travellers throughout the land."

Violet nodded and began to wonder how much the people from this land differed from those in her own. They did not seem to be as technologically advanced, there were no cars or any communication devices, but they seemed to have made do with what they had instead of inventing devices to life 'easier'. She thought that diverting part of a river seemed to be a much more effective use of resources than digging in plumbing across the land.

Suddenly, a shadow passed overhead and a terrifying screech tore through the silence of the clearing.

Violet stayed crouched by the river, too scared to look up and discover what had made that ear-piercing racket. A sound like the crack of sails on a yacht followed, and she could tell that, thankfully, it was receding.

Markham must have been watching her as she cowered.

"Don't worry, Lady Violet. The treaty with the dragons has been in place since shortly after the Kingdom was established."

Violet's stomach plummeted as he said this, *What on Earth have I gotten myself into?* She stopped herself from letting out a little hysterical chuckle as she corrected herself; *I'm not on Earth at all!*

"Is that meant to be *comforting* information?" she asked as she stood, still hunching her shoulders a little.

Another long moment passed before she dared to look up. All she could make out was a tiny speck wheeling in the distance. It did a full circle before it dove, plummeting to the ground some distance away. Violet shivered as it disappeared below the tree line. Treaty or not, she didn't think she would like to see a dragon any closer than that.

"Come, it is only another hour's ride to get to the castle, if we leave now we might get there in time for lunch. No doubt the staff will have whipped themselves into a frenzy to welcome the prince home. It has been several months since they have seen him."

Violet felt a little shiver of guilt on hearing this, certain she was the reason Daniel had spent so much time away from his home. *Wait a minute, why should I feel guilty? It's not like he ever told me any of this.*

Violet walked over to the mounting block to meet Markham with Star. She sighed as she resigned herself to more time in the saddle, and stepped up onto the block. Star whinnied as Violet grabbed the saddle, but she managed to mount with a little more grace than the first time. Markham passed her the reins and waited for Violet to get settled before taking the few steps to his horse and vaulting up with as much grace and precision as a gymnast. Violet managed to stop herself from snorting derisively at the display.

Double show-off.

Markham turned his mount around and asked if she was ready to leave. Violet shifted in her saddle to try to ease the tender spots and signalled that she was ready to go by nodding towards the road.

Violet did not enjoy the second leg of the ride two reasons. First, she was beginning to feel some discomfort in the regions which were in contact with the saddle and second, she was now spending quite a lot of time glancing upwards, scanning the sky.

While simultaneously trying to sit relaxed and tall in the saddle.

If Markham noticed her discomfort, he showed no sign of it. Instead, he had started to whistle a merry little tune to pass the time. Violet noted the change in his attitude and wondered aloud if Wynbourne was the place he called home.

"Indeed," Markham said. "My home is within Wynbourne village, and there is a young lady who I am looking forward to seeing. I had not expected to return here for several weeks, so I should be thankful to you for giving me reason to come home so soon."

With that comment, he resumed his cheerful whistling, effectively ending all conversation.

Chapter Four
VIOLET

About three quarters of an hour after their stop, they rode over a crest, finally revealing the land before them.

Ahead, Violet saw a large open valley, with a clear river running through it. The river was wide, but looked fairly shallow, and lined with great grey boulders and the small pebbles that were glacial litter. The rough belly of the river caused droplets of water to splash and leap and the sun turned these into jewels that made the waterway sparkle like a diamond collar across the throat of a young siren. The river was surrounded by a disc of green, with fields, copses and a few hedges scattered in a haphazard pattern. A crop of green wheat shimmered in the distance as it rustled in the breeze.

In the middle of the dell, was a village.

The effect of the peaceful dell would have been ruined by the presence of the ramshackle buildings, if it had not been crowned with the glory of Wynbourne Manor.

The royal home was not overwhelmingly large, indeed, it seemed to only have two storys, but it had the look of an old English manor to Violet's eye. There was elegance to the delicate silverwork around the windows that seemed to bring the building to life. It was built of sandstone, which had a distinct sheen about it and looked as though it was scrubbed on a daily basis. The roof was shingled with grey slate that gleamed as though it had just been rained on, and a figurehead at the peak held a blue flag bearing a white lily. Two great white doors were positioned directly below the figurehead and were tightly shut. The remaining façade bore a great deal of windows.

The palace was the pearl at the centre of the oyster shell formed by a range of mountains circling the whole dell. The effect was breathtaking.

Markham spoke, bringing Violet out of her reverie.

"That's strange. There does not seem to be much movement around the village, I expected that with the return of the prince, the villagers would be preparing a great feast to celebrate his arrival, for he is much beloved. Perhaps his homecoming was not as happy as he expected it to be and Prince Daniel has not yet made his arrival known." Markham looked sidelong at Violet as he made this last comment.

Violet just shrugged, she wasn't sure if she knew Daniel well enough to explain his actions. *And if I did, I probably wouldn't share them with you at this point.*

Markham led them along a path that went straight through the middle of the village, directly to the doors of the manor. After a few minutes of riding, they had sunk to the lower level of the dell.

"You certainly have a very beautiful country," she said.

"Well, you have just been treated to one of the greatest views in the land. There are not many who get to see this dell in such perfect conditions, except the locals. There are a few other places which are breathtaking, but the Wynbourne dell is certainly the most remarkable."

Although his voice had finally sounded warm, Violet did not feel that this speech invited conversation, and they lapsed into silence again as they descended into the valley.

They had kept the village in sight from the moment they first saw it, and after a short time, they came close enough for Violet to hear the sounds of people within it.

Dogs yapped playfully, accompanied by the calls of young children, and the rhythmic thump of an old woman beating the dust out of a carpet. They were accompanied by men calling to each other as they passed on the main streets, driving wagon loads of goods.

As Markham had said, there really wasn't a lot of activity around. Violet breathed in deeply and caught the rich smell of soups and stews. *Maybe it's lunch time,* she thought, imagining the village people gathered around their kitchen tables with bowls and plates set before them.

Her stomach kindly punctuated that thought with a deep rumble.

The first village buildings they passed were cottages with big gardens in front of them, some with chickens or rabbits scurrying in the picketed oases. After they had passed about a dozen such homes, they reached the businesses, housed in a group of two-story brick buildings. They traders comprised of a store, a haberdasher, a hotel and a few others that Violet couldn't discern from the outside. These were interspersed with a few other large, solid, wooden buildings that looked like warehouses to Violet's eye.

At last, they drew up to the manor and Violet was struck anew by its beauty.

"Come, the stables are this way," Markham said. "We will get you off that horse, and I will find a maid to help you clean up. You cannot be presented you to the royal family dressed like that."

Violet followed, a little irritated with his attitude towards her, but she understood his meaning. Her pants were grubby and she smelled like horse.

They arrived at the stables, which were to the left of the manor, and were greeted by a fairly highly ranked soldier.

"Lieutenant Markham," he snapped. "What brings you back to Wynbourne so soon after you were sent to your post?"

"Sir," Markham returned sharply. "I return to Wynbourne to bring a visitor who came through the portal seeking the prince."

"What nonsense is this? You know as well as I do that the prince has not yet returned from his trip," the officer returned. "And who is this woman you have brought with you? She looks like a peasant."

Violet did not appreciate the pompous attitude of the guard, Lord, she knew well enough how to handle his type. By throwing his attitude right back at him.

She flicked her necklace out from where it had been hidden under the collar of her shirt before she spoke. "I am Violet Truman, a personal acquaintance of Prince Daniel. The soldiers at the portal gate were told by the prince himself that he would be returning here," Violet said. "If he has not arrived yet, I am sure that he will soon, and I would appreciate it if you could arrange for a bath and some clean garments so that I may greet him as soon as he arrives."

The guard's chin slackened at her tirade, but it dropped completely when his eye was caught by the sparkling of the gem around her throat.

"My lady." He gulped. "Please accept my sincerest apologies, we were led to believe that the prince would not return for some time, but I am not privy to all the royal counsels. If you would proceed into the stable and dismount, I will arrange for someone to meet you to assist in preparation for your audience with the prince."

He bobbed his head and walked off. Violet looked around when she heard a slight cough, and saw that Markham was fighting very hard to hold back laughter.

"And what is it that you find amusing?" Violet asked.

"Well, it's just that old Firebreath has had that coming to him for years, but no one has ever been able to get away with saying a bad word to him. He is the Captain of the Guard here, and because of that, he knows everything and acts accordingly. He hates it when anything does not go exactly to the perfect plans that he sets out. I had hoped that he would not be on duty when we arrived to avoid any complications, but I think you dealt with him quite well."

"Thank you." Violet smiled. "I have had a lot of practice at getting people to do things that they don't want to do."

They now stood in the centre of the stable and Markham stopped and whistled. A small boy ran forwards with a step that he placed next to Violet's horse. Markham dismounted, then walked around to stand behind the step to catch Violet in case she fell.

Just as Violet's feet touched the packed earth floor, a maid in a periwinkle blue cotton gown came running into the stable, and stopped with a curtsey in front of Violet.

"Please ma'am, are you the Lady Violet?" the maid asked.

Violet nodded to her.

"I'm Mary, please come with me. I will take you to clean up and we will find something more ladylike for you to wear."

The maid led the way out of the stables, and Violet called back to Markham when she realised he was not following them.

"Thank you for bringing me here, Markham," she said.

"It was my pleasure, Lady Violet. As I told you, I am ever grateful for a reason to return here." He bowed to her as he finished speaking and she walked out of sight.

The maid giggled as she led Violet across an open courtyard and Violet was worried that she may have broken some unknown protocol already.

"What is it that you find funny?" she asked. "Did I say something wrong?"

"Oh, no, my Lady" replied the maid. "It is just that the soldier who brought you here is betrothed to my sister. Our whole family knows that he is always happy to come home."

Violet smiled. Although her stomach coiled in knots at the thought of meeting the royal family in a world that was not her own, she thought that this girl might be able to stop her from committing any major faux pas.

She stubbornly pressed down the thought that these royals were also her boyfriend's parents. Was he even still her boyfriend?

Mary led Violet across the packed earth courtyard and through a rear door into the manor. The door opened onto a short corridor with polished wooden floorboards and only three doors leading from it. The single door on the left was open and issuing from it was the sound of pots clanging and the distinct aroma of frying onions. The two doors on the right were closed, but as they walked past, a girl opened the closer door and the smell of lavender and steam followed her into the corridor. *The laundry,* Violet guessed. They walked to the end of the corridor, where the way opened out to left and right. They went to the left, towards a flight of stairs.

"I apologise for taking you through the servant's corridors," Mary said. "But I'm afraid I would be in trouble if I took you through the main entrance dressed as you are."

"Don't worry," Violet said. "I don't think I really want many people seeing me covered in dirt, sweat and horse anyway."

Mary laughed quietly as she led Violet up the stairs. They climbed to the first floor of the southern wing of the manor, where afternoon light shafted through a tall window onto the landing. This passageway was still narrow and there were four bedrooms, each with two beds, leading off it. Mary opened the door at the end of the corridor and Violet saw the true luxury of the manor for the first time.

In this portion of the house, the wooden floors were covered with rich carpet runners and bright paintings decorated the walls. To the left were large, open sitting rooms with windows that lit the corridors as well and to the right were short passages, leading to suites of rooms.

"This way," Mary said, leading Violet into the first nook, and opening the first door.

They entered a large, plush suite with a double, four-poster bed in the middle. To their left, beneath the window, was a sofa and a table with two chairs. The walls were painted white, with a waist-high border in delicate pink floral pattern. The bed was centred on a deep blue rug and made of walnut wood carved into a twisted pattern and had thick curtains to draw at night for warmth. There was a wardrobe against the right wall which Mary ignored, instead leading Violet towards the window nook.

Violet was curious as to why she was being led to a dead end, until she spotted the door behind the table. Mary opened this, revealing a two-way bathroom tiled in white with a large white porcelain bathtub in the middle.

Mary drew back a screen in the left hand corner, revealing a toilet.

"I will start the bath filling and you may relieve yourself if you wish," she said.

Violet wandered over towards the toilet, feeling a little self-conscious about a complete stranger being in the room while she used it, but her qualms were eased when she heard the bath start to fill.

When Violet emerged from behind the screen, the bath was half-full of water, and a quarter-full of floral-scented bubbles. She washed her hands in the basin just as Mary returned, carrying a silky dressing gown. She turned the taps off and placed the gown on a bench next to a plush bath towel.

"Your bath is ready now," Mary told her. "If you prefer, you may put the dressing gown on after and meet me in the bedroom where I will find something for you to wear."

Violet nodded her agreement and Mary left her to the

bath. She sat on the chair to peel off the boots. Ultimately, she had to pull so hard that her socks came off with the shoes. She grimaced when she found her feet a little pruney from the sweat-soaked socks. She had not realised that she had been so hot while they travelled. She peeled off the rest of her clothing and stepped into the tub.

The warmth seeped into her muscles and eased out the kinks she had earned for her first time in the saddle. She could smell rose oil in the water which she thought would help to relax her as well. After a few minutes of relaxing, she sank back and started scrubbing off the road dust. A stand next to the bath held an assortment of bottles with varying labels. A bottle marked for hair smelled gloriously of jasmine and she relished in the scent as she massaged the gel through her silky locks.

To Violet, the soothing bath added to the whole unreality of the situation.

Just a few short hours ago she had been shattered as the man of her dreams told her he was leaving her. Then she had been transported into this totally different world where she had found out that he was a prince and was now about to meet his family. She heaved a deep sigh and decided to leave it to Daniel to explain, as she might go crazy if she tried to work it out herself.

If I'm not legitimately crazy already.

When the tension in her muscles had eased, she stood and reached for a towel. It was luxuriously soft, as was the dressing gown she slipped on when she had finished.

She returned to the bedroom to find Mary sifting through an assortment of miscellaneous clothing. There were underclothes set out on the bed: cotton shorts and a light singlet. Mary asked Violet to pull the dressing gown tight to show off her figure to help Mary select some clothing. The maid looked Violet up and down and then asked her to put on her underclothes while she looked through the wardrobe.

Violet slipped on the soft cotton clothing, which also bore the now-familiar scent of lavender.

Mary finished pottering around in the wardrobe and returned to the side of the bed where Violet waited.

"Okay," Mary said. "Corset now."

Violet's heart rate picked up at her excitement. She had always liked the costumes she'd seen in period films, especially the bouffant effect of the petticoats and skirts. Mary picked up the boned and stiffened garment and loosened the lacing so she could pull it over Violet's head. Violet put her arms out so the other woman could slide the corset onto her torso. Mary jiggled it around a little to get it sitting in the right spot.

"Thank goodness the current fashion is only to have the support and not have everything cinched in until your waist is only two inches wide," Mary said.

"I think I am very glad about that," Violet said. "I don't really like restrictive clothing."

The corset had lacing at the back as well as the front, which allowed Mary to make sure that it fitted Violet snugly. She laced from the bottom up, with the lacing running in a straight line up Violet's spine. When she finished the back, Violet found that she had only a few centimetres of free space in the front to move around. Mary spun her around and went to lace from the front.

"It's alright," Violet said. "I can do that."

Mary stepped back with a slightly smug look on her face. Violet could just reach the bottom laces when she stretched, but found that the corset itself actually hindered her. She was stubborn though, and once she had started something she was always determined to finish it... regardless of the laughs that might be directed at her in the process.

Violet managed to get the lacing done up all the way with the help of a few carefully chosen curses and was then nearly blown away by her cleavage. The corset certainly did a lot of work in that area.

"How is that?" she asked Mary.

"Very good, ma'am," Mary said. "Now for your clothes, we aren't finished yet."

She delved into the pile of clothing on the bed and came out with a layered white petticoat, which she slipped on over Violet's head and secured at her waist with a drawstring. Next, she fiddled with the shoulder straps of the shift that were still visible above the corset, folding the straps in half so that there was less fabric to hide. The outer layer of clothing was a gown in a deep periwinkle blue, with a delicate floral pattern worked in yellow and green silk ribbon along the cuffs and hem. The dress had short puffed sleeves and a full skirt, and Violet spied a row of lacing on either side of the dress running from just under her armpit to her hip.

Mary slipped the dress over Violet's head and laced her into it. The dress fit perfectly and accentuated her small waist before flaring out over her hips into a full skirt.

Violet picked up her skirts and swished them around, giggling as she did so. She had always wanted an excuse to dress in period clothing, but none of her friends had ever been kind enough to have a fancy dress party.

She looked up from her swirling skirts to find Mary looking at her strangely.

"Oh," Violet said, a little embarrassed. "Sorry, it's just that I have always wanted to dress like this."

"What do you mean?" Mary asked. "This is how everyone dresses."

Violet caught her breath, she suddenly realised that the presence of the portal was probably not known to everyone in the Realm of the Lilies. She thought fast.

"I meant being dressed in a fine enough gown to meet the royal family." She covered quickly.

"Oh." Mary nodded her understanding. "Of course, it must be pretty daunting. I mean, I see the king and queen all the time, but they hardly ever actually direct their full attention at me. As a friend of Prince Daniel, you will surely be subject to their full scrutiny."

Crap, I hadn't thought of that. She considered her situation. *Getting nervous won't do me any favours. I may as well just walk in like I belong there and try not to stick my foot in my mouth.*

"I should be fine," Violet said. "Can you give me a quick review on how to address the king and queen?"

Mary chattered at Violet while she finished dressing her, telling her all the correct ways to act, and how to defer to them. When her dress was settled to Mary's satisfaction and Violet's necklace secured, Mary massaged a honey serum through the other woman's hair, setting it in delicate ringlets.

"Lovely," Mary pronounced. "Are you ready to meet the royal family?"

Chapter Five
VIOLET

Mary led the way out of the bedroom and down the hall. They passed a grand staircase that Violet thought must be the main feature of the entrance hall and she caught a glimpse of the massive doors she had seen from the road below them. They came to the final nook off the passageway and Mary opened a door beyond.

Violet found herself in a large drawing room, with bookcases containing large, leather bound volumes lining the walls. A mahogany desk with a leather inset sat in the middle of the room, an open book upon it, but there was no one reading it. Facing out of the window were two wing-backed chairs, one of these was empty, but Violet made out the figure of a woman in the other, and a man stood protectively behind her.

The woman was largely concealed in the embrace of the chair, but the man was tall and muscular. He wore loose, dark woollen pants tucked into a pair of sturdy leather boots and a linen shirt, cut as simply as the one Violet had worn earlier, but the fabric had a richer weave. The shirt collar was loose at the back of his neck and lead up to a head of thick, dark hair sprinkled with white. He turned as he heard the slippered footsteps of the two women approaching and saw his face for the first time.

The man's face bore the signs of a deep sadness; deep lines around his eyes indicated his anguish. Once he had turned and realised that he did not know the person who approached him, he let a mask slip into place and a friendly smile came across his face, changing his appearance completely.

When he smiled, Violet noted his resemblance to Daniel, they had the same rosy cheeks and their eyes were the same colour. Although he was now smiling, Violet sensed that something was not quite right. *He looks... haunted.*

"Hello, there. You must be the young lady who claims to know my son," he said.

As he spoke, the woman in the chair, but did not turn.

"King Cameron," Violet said. "What a pleasure to meet you. I am indeed an acquaintance of your son. We met in my home town..."

"That's enough," the woman interrupted from the chair. She rose and turned a piercing gaze on the two younger women. "Mary, you will not be needed here any longer. Thank you."

Mary bobbed a small curtsey and left while Violet studied the woman. She had light golden hair with a tracery of silver, pulled back into a loose bun. Her face looked kind, but at the moment she looked haggard. What Violet took to be a regular peaches-and-cream complexion was mottled red and dewy with tears. She was in her mid-fifties, but was still slender and wore a deep purple velvet dress trimmed with white lace.

When Mary was out of earshot, she spoke again.

"Be wary of you what say around here girl. Not everyone knows of the existence of you world, and that is something we think is good for our realm."

Crikey Moses, what crawled up her nostril and laid eggs?

"Queen Astrid," Violet said, giving a curtsey and brushing off her annoyance at the brusque reception. "I apologise for my lapse. I can assure you, no-one in my world knows of the existence of the portal, which is probably also very good for your realm."

Astrid nodded, and then folded back into the chair she had occupied earlier, the fight seeming already knocked out of her by that small exertion of will. King Cameron gave Violet another smile and gestured for her to sit in the chair next to his wife.

"Please, sit," Cameron said. "You are Violet, aren't you?"

"Yes, I am," she murmured as she took the seat. "How did you know?"

"Our son has told us many things about you that could make it easy to recognise you. But truly, I recognised the necklace he had made for you." He gestured towards her throat with this last comment.

She reached up to the pendant, and clasped it tight. *This is probably one of the weirdest meet-the-parents moment ever.* She wished Daniel was there and could not imagine what would be keeping him.

"Of course," she said. "He must have shown it to you before he gave it to me."

"There's more to it than that," Cameron said. "The design is a copy of a family heirloom, but that is a story for later. Now, we would like you to tell us of our son the last time you saw him."

"The last time I saw him?" She asked, baffled. He nodded and she continued. "Well, we were in a park and he told me that he wouldn't be able to see me anymore, because he had to return home to his family. Then he walked off and disappeared into a tree. I followed him, and I think I ended up coming through to this realm about half an hour after he did."

"And when was this?" he asked.

"This morning," Violet replied. "Why are you so worried about him?"

Cameron sighed and pulled up a footstool to perch on.

"Daniel told us that he was going to see you for the last time. We knew he loved you, but was willing to give you up to protect the Realm. He did not think you would follow him, and he told us he would not tell you about this world. It seems as though he did not tell you, but he was to let you see him pass through.

"However, what's done is done. Markham told us you seemed completely clueless, so I am satisfied that Daniel kept his word to us."

Clueless? Ouch.

"Truly," Violet said. "I had no idea. Either of the presence of this realm, or the position he holds within it."

Cameron nodded and shifted himself into a more comfortable position. Violet's attention was momentarily drawn by the sound of rustling fabric from the other chair, but Astrid seemed as impassive as ever.

"The problem that we face now is this," Cameron said, "Both yourself and the soldiers guarding the portal state that Daniel passed back into this realm a short time before you did. Judging by the pace at which you travelled, he should have been back two hours ago, at the latest. He promised that he would return to Wynbourne as quickly as he could after returning from your world, yet here we sit without him."

"So, you're worried because the Prince is a few hours late?" Violet asked. "Perhaps he felt that he needed some time to himself before returning to his duties."

"Unlikely," said the cold voice to Violet's left. "It is unlike my son to dwell on past mistakes. He would have returned immediately, as he said he would. He has always been true to his word."

The words stung Violet in a way she could not explain. Was Astrid inferring that his relationship with Violet was a mistake or was something else at play?

"Please forgive my wife, she is worried and angry, but

not at you. We believe that Daniel would have returned here at speed, because he knew of my need for him. We have not yet heard, but we believe he may have been ambushed."

Overreacting much? Violet thought.

"I don't understand," she said. "Why do you think that?"

Cameron rested his elbows on his knees, rubbed his head in his hands and let out a deep sigh.

"I'm not sure that I really have the time to tell you," he said. "But I feel as though I have some duty to, as it will explain why Daniel left you in such a way. The Realm is in a dire situation and I fear that only a strong front from my son and I will be able to protect our people."

"Come, I'll show you," Cameron instructed. He crossed to the desk and picked up a scrolled paper, unfurling it and weighing the corners down with heavy, coloured-glass paperweights.

"Our eastern and southern borders are formed by vast mountain ranges." He traced our the ranges on the map as he spoke. "Immediately beyond them is wilderness, but if you ride east for a few days, the land becomes more habitable, with flat plains and well-running rivers."

"Aramalia?" Violet read out the name inscribed across the region he'd circled.

"Yes. The country is ruled by a woman, the Sha'a, who wants to annexe this land and send the current inhabitants to the Realm. Naturally, they're against that, and want to form their own nation, Mellanastia, instead."

Violet traced the map, identifying the capital city and the road leading out of it, east and into the mountains.

"How many people are in these lands?" Violet asked. "The Realm of the Lilies, Aramalia, Mellanastia."

"There are hundreds of thousands people in our Realm, and Aramalia has approximately double that. There are only several thousand people in Mellanastia as the land is largely uninhabitable."

"Why do the Aramalians want it then?"

"There's a large spider native to the land that would become Mellanastia. Fabric made with its web fibre woven with wool is durable and waterproof."

Violet nodded, then took a moment to study the area of the map that showed the Realm of the Lilies more carefully.

"And you're on the side of the Mellanastians?" Violet asked.

"Naturally," Cameron said.

Violet looked up and studied the king's face. "Do you want to claim the lands of the Mellanastians for the Realm so you can use the spider's webs?"

A gasp came from the chair cocooning Astrid.

Cameron, who had been leaning forwards over the map snapped straight, a flush rising up his cheeks.

"I don't like your implication," Cameron said with a glower. "No. I don't want that land, but I will help them form their own nation, as my great grandfather did for the Realm of the Lilies a seventy-two years ago."

Violet simply nodded and Cameron took a deep breath before crossing back to stand with Astrid near the window.

"Mellanastia has already become stronger with our help and we travel to Aramalia to help them put forwards their case in a few days. However, the Realm of the Lilies needs to show a united front in this. Following our traditions, Daniel will become king in the next few years. It is imperative that he travel with us to Aramalia."

"So someone might want to stop him from going with you?" Violet asked, her heart suddenly pounding hard in her chest. "Is he in danger?"

"We don't think so," Cameron said. "They know that if any harm comes to him, it will be taken as an Aramalian plot and a declaration of war."

Violet dropped her gaze from Cameron's, back to the map. Then crossed the room to sit down again, her legs suddenly weak.

"Having said—" started Astrid, before pausing to compose herself. "Having said all that, we believe you may be the only one who can help him."

Chapter Six
VIOLET

Um, what the what now?

Violet was silent for a few minutes while this statement sank in. Dazed and confused barely covered the feelings Astrid's words had aroused.

"You think a complete stranger who didn't even know your country existed half a day ago is the only person who can help your kidnapped son?" Violet finally said, then cursed herself. *Dammit, Violet. That was an inside thought.* "Sorry, I'm just a little... what do you mean?"

Cameron heaved a deep sigh and looked out the window into the valley, before turning back to Violet.

"If what we suspect is true and this is an Aramalian plot, I believe Daniel would have immediately been taken towards the mountains. By tomorrow night, they should have passed through Aquilegia. I cannot call for a widespread search for Daniel as it may cause panic within the realm. The only way to rescue my son in time for him to attend the meetings in Aramalia is for someone to outrun his captors through the pass and release him before they can get there."

"Okay," Violet said. "And you're telling me this because... ?"

This time Astrid spoke. "We cannot send a whole troop of soldiers through the mountains, it would look as though we were preparing an invasion or to defend ourselves from one. We need to send a small team of only two or three people over the mountains to surprise the group of brigands and release our son."

"Do you have any proof that this is the path they have taken or are you relying on instinct?" Violet asked.

"We were hoping that you would be able to provide the proof," the Queen said cryptically.

Seriously? Violet studied the Queen, wondering if some form of magic or mysticism was about to be suggested. She generally would have scoffed immediately, but she had just been transported to another world through a magical tree, so she decided to roll with it.

"What do you need me to do?"

"The necklace my son gave you, may I see it?" Cameron asked.

Violet acquiesced, removing the necklace from her throat and handing it to the king.

"Daniel had this necklace made to match an ancient design known to my family. Its purpose is to link two people to each other. It should allow you to locate him, or at least find the general direction in which he is travelling."

"If you say so," Violet said, with a half-shrug. "How does it work?"

Cameron slipped the pendant off the necklace and handed it to Violet.

"Cup this in your hands," he instructed. "Now, close your eyes and think of Daniel. Think of times you have spent together, things you have done. Gently shake your hands, so that the pendant twists around in your palms. Think carefully of Daniel, and when it feels right, stop shaking."

Violet felt a bit silly, but she did as she was told, gently agitating the pendant within her palms while thinking about Daniel. Suddenly, a flare of heat passed through her palms and into the pendant and the weight lifted. She stopped shaking, took a deep breath and opened her hands.

The heart glimmered where it was suspended in the air before her, the pointed end aimed over her right shoulder.

Cameron sighed. "It is as we suspected. Aquilegia is that way."

Violet and Astrid followed Cameron as he made his way back to the desk and map of the Realm.

"Wynbourne is here." Cameron pointed out. "Up here, to the north east is Aquilegia, the capital of the realm. Daniel was intercepted somewhere between the glade and here, and will have been travelling at a fast pace both before and after the ambush. He has been travelling for roughly five hours, which probably places him a quarter or a third of the way between here and Aquilegia."

Cameron traced paths on the map as he spoke.

"From about here—" He pointed to a place on the map slightly north of Wynbourne. "—they will have to slow down or risk drawing too much attention on the road. If they break tonight, they should reach Aquilegia by sundown tomorrow."

Violet looked to the windows that overlooked the valley. The late afternoon light was waning, it would be dark soon. Daniel would be in Aquilegia in less than twenty-four hours. *Assuming days on this world are the same length as at home.*

"We want you to ride with Markham to find Daniel," Cameron said. "He will need your help, with your necklace, to keep track of Daniel's location."

"Okay."

"It could be dangerous," Astrid said. "Their need to keep Daniel alive may not extend to you or Markham."

Cameron jumped in quickly. "But Markham and Daniel will do everything in their power to keep you safe."

"I understand," Violet said, then took a moment to think.

Head of on an adventure to save the prince in a world with dragons and sword-wielding soldiers or go home to keep treating people with random things shoved up their butts in the ED? Can I even go back now?

"Well, I became a nurse to help people. It would feel a little hypocritical if I didn't join the search for Daniel. He undoubtedly needs help.

"Plus, I might have a few pressing conversation points."

Violet met the eyes of Cameron and Astrid in turn, spying a sheen in other woman's eyes.

"Thank you," Astrid said simply, "Let me ensure that you have everything you need for your journey, I will organise for the seamstress to come up to prepare clothes that fit you well and make sure the bootman makes you some shoes. Please, come with me, we have much to prepare."

Chapter Seven
VIOLET

Violet finally found herself alone an hour or so later. She had been prodded and poked and measured all over before being given this momentary reprieve.

Unfortunately, Astrid had been against the idea of Violet travelling in men's attire and only reluctantly allowed her to have a few pairs of trousers made. Consequently, Violet was now awaiting delivery of a rather large wardrobe. Astrid would not even be dissuaded by the fact that Violet wouldn't be able to take all the clothes across the mountains.

"We'll just take them to Aquilegia and then on to Aramalia in our entourage. You'll have to come on to Terisha with us after you—" Astrid had looked sidelong at the dressmaker then. "—meet with Daniel. Now, come and take a look at these boots..."

Violet sighed, it was very kind of Astrid to look after her so well, it had been a long time since anyone had done so. *So long in fact, that I don't really remember what it is like.*

Her room now looked bare without the clutter of fabric swatches, design books and lace samples, and it was oddly quiet without the bustle of the seamstress and her assistant.

Violet knew she should be using the time to prepare for dinner with the royal family, but was too exhausted to think about it. She had started the day with an early morning jog and a plan to have brunch with Daniel, but that plan had gone a long way astray. *Dragons and kidnapping were not on my bingo card this year.*

She flopped down on the bed with her legs hanging over the edge, the weight of her skirts pulling at her knees. She laughed to herself, *What would Astris say if she caught me in such an unladylike pose?*

The mattress was very soft and Violet found that she was quite comfortable there, despite her cumbersome skirts. She closed her eyes, telling herself it would just be for a moment.

A few minutes later, the sound of the door clicking closed woke Violet from her doze and she jolted upright.

"Oh," she cried, spying the young maid near the door. "Thank goodness it's you, Mary. I thought the queen had busted me."

"You do have a funny way of saying things." Mary laughed. "Let's get you ready for dinner."

She walked to the wardrobe, talking as she went. "Your new clothes won't be ready until the morning, but there should be something more formal in here for you to wear. Captain Markham told me that he is to escort you to see the Monks at Oakville and meet Prince Daniel."

While chattering, she had pulled out a selection of dresses, one in deep purple velvet that was simply cut, an emerald-green velvet one with a richly embroidered bodice, and a blue-shot-black taffeta. "Now, which one?"

"It is ironic that although my name is Violet, the colour does not suit me at all," she said, pointing to the purple dress. "I think the green velvet."

Mary nodded her agreement and walked around the bed to help Violet out of the periwinkle dress.

"You can always tell the clothes of a noble," Mary commented drily. "They are always such that you could never get into them on your own."

Violet laughed, the description seemed quite apt to her

as she stood with her arms out so that she could be extricated from the volumes of fabric. Mary finished unlacing the sides of the dress, then gently pulled it over Violet's head.

"Of course, these dresses were designed to be cinched to fit a variety of bodies. Your dresses will be made to fit you and should be easier to get into."

Violet shook her muscles out. Her work scrubs were usually loose and she generally wore baggy T-shirts and track pants at home. Suddenly switching to so many layers was a little constricting. She tried to flex out some of the stiffness in her torso, surrounded by the corset, but was unsuccessful.

Mary noticed her discomfort.

"Are your laces too tight?" she asked.

"Maybe a little bit," Violet said. "In truth, I am not used to wearing a corset like this."

"No," Mary said, then gave Violet a knowing look. "They're not common on your world are they?"

Violet straightened as quickly as if she had been given an electric shock.

"Please don't tell. Markham has told us of the mysteries of the thicket he protects. Well, he told my sister in secrecy and she told me in wonder. You don't need to tell me anything, but let me give you some advice on how to dress yourself and act here, you can be sure that the secret is safe with me, I would not want my sister's fiancée in trouble."

Violet simply nodded, she did not feel that she should tell Mary anything of her world, but she did need to know how to put her clothes on in the morning.

Mary picked up the green dress from the bed and walked back to where Violet was standing.

"This is the sort of dress that you definitely wouldn't be able to get into on your own," Mary told her, sliding the green dress over her head

The size was a much better fit to her than the one she had worn earlier, but it was tightened with a row of lacing down the middle of her spine. The front of the dress was modestly cut, but sat nearly below the tips of her shoulder blades at the back. Mary quickly set about doing up the lacing to cinch the dress in.

"You will not be the only visitor at dinner tonight," Mary said. "Prominent villagers are often invited to share a meal with the king and queen while they are in the area. Tonight there will only be a few businessmen and their families. You will be the centre of attention as a friend of the prince.

"Rumours have been flying lately as to when he will wed. His father and grandfather were both very young when they were married. However, you will draw attention on your own when you are seen in this dress!"

Violet looked down to see her torso swathed in embroidery picked out in bright colours, it was mostly a floral design, with red and yellow daisy-like flowers on a vine stitched in a brighter green than the velvet. The embroidery ended in a point just below her waistline and a broadly cut skirt flared out below. Her red-brown hair still sat in loose curls over her shoulders and just covered the part of her back that was bare from the low neckline of the dress. The heart-shaped pendant was again nestled in the nook between her collarbones.

"Lovely," Mary pronounced.

She produced a pair of green velvet slippers with soft leather soles and Violet lifted her layers so Mary could slide them onto her feet. Violet stood and mentally prepared herself for the evening.

They headed down the corridor towards the broad staircase they had passed earlier.

Just before they reached the stairs, Mary said, "I'll be there at the dinner tonight too, so I can help you."

Violet released a long breath. "Oh thank my lucky stars."

"I'll see you soon," Mary gave one of Violet's hands a quick squeeze, then gave her directions to the parlour before scurrying off to get ready for dinner herself.

Violet walked slowly down the stairs, worried about getting a foot caught in the long skirts and tumbling to the bottom instead making the graceful entrance she was hoping for.

The stairs wrapped around the sort of grand entrance she'd seen in large Elizabethan manors. Opposite the top of the stairs on the ground floor were the large entrance doors, and at eye level was a row of windows that allowed the brilliant sunset light to sparkle on the marble surrounds. The stairs themselves were lined with thick red carpet and ran down to a landing before diverging to either side of the room where they curled out and around to face the doors.

Violet turned left at the landing and reached the bottom of the staircase without mishap. Even from where she was standing, the entrance hall was remarkable. She imagined that when viewed from the doorway, the effect would be breathtaking. Above her head, a vaulted ceiling housed a great chandelier which was lit, at the moment, by sunlight streaming through portholes, resulting in arrows of dusky peach light being thrown across the room, illuminating the marble columns that flanked doorways to the left and right, and the intricate carvings around the passage that went under the stairs.

A gentle floral scent in the hall came from great bunches of wildflowers on plinths scattered around the walls and possibly the candles in sconces flanking all the doors.

Directly beneath the chandelier, a round, red carpet echoed the opening above and a carved marble bust sat on a simple wooden plinth in the centre of the carpet. As she crossed to it, she noticed that the bust was framed by a black velvet curtain covering the entry under the stairs. This final element made the whole room startling in its beauty and Violet found herself lost to the world for a moment as she absorbed the whole effect.

Light footsteps to her left woke her from her reverie and she turned to see Captain Markham heading towards her.

"Are you lost, my lady?" he asked.

"No," Violet said, "I was just taking in the view. I was also wondering how on earth you light that chandelier."

Markham laughed. "It is a trick. We do not light the chandelier itself, instead there is a walkway in the cupola above it, and we have candles surrounding that, the facets of the crystals in the chandelier catch enough light from them."

"Ingenious," she said. "And who is this fine fellow?"

"That would be Alexander Pollthrop. He was a doctor who hailed from Wynbourne and flagged the importance of clean drinking water and keeping sewage away from the water sources."

"Ah, yes." Violet nodded. "I can see why he would be respected by the royal family."

Markham led them through the column-flanked doorway to the left of the stairs. The room had wood panelling on the lower half of the walls and cream coloured wallpaper with a pattern of tiny pink roses above. A couple of bookcases held ornaments along the wall and some ornately carved couches with softly patterned upholstery sat in front of them. A large fireplace dominated the far wall, a quietly crackling fire burning in the grate.

A small group stood around the fireplace and turned when they heard the door open. Violet saw King Cameron standing between another middle-aged man and a woman who was probably a few years younger. The woman wore a deep purple taffeta outer dress, cinched at her waist, over a white shirt with a frilled collar. A black underskirt peeked through slashes in the taffeta and the dark, pointy toes of her boots poked out from under her skirt. The men wore full length trousers, light-coloured shirts with square collars and waistcoats with three buttons done up over their portly bellies.

Cameron gave Violet a broad smile and waved for her and Markham to join him and his companions.

"Lady Violet," he said. "I would like you to meet Mr and Mrs Courts, they own the grocery store in town. Mr and Mrs Courts, this is Lady Violet Truman, she is a close friend of my son."

Wait, should I actually be lady? Why not Miss Violet?

They exchanged warm greetings and the couple smiled broadly at Violet. While they were still talking, the door opened again and Violet turned to see a grinning Mary walking towards them.

The maid had changed into clothing of a richer fabric and finer cut than the simple clothes she had been wearing earlier. She had let her hair out of its sedate bun and the rich brown tresses now cascaded behind her shoulders. She wore a dark blue taffeta dress, which Violet thought was very similar to the one that had been laid out on her bed earlier.

Mary entered the circle and then crossed it to the woman on the other side.

"Mother," she said, kissing the woman on the cheek. "How are you this evening?"

Violet was momentarily stunned. The girl who had been waiting on her all afternoon was the daughter of one of the most influential people in town.

She missed the response from Mrs Courts, but watched as Mary greeted her father in a similar manner. The exchange had barely finished when the door opened to allow another five people, including Queen Astrid, to enter.

The Queen elegantly swept toward them with the two couples following along behind. Mary had returned to Violet's side, with a cheeky grin lighting up her face.

53

"Oh, hello," Violet whispered. "Is this a different Mary to one I met earlier?"

Mary stifled a giggle as Astrid introduced Violet to the rest of the group. The Sergeants owned the mill, and the rosy faced wool merchants were the Higgets.

"Well then," said Cameron. "Now that we are all assembled, let us move on to dinner."

Chapter Eight
VIOLET

Mary hooked her arm through Violet's and they walked together at the back of the group as they headed through to the dining room.

"Captain Markham," Mrs Higget said. "Where is your lovely betrothed this evening?"

"Ah," said Markham. "Sadly, she was taken ill a few hours ago. My Sarah is usually quite a healthy girl, but there seems to be a breathing trouble in the village at the moment and she was suffering quite a bad headache when I called upon her this afternoon. I convinced her that she would be better off in bed than coming out this evening."

Mary looked a little worried. It seemed she'd not had time to go home before preparing for dinner. Violet tried to give her a comforting smile, as she and Markham obviously cared a lot for the girl's sister

"I wish her a speedy recovery," Violet said.

Further thought of the family was momentarily wiped from Violet's mind as the double doors to the dining room were opened by two porters on the other side. Even from her first glance through the framed doorway, Violet knew that the room beyond was one of the grandest she had seen. It was not overly large, being about ten metres wide and twenty long. However, just beyond the entrance were columns that supported the vaulted ceiling and the narrow area behind the columns was dimly lit, making the halo of light around the table even more welcoming. The vaulted ceiling held three crystal chandeliers which, Violet could see by looking closely, were lit in a similar way to the one in the foyer.

Mary tugged on her arm and Violet realised that she had been standing still and practically gawking at her surroundings. She collected herself and started to walk towards the centre of the room.

The table was simply set, with a white linen table cloth hanging over the edges and gleaming cutlery in front of each of the eleven chairs. The table was only decorated with a few small vases containing bunches of lily-of-the-valley, their delicate white blooms emphasised by a ring of violets around their stems.

The others had reached the table and were taking their seats. King Cameron sat at the head of the table with Queen Astrid to his left, on the side of the table furthest from where Violet stood. Mary's mother and father sat next to the queen and the Sergeants took the last two seats on that side of the table. The Higgets then sat opposite the Sergeants, leaving only three empty seats on their side of the table.

Violet realised that the king was beckoning to her and Markham had pulled the seat next to Cameron out from the table for her. Violet took her seat and was relieved when Mary sat next to her.

Within minutes of them sitting, a group of neatly dressed waiters sat a pastry covered ramekin in front of each of the diners.

"Violet," Mary said quietly. "Just copy me."

Violet nodded and copied the other woman, picking up a fork from the outside of her array and delicately stabbing it into the pastry. A swirl of steam arose from under the crust, carrying an inviting aroma of fish and onion. She looked to her right and noticed that Mary had broken off a piece of the puff pastry and was using her fork to get some of the sauce from the pie. Violet had some trouble breaking the pastry, but managed to get a piece of it free and dipped it into the creamy sauce. The sauce was delicious, but the piece of creamy fish she found a few mouthfuls later was even better.

The table was quiet for a few minutes while everyone ate their first dish, but conversation began as the diners finished their pie. Violet was intrigued and listened carefully.

"So, I hear you have recently started a new cooperative venture?" Cameron asked.

"Yes. We used to have trouble getting grain to our mill," Mr Sergeant said. "Sometimes farmers couldn't get their loads to us until they'd finished their harvests, and sometimes moisture or vermin had then gotten to their crops."

"And we had several lull times in the year when our carters would spend time without employment," added Mr Higget.

"Well, we worked out that their lull times lined up wit' the harvest times, so we decided to work together and hire the same carters."

"Brilliant," said Cameron. "And how is that working out?"

"Quite well, so far," said Mr Sergeant. "We had much greater quantities of grain brought in at the end of last season than we'd had previously and it came it at a steady, more manageable rate, rather than all at once when everyone was done harvesting."

The next course interrupted their conversation. The presented plates held steamed baby carrots and beans with a roasted chicken breast garnished with rosemary and garlic.

The conversation continued sporadically while they ate

their main course, but everyone quietened as their stomachs grew full. Cameron kept grilling the two couples about their success and Violet wondered if he was collecting knowledge to share with people in different regions when he travelled there later in the year.

A short while after they had finished their main courses, Cameron suggested that they return to the parlour where some refreshments had been served. They stood and walked back towards the door they had entered through.

The chairs had been arranged into a couple of small groups around two tables which held and array of sweet pastries, cheeses and fruit. Violet sat with Markham and Mary and the others sat around a larger table closer to the fire.

"Have you spoken to my sister today?" Mary asked Markham as soon as they were alone.

"I have," the soldier said. "We spent part of the afternoon together. I had to tell her that I am to travel to Mellanastia, then Aramalia, so it will be some time before I return. Your sister took the news quite well, but came over with one of her nasty headaches. I am sure she will be fine when you return home."

Mary nodded, but worry lines still creased the edges of her eyes.

The trio sat, filling the corners of their stomachs with pastries and cheese, until Markham stood and addressed the members of the dinner party.

"I am sorry, but we leave early for Oakville early in the morning and I think it would be wise for the Lady Violet and me to retire," he said.

Cameron nodded his agreement.

"If my parents agree, would you escort me home, Captain Markham?" Mary asked. "I would like to see if my sister requires anything."

Her mother nodded and the three younger diners bowed

and curtseyed their way out of the presence of royalty.

They walked the length of the drawing room into the entrance hall and stopped.

"I will be up to help you prepare to leave before dawn," Mary told Violet. "Try to get as much sleep as you can. Will you be able to find your room?"

Violet nodded and bade the two others good night before turning and heading up the stairs, she heard the great doors close behind her as she reached the first landing.

It wasn't until she reached her bedroom that she realised she wouldn't be able to undress herself. Her worries were eased when she opened her door to find another maid sitting in a chair embroidering while she waited.

It only took ten minutes for Violet to change into nightclothes and fall fast asleep in the thick, downy embrace of the bed.

Chapter Nine
VIOLET

Violet awoke to soft light coming through her eyelids. She was determined to get more sleep so she rolled over and kept her eyes closed, hoping to drift off again.

She lay there for a moment while the fuzz slowly lifted from her mind and she gradually realised that something wasn't quite right. The bed was too soft and the quilt was too thick and the pillows felt wrong. She opened one of her eyes to peer into a room that was definitely not her own and then clenched them both tight shut again as the flood gates in her mind gave way and reality came crashing in.

She sighed and rolled over so that she was facing towards the window again. The sky was only just light enough to make out the shape of the horizon, the jagged peaks of the distant mountains a deeper grey than the clouds that hung menacingly above them. Clearly the weather had changed overnight and they would not be in for a sunny day of travel like the day before.

She realised that it must have been Mary who opened the curtains when the girl came walking over from the corner of the room.

"Good morning," the maid said brightly. "Time to get ready to go."

Violet grumbled and sat up in the bed, throwing all the blankets down to her feet.

"Ooh, it's chilly!" Violet said. "How is your sister this

morning?"

"She is fine, thank you, nothing a good night's sleep couldn't fix. I have filled the bath for you in case you wanted to have a quick scrub before you go. I'm sure that you will be travelling in relative comfort, but it may still take a few days for you to reach somewhere with a bath as big as this one."

Violet took her advice and felt much better for the soaking when she returned to the room ten minutes later. Mary had laid out some clothing on the bed for her and Violet noticed a platter with some toast and spreads set out on a table near the window. She ate while she was still in her undergarments and dressing gown.

Mary returned as Violet finished her breakfast and gave limited assistance while Violet dressed. This outfit was much less formal than the ones she had worn the day before. She still wore several thick layers of petticoats and a boned corset, but at least this one fitted properly and only needed to be laced at the front. The next layer was a pale blue full-length dress with long billowing sleeves that Violet cinched at her wrists. She then slipped on a dark blue overdress and did up a row of hook and eye fasteners behind an embroidered strip of fabric that extended beyond her collar. The dress fit her perfectly, emphasising her slender waist and flaring out over her hips. *Damn, looks like I finally found a clothing style that suits my body type.*

"There you go," said Mary. "That outfit was a lot easier to get on. You will manage. Plus, you can switch to trousers after your first day of travel."

Violet nodded and adjusted her posture, pulling her shoulders back so the corset sat correctly. She already feel a strain in her lower back and didn't know how long she would be able to maintain it.

Both girls started at the sound of a bugle cry from below the window, Mary rushed over to look out.

"Quick, the party has assembled. We need to hurry downstairs," Mary said.

Violet picked up the last item of clothing from the bed, a velvet cloak of midnight blue, and flung it over her shoulders, hastily tying the strings at her throat. She automatically turned to see if she had left anything behind in the room, but she had only entered the Realm with the clothes she was wearing and didn't know what had happened to them after she'd arrived in Wynbourne. She had nothing to take.

They dashed down the back stairway and into the rear courtyard to find a group of about twenty soldiers assembled ahead of a couple of carts. King Cameron and Queen Astrid waited for Violet just outside the door and beckoned to her as soon as she emerged from the manor.

"Best wishes for your travels," Astrid said. "We hope you have a safe journey under our protection and will see you after you have been reunited with our son."

Cameron simply nodded his agreement. Violet noticed the lines of tension etched around his mouth and eyes and suspected he had not slept since she saw him at dinner.

"Thank you for your hospitality and protection. I look forward to meeting you again soon and I am sorry that I must take my leave of this town, but I feel a great need to meet with Prince Daniel," Violet said, keeping up the ruse that she was headed to Daniel at Oakwood.

A porter came up behind Violet.

"My lady, we have prepared a seat in the cart for you," he told her.

Violet turned back to the hills to see that the sun had lit the clouds from beneath, limning them in a brilliant tangerine edged with a deep purple. She drew her eyes away from the display and walked towards where the cart waited, her horse tethered to the rear.

A young woman with deep chocolate curls sat on a bench

seat behind the driver of the cart. The woman gave Violet a wide, vivid smile as she approached.

"Hello," she said. "My name is Sarah Courts. I am Mary's sister and will be riding with you to Oakville."

Well, that's unexpected.

"It is very nice to meet you, I hope you will be as much help to me as Mary has been and look forward to spending some time with you," Violet said.

She had not been briefed about Sarah travelling with them, but knew Markham would not put his betrothed in any danger.

She moved to the back of the cart and gave Star a gentle rub on the nose. The horse whinnied in response and Violet nuzzled her velvet face.

"My lady, we are to leave shortly. Please come and sit with me," Sarah said.

Violet nodded and quickly walked around to the steps of the cart. Violet collected her skirts in the most ladylike manner she could muster before climbing the three steps up to the buggy to sit next to Sarah. She thought she heard Sarah stifle a giggle while she was arranging her skirts, but if so, the girl hid it well when Violet eyed her questioningly.

Violet looked back towards the king and queen and saw them in quiet conference with Markham. The soldier then executed a brisk bow and walked to where a page was holding his horse and, with all the elegance he had shown the previous day, mounted with one swift, smooth movement. He then rode to the front of the line of soldiers and signalled to a boy with a bugle. One short, shrill blast later, the convoy moved off, heading out of the mustering yard at a sedate pace.

Violet let herself be soothed by the gentle rocking of the cart and the clopping of hooves as they headed out onto the road and picked up a bit more speed.

"Are you feeling alright?" Sarah asked, obviously

worried.

"I am fine," Violet answered. "A lot has happened since I left home yesterday morning and I guess I am just trying to make sense of it all."

"I think I can understand a little of what you must be feeling," Sarah said. "And I suppose you probably didn't sleep too well either."

"I actually had quite a restful night. I am not used to it being so dark or quiet outside, but I found it very peaceful."

Sarah nodded her agreement and they lapsed into silence for a while as they listened to the birds along the roadside chirruping their wake up calls. Violet turned to again look at the sky, the richness of colour she had seen before had faded and now there was only a faint pink tinge along the horizon, while the sky had turned a pure blue. Violet took in a deep breath of the crisp morning air. She had always loved getting up before the sun had warmed the dew off the grass so she could still smell the moisture in the air.

"Markham said that you should try to rest as much as you can today," Sarah said after a time. "I think there will be fast riding in the days ahead and this will be the only day you can spend in the buggy."

They progressed at a fairly steady pace throughout the day, stopping only a few times to water the horses and let the riders take in a couple of hasty meals. Violet tried to let the soft sunlight relax her as they travelled between paddocks and through small towns.

As the day headed towards evening, a larger town appeared on the road ahead. There was a lot of horse, cart and foot traffic, both on the road that Violet's party travelled on, and on the faint ribbons of road heading out of the town in two other directions.

"This is where we will stop for the night," Sarah said, pointing towards the town. "There are several boarding houses there and the king sent word to the largest one this morning, so they should be expecting us. We will share a room so that I can help you, my lady."

Violet was about to tell the girl that she wouldn't need the help, but something in the girl's expression stopped her.

"Thank you," Violet said instead. "I would appreciate that."

The group rode into town and pulled up outside a two story building with a wide verandah encircling both stories and large windows all round. A pair of double doors on the lower level were flung open and a middle-aged woman with round rosy cheeks came out and greeted them.

"Hello and welcome to our fair town this afternoon," she said cheerily. "I am Mrs Goodwin and this is my boarding house. Ladies, please come with me and I will show you to your room. Gentlemen, if you would head around to the back of the building you will find stables and food for your horses and I've a couple of boys round there who will help you."

The two young women climbed down from the cart—Sarah elegantly and Violet stumblingly—and walked to the entrance where Mrs Goodwin waited. The ample landlady fetched a page to collect their bags from the cart before the driver followed the orderly procession of horsemen to the stables.

"Come along, then," Mrs Goodwin said, leading them into the house and up a straight staircase along the side of the entrance lobby. "I was told you would be leaving early, so I have already asked for a meal to be prepared for you. I will have it sent up in about an hour when you should have had a chance to refresh yourselves."

"Thank you," Sarah said for them. "That will be lovely."

They turned right and headed down a corridor which was flanked on either side by doors, most of which stood open to allow the late afternoon sunlight to flood through the windows on their left and light their way. They walked straight down to the end of the corridor where they entered a large room with a bed at either end, a small dining setting in the middle and several comfortable chairs by the northern windows. Violet could smell a fresh warm fragrance and scanned the room to find it. Finally, she spotted a large brass bathtub tucked away in the right hand corner, merrily steaming away.

"I thought you might like to freshen up," the landlady told them. "So I had the boys fill up the tub for you when I saw your party on the road, the water was near to boiling when they brought it up so it should be cool enough as not to scald you by now."

She directed the page boy to place their bags in the middle of the room and closed the door while the girls called out their thanks. Suddenly, Violet found herself alone in the room with Sarah, a girl she had only met that morning, yet apparently she was about to bathe with her in the room, she found the thought quite confronting. The other girl must have picked up some of her tension and tried to ease her qualms.

"If you like, I can unpack some fresh clothes for you and then leave while you bathe," Sarah offered.

"No, it's ok. Are you sure you are happy for me to bathe first, I think I have quite a few aches to soak out."

"My lady," Sarah said, gently reminding Violet of their positions. "You are very kind to offer, but it would not be right of me to accept."

Violet nodded and moved over to the bed where Sarah was setting out some clothes for her. She had pulled out a soft green cotton dress and some undergarments and laid them on the bed closest to the bath. The other girl walked over to the chairs by the window and sat looking out, ready to offer assistance if she was needed, but staying out of the way to give Violet some privacy. Violet realised that the task of undressing would be colossal, but was determined to manage it on her own.

Her cloak had been discarded earlier in the day, so she only had the two dresses to contend with. She started by undoing the hooks and eyes that fastened her bodice and, rather inelegantly, tried to haul the heavy fabric over her head. After a few minutes, she had worked herself free of the overdress and set to work about pulling off the cotton dress underneath. Naturally, it wasn't until the dress was over her head and she was trying to pull her fingers out of the sleeves that she remembered she'd tied them around her wrists.

Get off of me! Violet thought as she wildly flapped her arms around in an attempt to break free.

A stifled giggle from the direction of the window indicated that Violet had drawn the attention of her roommate. She stopped flapping and tried to stand with as much dignity as she could manage. Despite the amazing self-control she had shown up until that point, Sarah couldn't help but laugh. Violet imagined Sarah's view of the situation. A wild, outlandish woman, standing in her undergarments, with a dress hanging from her wrists and her hair in a dishevelled mess.

Violet did feel a little silly and smiled at the other woman's mirth.

"Maybe I need a little more practice with these clothes," she said. As the other girl began to rise, she continued, "Don't worry, I will manage."

Sarah turned back to the view and Violet managed to undo her sleeves and extricate herself from the garment. The corset was the final barrier to the bath tub and Violet knew she could get herself out of that. As she had done the laces herself, the garment had not been as restrictive as the one she had worn the previous day, but she was still not entirely used to it. She undid the laces and pulled it over her head, then slipped off her shift, petticoats and undergarments and slid into the tub.

The warmth enveloped all of her aching muscles and the gentle aroma of lavender and jasmine seeped in and soothed her body and spirit. After a few minutes, she reached across to the table that held soap and shampoo and began to scrub the road dust from her skin. Now that they were off the road and away from listening ears, she felt that she could start to ask about their plans.

She knew that the group must be set to divide at this fork in the road. This was the point where the road to the Abbey led off to the north-west, while Violet and Markham must travel east. What Violet could not work out was how they were going to separate. *Surely it will be too obvious if the party simply splits up at this point*?

Violet finished scrubbing and shivered, the water was not yet cold, but it was no longer as hot as it had been and she hurriedly climbed out so that the Sarah would not freeze. The floor under the bath was lined with terracotta tiles and she walked a couple of steps to where there were some towels and dressing gowns. She quickly wiped herself dry, then cocooned her hair in the towel and wrapped a gown around herself. She called out to Sarah that the bath was free.

Sarah had not been idle while Violet had been bathing and now walked over to the tub clothed in only a dressing gown, carrying several small, opaque bottles. She placed the bottles on the soap stand, then unashamedly slipped out of her gown and into the tub. She wasted no time, or warmth, and quickly submerged her head, soaking all of her deep brown tresses. She reached for the first bottle and poured a clear liquid into her palm and began to massage it through her hair. After a few minutes of vigorous scrubbing, she dipped her hands in the water and rinsed them, then thoroughly dried her fingers on one of the remaining towels.

Violet now watched curiously from the window as Sarah reached for the second bottle and poured a brilliant red powder into the palm of her hand before spreading it on her scalp. She rubbed this through her hair as well, working from her scalp to the tips. After a few minutes of this treatment, Sarah again slid down the tub and dipped her head down to the level of the water, allowing her hair to fan out around her.

Suddenly realising she was staring, Violet turned away. A moment later, she heard the sound of sloughing water and assumed Sarah was emerging.

A few minutes later, Sarh said, "What do you think?"

Violet turned as Sarah shook her hair out, allowing it to cascade down over her shoulders in a distinct copper wave.

"It is all part of the plan," Sarah said, smiling at Violet's confusion. "Markham will be dining with us this evening. He knows the plan better than I, so he will explain it to you then. Now, they will bring up our food up shortly, we must make ourselves decent."

Violet crossed the room to the bed and started to dress. She was loath to put the corset back on yet as her muscles still ached from being cinched into it all day. Even though she had not had it done up tightly, the restraint was still foreign to her, and she wasn't entirely sure she liked it. She begrudgingly pulled the offending item over her head and laced herself into it, but stopped short at the petticoats. She always bought hipster pants and even though she knew she wouldn't feel the waist tie of the skirts through the corset, she still did not want to put them on.

Sarah turned when she had finished dressing to find the slim form of Violet in front of her, the green cotton dress falling into full, soft folds from her hips where normally the layers of petticoats would hold it out. Sarah looked the other girl over with a stern look on her face.

"Well," she finally said. "I'm not sure that they would let you dress like that at court, but I won't argue. If you will go around without your petticoats though, you will need all of your skirts taken up."

Violet pulled her skirts out and did a polite curtsey, but was interrupted by a knock at the door.

Sarah opened it to find that a page wheeling a trolley with their dinner, accompanied by Captain Markham. Markham looked over Violet and his expression became one of slight disapproval when he reached her hips, but he did not say anything. Violet found the social turmoil she had created by leaving off her petticoats amusing, but managed to keep her mirth from showing.

The three sat at the table once the page had finished setting out their meals and left the room. Markham looked at his fiancée and asked her to turn her head so he could see the full effect of the dye that she had used.

'Very good. That has worked well and should suit our purposes nicely." Markham turned to Violet. "I must apologise that you have undertaken this part of the journey without really knowing what our movements would be, our plans were not finalised until very late last night and the king and I did not feel that we should wake you."

Violet nodded to show that she had no ill feelings for the soldier.

"Our plan is quite simple," he said. "Although it puts both myself and my future wife into disrepute." He smiled at Sarah, who responded in kind. "I arranged to have Sarah accompany us so that she may be your lady's maid on the trip to Oakville. However, as you may have guessed, there is also an alternate motive. Sarah has coloured her hair tonight so that she may take your place as the rest of the convoy journeys to Oakville.

"The king and I agreed that your presence will have certainly been noted and you will have been associated with

Prince Daniel. We cannot let whatever parties are at work here suspect that we know he has been captured. At this time, the prince should be finishing some research with the monks, so it is very reasonable to be sending you there to see him. If we drop this convoy, it would be as good as shouting that we know his safety has been compromised."

Markham paused so that Violet could take all of this in before continuing.

"Our plan is that you and I shall leave this town and travel towards the mountains in the middle of the night and Sarah will continue on to Oakville in your place. It will effectively look as though I have deserted my post to elope with my fiancée instead of continuing on the short journey to Oakville and long one to Aramalia after. It will be scandalous and I will be painted as a deserter and Sarah's reputation will be in shambles, but we have been promised great concessions in return for our sacrifices."

The couple looked at each other and smiled with a heat that Violet could almost feel. She could tell they would sorely miss each other in the coming weeks and could only imagine how worried Sarah would be for her future husband.

"Sounds like a good plan to me," Violet said. "When do we leave?"

"In a couple of hours," Markham said. "I recommend that you get some sleep if you can. We have a hard ride ahead of us and will probably not have the benefit of a bed for some time."

Violet looked down to her now-empty plate and nodded.

"Is there anything else you think I need to know," she asked.

Markham shook his head. "Nothing that I won't be able to tell you on the road."

"Thank you," Violet said, then looked to each of them in turn. "I appreciate all that both of you are doing for me, and for Prince Daniel."

With that, Violet stood and left the table, leaving the other two on their own. She pulled the curtain around the side of her bed closest to them closed so she could stand behind the bed to change. Within minutes, she was tucked up under the thick covers, looking out towards the wall. The flickering candlelight from the table shed an eerie red gleam on the wood-panelled walls and Violet tried to let it lull her to sleep. She did not feel particularly tired, but she let her thoughts drift towards Daniel, wondering where he was as she fell into a light sleep.

Chapter Ten
DANIEL

Daniel was not sleeping. He was desperately trying to work out where he was based on the noise trickling through the hessian sacks he was buried under. His head ached from the blow that had knocked him unconscious when had been ambushed.

Damn my inattention, I should know better.

He'd been hurrying along the road from the thicket toward Wynbourne, thinking about the woman he had left behind. His parents had asked him to stop splitting his time between their own world and Violet's, but had forbidden him from telling her about the Realm.

To get around the edict, he'd told Violet that they were from different worlds and he could no longer see her. The disappointment and hurt on her face when he'd said that twisted his stomach tight, but she was a very curious woman. He knew if she saw him return home, she'd be drawn to follow him and they would be reunited.

He had been absorbed in these thoughts, wondering if she'd crossed through yet, as he thundered towards his family's spring home. Therefore, he spared no thought of wariness for the group of workmen huddled alongside a loaded cart on the side of the road. As he drew closer, one of the men hailed him to stop. He did not think he would be recognised as he wasn't wearing formal clothing.

"What can I do for you, gentleman?" Daniel asked,

reining in his horse.

"We could use an extra set of hands to repair this wheel," one of the men said. Daniel would later reflect on the strange lilt to his voice.

The man who spoke was on the other side of the cart to where Daniel sat on his horse and he and his companions were well-muscled men. If Daniel's mind had been on his surroundings instead of several miles down the road behind him, he probably would have noticed that the muscles were formed by hours of wielding a sword and not from swinging a scythe as the men were dressed to imply.

Daniel dismounted and headed around to the other side of the cart, followed by the fourth man of the party. He rounded the end of the cart and looked at the wheel, which was whole, unbroken and still attached to the cart.

"What's the problem..." He trailed off when he noticed that the three men in front of him all had their attention fixed over his left shoulder.

Daniel suddenly felt a prickle of fear and spun around just as the fourth man slammed a piece of wood against the side of his head.

Daniel had awoken slowly, attention immediately drawn to all of his aches. He's been unceremoniously shoved in a space barely big enough to hold him, with his knees pushed uncomfortably into his chest.

He had no idea how long he had been unconscious, or the time of day, despite the few stray beams of sunlight slipping in from the corners of the sacks of grain that held him imprisoned. He was relieved when he discovered there was space to stretch into. He grimaced in the dim light as he shifted his stiff muscles, but managed to wriggle straight enough to relieve the pressure on his chest.

Next, he mentally assessed the rest of his body. Thankfully, his hands were not tied and apart from the tender spot on his head, he was largely unhurt. He presumed he was in the same cart he had been waylaid to "fix" as he was surrounded by the same hessian bags. A lattice-work frame had been laid when the stack reached four bags high and then bags were stacked on top to form the hidden cavity.

Lucky I'm not claustrophobic, he thought.

The cadence of the horses hooves and creaking of the axle told him they were moving at a moderate pace. Muffled voices filtered through his musty surrounds, but he could not make out the words. He listened for a few minutes before realising his stupidity. These were not people of his own realm. The accent he had heard earlier, but not recognised, identified his kidnappers as Aramalians.

The shock of the realisation made his head spin, although that could have also been a lack of oxygen. This must have something to do with the alliance between the Realm of the Lilies and Mellanastia.

He his stupidity again, using a few choice words he had picked up in Violet's world. He had put his parents in a very awkward situation and must free himself. The gentle jostling of the cart, though, was oddly soothing and he let his mind wander to try to work out what his captors might have planned.

After another hour or so in the cart, the air began to chill and the light coming through the cracks started to fade. The men outside the cart had started chatting again, some calling loudly as if they were hailing someone. The cart slowed and Daniel rolled to the left as they turned. Their new path was bumpy and set the cart rocking. Wherever they were headed, he would be lucky if he escaped with only a few bruises from this part of the journey.

After a few minutes on the bumpy track, the cart stopped. Then, there was a loud scraping noise before the cart moved forwards again and their movement gained an echoing tone before they stopped. He heard the scraping noise again, followed by footsteps approaching the cart. There was a creak and a bang as the tailgate was loosened and fell free.

The face of the man who had spoken to him earlier leered through the gap. "I must admit, Prince Daniel, your capture proved to be much easier than I thought it would be."

"Yes, well," Daniel said. "I must apologise for that, my mind was elsewhere at the time."

"May I help you out?" The man did not wait for an answer before hauling Daniel out of the cart by the shoulders.

Thankfully, two more henchmen supported him while the blood trickled back to his toes.

"It is not our intention to harm you. However, it is in the best interests of my employer for you to not be seen for a few weeks. Once the time is right, you will be released and assisted to travel wherever you wish, even to the middle of your capital if you so desire."

Daniel studied his captor, the man wore the typical plain-dyed clothing of his realm, but had slightly darker skin and coarser hair typical of Aramalians. Daniel decided that it was pointless to deny his identity. These men had obviously done their research well.

"And what assurances can you give me to this end?" Daniel asked. "I am aware that I am not in a particularly good position to negotiate at the moment, but you have not exactly treated me with the correct level of respect."

He pouted to highlight the persona he wanted show. He was hoping that if he played the role of primped fool they might believe him.

The leader laughed. "Oh dear, the Little Prince is not happy with his treatment at the hands of his nasty captors. Well, I do apologise. I didn't think that you would be kind enough to climb into the cart with only the threat of a sword on your neck."

You're correct on that. Daniel thought. *Let's play the spoiled brat a little further.*

"Well, never in my life have I been treated this way!" he exclaimed, but he was careful not to draw attention to his full height or musculature. "I demand that you at least give me your name and address me in the correct fashion."

"My Lord Prince," the man said, executing an exaggerated bow with much hand flourishing. "Please accept my humble apologies. You may address me as Loucius."

The other members of the chuckled at the exchange. Daniel knew that they would not expect too much trouble from him now. He was pretty certain of why he had been captured, but he thought it would be suspicious if he did not ask. The person he was trying to paint himself as would not have the capacity to work it out for himself.

"I demand you tell me why you have captured me at once," Daniel said. He used his most pompous voice, which he had perfected over hours of boyhood play with Markham

"Prince Daniel, you are dumber than you appear if you think I will tell you that," Loucius said, simply. "Suffice to say, you will be enjoying my hospitality for a few weeks.

"Enough of this now," he continued imperiously. "Take him to the stall and chain him to the post by the ankle. We would not want to damage the royal wrists. You will be brought food and drink later, do not try to escape, we are not the only ones watching you."

Daniel allowed himself to be led away and chained, but shot sullen glares at his captors, catching each of the four men in turn. He was careful not to let his sulking expression slide while he was left alone thinking.

He tried to think clearly through the dull ache of his head and the spikes of his straw bed poking through his clothing. He had been captured only few miles from the thicket. *How long did they have to wait?* he wondered.

He had travelled to the thicket only the day before, planning to cross into Violet's world just before meeting her there one last time. The barracks there was also the main training post for the elite soldiers who protected the royal family, and his trip down there had been passed off as checking the readiness of the troops for their planned travel over the mountains. Daniel was sure that if the Aramalians knew of the portal between worlds they would have stormed his realm to gain sole access. The history of their nation was steeped in tales of war and deception and the temptation of the bounties beyond the portal would have been too much for them to resist.

They must have known he would be returning to report to his parents today and had waited for him to travel past them. Daniel only hoped they were the only party waiting along the road so that if Violet had followed him, there would be no-one waiting to cause her any harm.

As he was sitting there, seemingly sulking, Daniel felt warm tingles press against his skin, a few at first, then a full assault relentlessly pricked every square inch of him. For one worrying moment he felt as though his whole body was being compressed, then a sudden flare of heat and a release of tension allowed him to breathe normally again. He sat in his corner panting for a moment before he reached a sudden conclusion.

The necklace!

"There is something you must know about the pattern you have chosen," the monk had said, when they'd met a few weeks earlier. "The pendant, as you know, is made in the image of your great-grandmother's, which she used to find the first king while he travelled the Realm. Her locket had a ruby as the central gem, symbolic of the blood shared between them in their children."

Daniel nodded, he knew all this.

"What you will not understand, and I cannot explain, is how it works. This necklace has been tuned specifically to you, the lock of hair you provided, the blood, both were used in the creation, but the spell is not yet complete.

"Only when you have given this necklace to the woman you love will all of the seals be set and it be tuned to both you and her. You need only give it to her, place it around her throat. After a few days of wear the spells will work for her only. Keep this necklace close until you can give it to your lady, for if it were to fall into the wrong hands, who knows what enemies would find you."

"Thank you, I will protect it 'til then," Daniel said as he collected the velvet lined box.

"One last thing," the monk said. "A spell of this nature cannot be used without the object of interest feeling some echo. You will know when she is trying to locate you."

Chapter Eleven
DANIEL

Violet must have followed me.

Daniel sat abruptly upright when he realised the meaning of the strange sensations. Realising the danger of his position, he subsided so as not to draw attention to himself.

His captors were huddled together a few metres away from him, speaking their own language in low voices. He understand some of their conversation, but did not strain his hearing to learn their plans. It was more important to come up with his own.

Violet trying to locate him told him that she'd travelled to his world. More than that, she'd me his parents and they would not have told her how to use the necklace if they didn't know he'd been ambushed.

His parents would come up with a plan to rescue him, but he would not sit idly by like a maid in distress. There must be a way for him to secure his freedom on his own. Then he would either get himself back to his family or they would locate him with the aid of Violet's necklace.

He sat for a while longer, assessing his temporary prison. He was inside a large, meticulously organised barn. There were hay bales stacked against the wall to his right, benches on the wall to his left, and two large sections of the wall opposite could be slid open. His prison cell was a horse stall, which was only half the height of the rest of the barn as there was a loft above him. Three stalls to his right, against the wall, was the ladder to the loft.

"Excuse me," he called out, when it looked as though his captors were to separate. "I believe you said you would provide me with food. I have not eaten for many hours and my throat has been scratched dry by the conditions in the cart. I must say, if you want me to cooperate, you will have to treat me better than this."

Loucius swaggered over and the other two louts followed, flanking him.

"My humble apologies, Little Prince," Loucius said, looming over Daniel and smirking. "I am afraid our catering is not up to the standards you are used to, but I will have something brought to you."

With that, the three men turned away, the other two captors looking a little disappointed by the exchange. They walked towards the door, and Loucius and another left the barn while the third remained to stand guard within.

A short time later, the door opened again and the other man re-entered, carrying a bucket that he took to Daniel in his stall. In his absence, Daniel had meticulously laid out his cloak on the hay covered floor of the stall so that he had a clean place to picnic. When the guard noticed, he smirked and unceremoniously tipped the contents of the bucket in the middle. A loaf of bread and a piece of hard cheese dropped out, along with a clay pot of quince paste, a butter knife and a tin cup. The guard executed a sloppy curtsey—the other guard rewarded these antics with a chuckle—before going to a pump against the wall of the barn and filling the bucket with water.

Daniel set about organising his feast, lining up the bread and cheese with the spread in the middle and his tin cup of water to the right. He was used to eating rough and ready meals and it did not bother him, but this show was not for his benefit. The two guards leant against the door, watching him with sly grins on their faces and making remarks to each other in their own tongue, so Daniel assumed his act was convincing.

The food was not fancy, but it was good. The bread was fresh and the cheese was a dry, tart cheddar, which contrasted well with the sweet quince paste. Daniel set about tearing the bread into strips, then wrapping it around cheese and spread, thoroughly enjoying the food. The water was fresh and cool and Daniel judged that they must be fairly close to Wynbourne. This water probably came from the river near that town.

Daniel looked towards the guards to find they had turned around and started chatting when it became apparent that Daniel would not be providing them with any more entertainment. They had removed his right boot to shackle him to the post, but had thankfully left it in the stall close at hand. His horse was on the other side of the barn and making his escape to walk barefoot across his realm was not something that appealed to him.

He adjusted himself so that he sat cross legged, the shackled foot on top of the free one. He slipped a finger inside the heel of his left boot and pulled out a small compartment containing several small metal objects. He carefully selected two picks and went to work on the exposed lock of the shackle on his right foot. After a few moments he was rewarded with a soft click and he hastened to return his lock picks to their hiding place, lest his freedom be discovered before he had time to conceal them again.

He sat back in the hay to casually look at the guards again, they were still absorbed by their conversation and facing away from him, but he did not trust them to remain that way while he tried his escape.

"I say," he called out in his pompous voice. "Don't you at least have any cards? You can't honestly expect me to sit here like a good little captive for you all night if you don't at least give me something to do."

The guards sniggered at each other, exchanged a few words and then one walked out of the barn. Daniel presumed he was going to talk to his leader about the strange behaviour of the prince they had captured.

The remaining guard resumed his pacing and Daniel made a show of burrowing down in the hay, while watching him closely. After a few minutes, the guard stopped watching Daniel and looked out through the gap in the doors to the night beyond.

Daniel took the opportunity to slip off his other boot, release his shackle and pick up both shoes. He stole from his stall and hurriedly ran the length of the others, his sock covered feet making little sound on the packed-earth floor. He said a quick prayer that the ladder wouldn't creak as he hurriedly made his way up to the loft, being careful not to let his boots knock against the rungs.

Within seconds of leaving the stall, Daniel was hidden behind some hay bales in the loft and the guard hadn't even turned around. He sat and listened for a moment, but could not hear any noise aside from dull creaks as the barn cooled and settled for the night. He looked towards the rear of the loft and thought he could see the outline of a door. He slowly made his way to the rear of the barn, only causing a few boards to creak on his way.

Finally, he reached the doors and sat on a nearby bale of hay to put his boots back on before daring to look out of the doors to discover if escape was possible. A sudden scrape behind him made him start.

"I'm afraid that you will not be able to leave the barn this way, Prince Daniel," Loucius announced through the darkness. "If you care to take a look out through the window, you will see there are four additional guards, including a bowman, ruling out this possibility."

Daniel's heart sank as he turned to face his captor. Loucius stood out only as a dark silhouette perched on a hay bale in the dim loft. He heard the scraping sound again and realised Loucius was sharpening the blade of a long, curved knife.

The foreigner stood, dropping his veil of darkness like an inky black cloak, exposing his smug countenance as he approached Daniel.

"You see, Little Prince," Loucius said patronisingly. "We have planned well and we have plenty of guards in each place that we will stop along the way. If you should manage another escape attempt, we will take any steps necessary to ensure that you do not return to your family before we want you to."

"I must commend you on your planning," Daniel said, with a nod to his captor. "Of course, this does not mean I endorse your activities at all, but I can acknowledge a worthy opponent when I face one."

Loucius merely nodded and gestured for the Prince to lead the way back down from the loft. When they reached the stall, Loucius pulled down a coil of rope which he then used to tie Daniel hands and ankles. He did not tie the limbs together, but left a small amount of rope between them, allowing Daniel to eat and walk, but not move freely.

"Now that I know you're impervious to shackles," Loucius snickered as he walked away. "Let us see how you fare against my knots."

Daniel sighed and flopped down in the hay. It seemed escape would not be easily achieved. He must bide his time and wait. At that moment, sleep seemed the best option. His thoughts went out to Violet as he fell asleep, he hoped his parents would not let her do anything foolish and that the woman he loved was safe.

Chapter Twelve
DANIEL

The next day started early for Daniel.

He was awoken by the two guards preparing the horses for their day's travel, the jingling of reins bringing him to wakefulness slowly, until he suddenly felt his bindings. He silently cursed as he realised he was in for another day stashed in the back of the cart, his muscles were already protesting about their treatment the day before and his rough sleeping arrangements had not helped matters.

Daniel sat up when he realised that a breakfast of apple and bread had already been set down by his feet, along with a cup of fresh water. It was a testament to the work of his family that although the poor did not eat the rich fare he was used to, the food he was served was wholesome. He relished the sweet juicy apple and tore strips off the bread, eating slowly as was his habit when food was in short supply.

His hunger satisfied, he sat back to study the guards as they prepared the cart, switching the grain bags of the previous day for hay bales. The burlier man, who had dark hair, used his left hand to do most of the fine tasks, yet seemed to favour his left leg. The other, taller and fair haired, was right handed and seemed to be fully capable, however a stray wince when he was tightening a strap gave away a possible shoulder injury. Confident that he may have found some weak points, Daniel relaxed. He was wary of looking too alert lest they lock him up longer than they needed too.

Loucius stumped in through the partially open barn doors a few minutes later, casting a glance at his men and the cart before walking towards Daniel.

"Good morning, Prince Daniel," he said, executing a sketchy bow. "I trust you slept well."

Daniel noticed the sly smile, but also that the leader had dropped the patronising tone and "Little Prince" diminutive.

"Ah, my gracious host," Daniel said with his own smile. "How kind of you to see to my wellbeing before I have even left my bed."

The two men assessed each other for a moment, each aware that they would have to give credit where it was due and begrudgingly respect their opponent.

"Come," said Loucius. "We must leave soon, it is a long ride to Aquilegia and I wish to be well past that town before we stop tonight."

Daniel nodded and rose, shuffling towards the back of the wagon to be helped in by the two other guards. Loucius proved that he did indeed mean the Prince no harm by passing in a skin of water, a loaf of bread and a couple of apples.

"We dare not risk your early discovery," Loucius said. "I am sure you understand what the consequences would be for us. We will refresh your supplies at midday, but you must make yourself comfortable here until we stop for the night."

With that, a thin bale was placed at the end of his enclosure, the tailgate was closed and Daniel was left to his own company. A few moments later the cart bounced as the driver jumped aboard, then Daniel heard the muffled scraping of the great barn doors being pushed wide. With a click from the driver to the horses, the cart was on its bouncing way down the track to the road.

Daniel had some hope of being found in the cart, his parents would not dare to cause a panic by making his capture well known. The only way they could arrange a search for him would be under the guise of rooting out smugglers, but even then the realm would be shaken if it were heard that the Prince was found unceremoniously shoved in the back of a wagon.

No, he thought, *they will not tempt such a course.*

The wagon could be searched as it left Aquilegia, but his prison had been well constructed. Only a very thorough search would spy out the concealed compartment. His rescue or escape would need to take place some other way.

After some time pondering this problem, he began to think of Violet. It had hurt to leave her standing there the day before, shattering her dreams of a life together. He should never have allowed them to become so emotionally involved and had been foolish to think he could continue their trans-world relationship. Still, when he thought of how he had felt her using the power of the necklace the day before, he was sure he had made the right decision.

Thank God I dropped the necklace for her. And that she does apparently love me.

Daniel thought back to the previous day and realised he didn't know when Violet had passed through the portal back to his world, so he had no idea how long she had been in his world, or how long his parents had known him to be missing.

He didn't even know how long they had travelled the previous day, or what time of day it was. Moist, cool air had begun to filter into the cart through the cracks between the bales, and some light peeked through, so he guessed it was a short time after dawn.

They had to be at least halfway between the thicket and the Realm's capital, but they would still have to make fast pace to get through the city today. It would be a long, rough ride and he wished asked for some padding.

Eventually, he curled himself up in a ball in one corner of his enclosure, with his cloak roughly bundled beneath him, and let the jostling and jolting lull him into a rough sleep.

Chapter Thirteen
VIOLET

Sarah woke Violet after she'd had a mere few hours of sleep. The air in the room had chilled while she slept and she was reluctant to leave her blanket cocoon.

"Lady Violet?" the more recent redhead enquired. "I'm sorry, but Markham is here, it is time for you to leave. Would you like some help dressing?"

Violet shook her head, both to indicate that she could dress alone and to clear her head enough to wake up. Sarah had set out some clothes for her and she hastily slipped into a cream shirt and loose brown trousers. Markham had told her the previous night that she could leave the boarding house dressed as a man as it was unlikely that they would be seen. Plus, it would only add to the disrepute of the situation if someone did happen to see them.

After she had dressed, Markham entered the room and bade Violet to pull her hair away from her face and cover it with her hood, so they wouldn't be immediately identified by anyone who may be out wandering in the dark. When she was ready, she stood by the door to allow the couple a private moment to say their farewells. They both had long days of travel ahead of them and it would be many days before they met again. Apart from the royal family, the couple sharing the room with her might be the only ones in the realm who understood the trouble currently facing the Realm of the Lilies and deserved the opportunity to say a proper farewell.

When the couple turned towards the door, Violet saw a brightness in Sarah's eyes that betrayed the depths of her fears for her fiancé. She gave Violet a fragile smile before bidding them to have a safe journey.

"Thank you, Sarah," Violet said sincerely. "I appreciate that both you and your fiancé are potentially heading into danger. You have left your family and have just bid farewell to your future husband, I will use whatever sway I have to ensure that your sacrifices will not go unrecognised by the royal family."

With that, Violet gave the other woman a squeeze and turned to Markham. Giving his fiancée a final kiss on the cheek, he opened the door just wide enough for them to slip through and made his way stealthily down the corridor. Violet following as quietly as she could behind him, lifting and placing her feet carefully as she was terrified she'd trip on the edge of the carpet.

They left through the back entrance of the boarding house, facing the stables, and moved through the darkness to find their horses. Violet waited, stamping and shivering, while Markham saddled their horses, talking to them quietly as he fitted their bridles. He collected a couple of small saddle bags from a shelf near the horses' heads and secured them to the horses. She'd been told the day before that the packs contained a map of the Realm, enough food for two days and supplies for camping, including a waterproof sheet that could be folded and worn as a raincoat or strung to make a tent.

When the horses were ready, Markham helped Violet mount and led both horses to the stable doors. He slowly scanned the yard through the stable door to ensure that there was no-one watching before leading them out and closing the door behind him. Markham mounted with the same agile grace that he had shown before and took the lead out of the yard of the boarding house.

The town looked different in the dark. The verandahs of the boarding house were deep in shadow, and mist gently kissed the roof. Violet's breath made puffs of steam in front of her face and it wasn't long before her nose was running from the cold. She estimated it would be a couple of hours before the sun rose and shivered. It would be a long time before she got some warmth into her bones.

They rode past the village green and turned onto the road out of town that led directly towards the mountains. They passed a few small businesses and some houses, most of these were still quiet, their occupants warm in their beds. They passed a few outlying houses and then were on the dark, misty road, travelling towards the sun, which was still itself abed behind the mountains.

After an hour of steady riding, Violet's fingers had become so numb that she was having trouble holding the reins and all of her aches and pains from the ride two days past were making themselves known. The bottom of her pelvis was getting very sore and her legs were so stiff she didn't even want to think about walking again. Markham seemed oblivious to her pain and had begun humming to himself quietly as they moved along the dark road.

Cheerful bastard. She groaned. *Why doesn't this world have thermoses and coffee.*

The sky faded from black to steely grey as they reached a small town along the road and the mist began to lift, allowing them to see more than ten metres ahead of them. Light was now showing past the curtains in the houses and smoke was beginning to lazily rise from chimneys, adding to the clouds which were still resting on the rooftops. They threaded their way to the centre of the village and saw an open green space dominated by a statue.

Violet smiled as she watched swallows darting around the statue, rising high and dashing low to catch the insects just above the surface of the grass. She could nearly imagine they were fairies, darting to and fro in an elegant dance to welcome the morning.

"Do you know who the statue is there?" Violet asked quietly.

Markham turned to study the park. "I'm not certain, but it is likely the first king, Raymond Reyne. He was from a village in this county. See the flowers at the bottom of the statue? They are lily-of-the-valley. They grow in every county and inspired the name of our Realm."

Violet had to squint to make out the smear of green dusted with white around the bottom of the statue.

Soon they were through the village and back on the open road, which began to roll gently as they approached the mountains on the eastern border of the kingdom. A short time later Violet's stomach gave a rumble that Markham heard from his position a few metres ahead of her.

"Goodness." He chuckled. "Remind me to make sure you have a good meal before we head into our ambush, otherwise your stomach will warn them of our approach!"

Violet smiled and was grateful when he told her they would stop soon to rest the horses, stretch their legs and fill their bellies.

They stopped at a small grassed area surrounding a well on the edge of a cliff. Violet dismounted with Markham's help and walked over to the edge of the cliff to survey the countryside. The sun had not yet fully risen and there were a few scattered villages and hollows still hiding in shadow and lingering mist.

From the curved cliff face, Violet could survey the land from due west around to the north-east. A thin band of trees flanked the foot of the cliff for a short way and before giving way to paddocks dotted with sheep. Distant stands of trees surrounding the odd chimney and skeins of smoke marked the locations of two or three villages, but the city of

Aquilegia dominated the view.

From the northern point of the cliff, Violet could see the distant wall surrounding the settlement and the early sunlight created sunbursts on the gleaming peaks of the castle towers beyond. It was too distant to make out any further details, but the shining towers sang to her of times gone by in her own world and mysteries as yet unknown. For a moment, she wished that she was heading towards the sparkling city, but a whinny from Star brought her mind back to her task.

"How much further do we have to travel today?" Violet asked when Markham brought her a cup of water and a crisp, juicy apple.

"Still a way, I'm afraid," the soldier replied. "We have further to travel today than yesterday, but we can move faster with just the two of us than we could with the wagons. We should reach Millswood by mid-afternoon. We'll rest there tonight and walk to Dragonhome in the morning. The prince and his kidnappers would have tried to pass through Aquilegia yesterday afternoon at the latest, so they will be entering the mountains sometime today. The road through the mountains is steep and winding, but it will only take a day to travel to the countries beyond."

After adding bread with fruit spread to their breakfast, Violet stiffly climbed back onto her horse, wincing as she settled her back in the saddle. She tried not to watch how smoothly and easily Markham mounted and turned Star back towards the road.

Chapter Fourteen
DANIEL

The second day of travel cramped in the back of the cart was not going well for Daniel's sore muscles.

He had bundled his cloak at least eight different ways so far to try, unsuccessfully, to get comfortable. Thankfully, most of the roads in the realm were well maintained and there weren't very many large potholes to bump and knock him about, but he was still jostled about quite a bit.

Piercing rays of direct sunlight were still sneaking through the gaps on the right hand side of the wagon when he felt them turn and head towards the mountains. The road they followed previously hadn't been completely straight, but Daniel had been travelling the roads of the realm for his entire life and knew the road to Aquilegia, even when he was crammed in the back of a wagon with no view of the landscape outside.

He spent the next few hours of travel imagining the roads ahead, the one to Aquilegia and the pass through the mountains beyond. He had travelled through the eastern pass a few times in his role as an emissary to the lands beyond and had spent several months working with the people of Mellanastia to help them build their nation. He remembered the road through the pass fairly well, but could not think of any good places to stage an escape, nor did he know how his captors would let him travel once they were beyond the capital.

Daniel had to assume that his horse had been left at the farm where they had stopped the first night as Loucius would not want to risk a someone recognising him. Daniel would need to be near somewhere he could get a horse when he snuck away from Loucius and his louts, otherwise he wouldn't get very far.

He guessed they were getting close to the capital when the rolling movement of the cart began to slow and eventually stopped. Daniel heard the muffled voices of his captors through the hay, but he could also hear other voices when he strained his hearing. After a few minutes, the cart rolled forwards a short way and then stop again.

After the cart had moved forward half a dozen times he heard voices speaking to the driver and guessed they were at the front of the line waiting to enter the city. He couldn't completely make out the words but he knew the guard would ask through the usual questions. Where the travellers were coming from and how long they were planning to stay in the city. Daniel knew the questions were more of a formality, but often merely being asked was enough to make travellers think twice about causing trouble within the city walls. The guards generally did not conduct exhaustive searches of the wagons entering the city.

When they hadn't moved off again after a few minutes, Daniel listened more closely to try to work out what might be happening. When he strained his ears, he thought he recognised the voice of one of the city guards. The man was in his early twenties with sandy blonde hair and had been noticed for his leadership skills and having an uncanny knack for detecting trouble. Daniel said a quick prayer of thanks for placing this soldier on the gate. If anyone would sniff out the trouble here, it would be him.

Daniel heard the scrape of the cart's tailgate being opened and prepared to push the bale of hay free, but thought better of it. Instead, he tapped a coded message on the boards of the cart. The soldier stopped talking, then came a quick, coded knock on the tailgate in reply.

Although his voice was muffled, Daniel heard the soldier's next request. "Would you please come into the barracks, bring your wagon and your horses."

Daniel held his breath for a moment, unsure of how his captors would react and then let out a long breath as he felt the cart slowly jostling through the gate and into the barracks.

Daniel's coded message had been short but to the point. "PDR, captive. Take team to guardhouse."

Daniel hoped that the young, bright soldier would understand that this was a matter that needed to be handled delicately. He heard a faint change in the sound of the hooves as they passed under the wall surrounding Aquilegia and felt the cart immediately turn into the yard of the guardhouse. Even though the light in the cart was not abundant, he still noticed that it dimmed further after a few minutes.

He heard the bang of a great door closing, followed by a shout directed at the soldier. They were enacting a well-practiced routine of senior captain berating lowly guard to put Daniel's captors at ease. While the senior officer shouted at the young soldier, making their suspects relax, other soldiers would be surrounding them. And the senior officer would be identifying any illicit schemes.

In this case, the charade was short. Within a minute, the two soldiers had gone around the whole cart with the senior shouting the whole time. The captain finally asked the captives to show their weapons before they would be allowed to head off to conduct their business.

A moment later, Daniel heard the catches of the tailgate being pulled released and the hay bale at the end began to wriggle from its place.

"Hey," Loucius shouted. "I thought we were free to leave."

"I'm afraid that isn't quite the case," Daniel called from inside the cart. "Sorry, about that."

Finally, the hay bale was removed from the end of the cart and Daniel inelegantly slid his way the length of the cart and half-rolled out of the end. His stretched his cramped limbs with a grunt and turned to find Loucius, whose face was red and puffed with anger.

"I'm very sorry, sir. This 'Little Prince' does not wish to be a member of your company any longer, but perhaps you would like to take advantage of some special accommodation of mine?"

Daniel turned to the captain on duty at the guardhouse and noticed his look of shock, which matched that on the face of the soldier who had become aware of his plight. Quickly, he summarised the situation for them and asked for a horse as he wanted to get to the palace as soon as was possible.

"Sir, if I might make a suggestion," said the young soldier, as Daniel's limbs were cut free of his Loucius's ropes. "It might also be wise to take a tabard and dress as a soldier, you are not exactly as... tidy... as you usually are for public appearances."

Daniel looked down at himself and noticed the layer of dirt and dust on his clothing. When he thought about, he could also feel bits of hay in his hair. He made a mental note to make sure that the soldier was promoted before asking for a cloak and helm to travel to the castle. Daniel left instructions for the Aramalian prisoners to be transported to the cells in the castle and set off in that direction himself.

Once again, Daniel found himself travelling absent-mindedly as he tried to decide where he should go from Aquilegia. He didn't know whether to travel back to Wynbourne to find Violet and his parents or stay where he was and let the Aramalian plotters think he was still in captivity. He needed to speak with the castle chief and find out what information his parents had given about his whereabouts.

He took a circuitous route through the city to the castle, to further throw off anyone who might suspect he was back, and finally entered the castle though a side gate, surprising the guard on duty with his appearance. Daniel stabled the horse and headed towards his chambers to refresh himself, asking a maid to send word to the chief to call upon him there.

He was just sinking into a steaming hot bath to soak out all the aches from the cart travel when he heard a polite knock on the door and called out for the castle chief to enter. A middle-aged man with long, wispy, fading brown hair and beard entered, his white shirt stretched across his ample belly and his trousers sitting beneath it.

"I beg your pardon, your highness. Would you like me to return later?" asked the man, when he saw that the prince was bathing.

"No thank you, Sir Whittington," the Prince replied. "I think I need to move quickly today and will only stay at the castle until I decide where I must go next. Please, tell me what has transpired in the Realm in the last couple of days and the nature of any messages that the king has sent."

Whittington took a seat in an easy chair a short distance from the bath, close enough to see the prince while he spoke, but far enough away to give him some privacy. Then began to detail what correspondence he had received in the previous few days. Daniel had only been held captive for just over one day, so there was not much to tell, but everything he told was important.

The previous evening, Whittington had received a message via carrier pigeon that he should ensure all of the guards on the gates into and out of the city should be extra vigilant for the new few days, but had not been told what they should look for.

That morning, he had received a message from the king and queen, saying that the Lady Violet was travelling to meet Prince Daniel at Oakville, with Captain Markham as an escort. Daniel could only assume that this information had been sent on the off chance that Daniel managed to get free of his captors as Violet's name was not known around the castle. He pondered why they might have chosen to send her to Oakville. *Maybe they wanted to keep her out of the way until I was found.*

Another message had come from the queen, asking her personal maid to prepare her wardrobe for travel to Aramalia and ensure that light dresses were packed for the hotter climate.

A final message had come late that day saying that the king and queen would set out from Wynbourne the following day to return to Aquilegia and prepare for the diplomatic trip across Mellanastia and Aramalia.

Daniel allowed all of this information to soak into his mind as he soaked his sore, bruised body.

"Thank you, Whittington," Daniel said. "I shall ponder on my plans from here. Could you please ask for some dinner to be sent up to my rooms in about an hour and a boy from the pigeon loft to carry a message for me at around the same time?"

The castle chief nodded to the prince and excused himself as Daniel finished scrubbing off the dirt from the cart ride before climbing out of the bath. A full-length mirror in his room showed that his hip and ribcage were bruised on his right side where he had been shoved into the cart on his first day of captivity. His left side only had a few sore spots thanks to the padding of his cloak, even though he had lain on that side for most of the second day.

He dressed in a loose shirt and trousers and sat down at

the writing desk in his study while he thought through his plans. Eventually he decided that he would travel to Oakville the next day to collect Violet and then they would return to Aquilegia together to await the arrival of his parents so they could work together on a plan for the upcoming diplomatic trip.

With that decided he settled in to wait for his dinner and wondered what to do with Loucius.

Chapter Fifteen
VIOLET

It was late afternoon when Violet and Markham reached Millswood. The barracks yard was dusty from soldiers finishing their drills and packing up to prepare for dinner, and only the two guards at the gates stood still amid the flurry.

The travellers stopped when they reached the gates and Markham twitched his cloak to show his rank and held out the letter detailing that he was on a mission set by King Cameron. The two guards made way for the pair and directed them to a two-story, stone building with a carved door and the fleur-de-lis flag of the realm at the peak of the building.

They crossed to the stables, dismounted and handed their reins to the waiting stable boys. Violet stretched her stiff back and side muscles and then tried to work out how to walk normally while keeping the discomfort in her legs to a minimum.

Markham was courteous enough to match Violet's slow pace as they crossed the marshalling yard to the two story building. They were greeted by a young lieutenant who led them through the lavishly appointed, but sparsely furnished, building to the office of the Lieutenant Colonel in command of the Millswood barracks.

The man behind the broad, darkly polished desk set an imposing figure with the late afternoon sunshine flowing in from the window behind him. He had a broad nose, set above a wide salt-and-pepper moustache and he was leaning his elbows on the desk with his fingers steepled in front of his face. Calluses on his fingers and muscular shoulders showed that he still spent time in the training yard on a daily basis and Violet felt sorry for the young recruits who came to him. He looked like a hard commander.

Markham led Violet into the room and snapped his heels together and his hand to his forehead in a smart, sharp salute. The Lieutenant Colonel acknowledged his deference with a nod, gestured for them to sit in two low-backed chairs opposite him and motioned for silence as he accepted the papers in Markham's hand and read them.

The Lieutenant Colonel cleared his throat.

"I would like to begin by welcoming you to our barracks here, Lady Violet," he said in a husky voice. "I am an old dog teaching new tricks to our young ones, but I know when to treat a beautiful lady with the honour and respect that she deserves. You may have rooms within this building for as long as you need to stay here with us. I will ensure that a maid stays on to assist you as you need."

Violet found herself blushing at the words of the old soldier who sat before her and thanked him for his consideration.

"My name is Graeme Wolfwood, I have been leading here at Millswood for nearly fifteen years. Prior to that I was a soldier in the king's household, much as this young fellow here is now. After training up some new recruits there, I was recognised for my ability to polish even the roughest street urchin into a reputable soldier, so I was sent here to train the new recruits and manage our relations with Dragonhome.

"And it is these very relations with Dragonhome that you need to rely on now, it seems," he said, turning to

Markham. "The king must see some great trouble rising in the Kingdom to ask the Dragons for help?"

"I am sorry, sir, but if the king did not detail the trouble we are facing in that letter, then I do not feel it is my place to say."

Wolfwood's moustache turned up at the edges as he smiled.

"As you should feel, youngling, I confess that I was testing you. What would you ask of me under the king's command?"

"I would ask to be conveyed to Dragonhome early on the morrow. We hope they will grant us some assistance in our task."

"Certainly," Wolfwood acceded, nodding. "But, if I might make a suggestion? The dragons tend to rise with the sun and leave to hunt shortly thereafter. They often don't return until quite late in the day. I would recommend that you make the journey there tonight. It will only take a few hours, they have beds to spare and someone can ask a dragon to stay and hear the request of the king in the morning."

Violet sighed audibly at the thought of more time on the road that day and slouched her shoulders as much as she was able to within the confines of her corset. Wolfwood raised his eyebrows querulously, prompting an explanation from Violet.

"I fear that I have spent many more hours on horseback in the last few days than I am generally used to and I hurt."

"Might I ask," Wolfwood began. "Did you happen to travel through a thicket in the south-eastern quarter of our Realm?"

Violet started and Markham stiffened.

"Don't worry," the Lieutenant Colonel soothed. "I spent some of my own young days down in that green swathe and nothing gave you away save a few differences in your bearing and mannerisms.

"I made many advances in my career by being observant and trusting my intuition. You look much more comfortable in trousers than many ladies from these parts would be. I am guessing you have recently entered our realm and were quickly introduced to horse riding and have barely been out of the saddle since."

Violet nodded tiredly.

"I will confess that a few of my old muscles now cramp and tighten on a regular basis and I have an excellent masseuse on my staff. I will loan you her services for a time this afternoon while supplies are prepared for the next stage of your journey," he offered kindly.

Violet could barely find the words to express her thanks but before she had time to fumble out the words she did have, he was shooing them out of his office to be shown to their quarters in the house.

Markham left Violet at the door to her chamber, explaining that they had a few hours to spare before they needed to leave. It was a two-hour walk, but it should be fairly smooth going and they would be able to travel after nightfall as it would be a clear night. He took his leave with a quick bow and Violet found herself in yet another unfamiliar room, but at least she had complete privacy in that one, unlike the night before.

She crossed the room and sat in a tall armchair in a bay window overlooking the training yard and past the gate to the village beyond. Soldiers were beginning to enter the dining hall as she tugged her feet free from her boots, wrinkling her nose as she caught a waft of sweaty feet from them. She sat back in the chair, upright, of course, thanks to the blasted corset. She felt dusty, dirty and in need of a bath and was ready to shed the trousers and shirt that she had donned before spending the whole day in the saddle. The cream coloured shirt was now light ochre and her trousers were crumpled and creased with sweat from human and horse.

Having realised this, Violet quickly stood and searched the room for her belongings, a tightly packed bag had rested behind her on Star as they had travelled that day and Violet thought it must be close. She finally located it on a small table near the door and went over to rifle through the carefully folded clothes to find a dressing gown.

Within minutes she was sitting in the armchair, this time wrapped in the soft, silky dressing gown and comfortably slouched. She spent a few moments doing her best impression of a sloth before calling her eyes back to focus on the world before her again. The yard was quiet now, with most of the soldiers in the dining hall, filling their bellies. Two new soldiers were replacing those on the gate, allowing those being relieved to eat their fill.

Beyond the gates was Millswood itself, a neat array of houses and businesses with another grand house, presumably another home for the royal family, nestled at the foot of the mountains which overshadowed the whole village.

Violet's gaze was just roaming up to find the top of the great monoliths before her, when there was a rap on the door.

Violet rose gingerly and stiffly made her way across the room. By the time she reached the door, she had managed to unfold herself, was nearly completely upright and almost walking normally. She made sure that her robe was covering the important parts and opened the door to find a little crone waiting for her.

An old, bent woman gave her a gap-toothed grin and asked the younger woman to follow her.

"I'm sorry," Violet started. "Where are we going?"

"We are going to make sure that you can still walk when next you climb down off a horse. But you are free to stay here if you prefer, Lady," said the crone, again flashing her grin.

Violet guessed the little old woman to be an assistant to the masseuse and closed the door to her rooms before following her, slowly, down the hallway.

Chapter Sixteen
VIOLET

The old woman led Violet down the stairs to a small, dark chamber which looked as though it was set up for torture. A miscellany of small bottles with shaped stoppers lined a series of shelves hung on the wall behind a workbench and dried herbs and leaves hung from the ceiling above. A mortar and pestle rested towards the rear of the bench, and bowls, knives and spoons were laid out on the workspace.

The opposite wall was set with shelves that held folded towels, sheets and blankets, but the far wall held an alarming assortment of wooden tools and implements. In the centre of the room was what Violet assumed to be the massage table. It was a large slab of wood, held at about hip height by great, thick legs. The top of the table was narrow and had a hollow carved in the far end with a hole to breathe through and a plush towel spread across the surface.

"Onto the table," commanded the wizened little lady.

Violet went to climb up on the table but the old lady stalled her.

"Take off the robe," she ordered, crankily.

Violet self-consciously removed her robe and lay face down on the table. While she waited, she heard scraping, the tinkling of little bottles and the leaves overhead rustling. After a few minutes, she felt the crone's bony fingers poking around on her back.

It quickly became clear that the woman was the masseuse when she started working her strong fingers into all the knots and painful spots in Violet's body. She massaged Violet's muscles with an oil that felt a bit rough and prickly on her skin, and smelled of oregano and eucalyptus. Her ministrations brought soothing warmth into her muscles, even as it also brought on sharp spikes of pain.

Over the course of about half an hour, the masseuse worked her way across the back of Violet's legs to the base of her buttocks. She then moved to Violet's shoulders, where she found every knot Violet had developed through her days in the saddle and worked them free.

She found a particularly painful spot on the right hand side of Violet's back, just below her rib cage. It felt like she poked around there for at least five minutes, sending pain shooting down Violet's spine before she moved on. Every place that she had worked on was left with a lingering dull ache, but also blissful warmth which Violet attributed to the massage oil.

Finally, after what seemed like hours of torture, the crone pronounced that she was done.

"Girl, you are going to ache for a while, but you should be able to sit the saddle better when next you ride."

The crone turned back to her workbench and pottered around with some pots and bottles while Violet slowly stood and put her robe back on. Her muscles did ache, but the tension in her shoulders and back had been relieved and she felt as though she could stand straighter than before.

The older woman shuffled to the door and led Violet back down the hallways to her room. She turned when they reached the chamber's door and offered Violet a small glass jar.

"Here," she said, sounding kinder than she had earlier. "This salve will help as well. Apply it wherever you can reach and it will work through your muscles. It won't be as good as a full massage, but it will help ease you at the end of each day and make it possible to continue riding."

Violet gave her a curtsey and her deepest gratitude for the kind, although painful, treatment of her sore muscles and closed the door to her room as the masseuse turned and shuffled back down the passageway. Violet could still hear the soft whispering of the old lady's feet as she made her way back through the building.

Violet was once again faced with a short time for rest and an unfamiliar bed, but she decided to make the most of it. Still in her dressing gown, she quickly crossed the room and dove into the bed, burrowing the still-warm muscles of her body between the tightly tucked sheets and burying her head in the gap between the three pairs of pillows. After a few moments, the air began to foul, so she pulled her head to the surface, tossed one pillow to the floor, then placed her head square on one and balanced another over her eyes so that she was blocking out most of the light, but could still breathe freely.

Despite the fact that she was terribly worried about their walk to Dragonhome and the travel that would come after, Violet felt her eyelids drooping. She had been up for a long time that day after having very little sleep and was tired to a point where she nearly couldn't think straight. Only a few minutes passed between when she closed her eyes and when she fell into a deep sleep.

An insistent knocking woke her up, the banging interspersed with Markham calling, "Lady Violet."

She rubbed her eyes, blinked a few times and rolled onto her belly before calling out to Markham that she was awake.

"My Lady," the soldier called through the closed door. "We must leave shortly, but the Lieutenant Colonel has had an informal dinner set for us. Please, prepare yourself and join us as soon as you can."

Violet called out her agreement and reluctantly climbed out of the plush nest she had created. The sun looked to only be about half an hour from the horizon and she guessed that she might have been asleep for two hours. *Still not long enough.*

She held an inner debate about whether to wear trousers or a dress for the evening outing. She knew they would be walking the rest of the way and that it must be a fairly easy walk for Wolfwood to suggest they travel at night. She thought that trousers should be acceptable, but didn't know who would be escorting them and whether they might take offence at such attire. In the end, she decided that a dress was the best option.

She opened the window briefly to get a sense of how warm it was outside and felt an oncoming chill in the air. She selected a thick cotton dress, light blue in colour, with simple embroidery at the cuffs and a demure neckline. She wore a light petticoat under it, but placed a thicker one at the top of her pack to add later if she needed it, although she doubted that she would as she always got quite hot when she was exercising. She placed her navy blue cloak over her pack and left them by the door of her room before heading to dinner.

The evening meal was much simpler than the one she had shared with the royal family, but still tasty. The single course meal consisted of roast lamb and vegetables. It was succulent, fresh and seasoned with thyme from the kitchen garden. Violet had always loved home-cooked food and she was well satisfied.

They did not linger at the dinner table after they had filled their bellies, instead taking their leave to collect their belongings and head for the stables. When Violet looked askance at Markham, he explained

"Horses don't like travelling near Dragonhome, but there are some ponies that they use to carry packs and supplies. We'll take one of them for our bags.

"It is not an arduous walk, but neither is it a short one. We should do anything we can to lighten our loads for the evening."

"We've also already had quite a long day," Violet added.

Star gave a little whinny of greeting when they entered the stables and Violet found she was a little sad to be leaving the horse behind. She walked up to the mare and gave her a rub on the nose and told her that she hoped she would be back to see her again soon.

Markham heard the quietly mumbled words and smiled as he walked towards them.

"I see that although you are not comfortable with riding yet, you have still found love for your horse," he said quietly as he drew alongside her.

"Well, I think she is a beautiful and kind-hearted girl, it's not her fault I don't know how to ride," Violet replied as she kept rubbing the mare on her face and neck.

Their guide called out to them that the ponies were ready and it was time for them to leave, pulling them out of their quiet conversation. Violet gave Star a quick kiss on her nose and Markham gave his horse a quick farewell too, then they left the stables and crossed the yard to the gate.

Lieutenant Colonel Wolfwood waited at the gate to wish them a safe journey in the twilight. The sun had just dropped below the horizon to their right, but there was still a pale glow across the sky and there were not yet many stars to see.

"Travel safely and best of luck with your journey. I hope the Dragons are receptive and helpful, and that you succeed with your mission." Wolfwood said to Markham, before turning to Violet and grasping her hand to kiss it in farewell. "Lady Violet, it has been a pleasure to meet you. I hope that I will get many other opportunities to host you in this humble village and learn more about you and your enigmatic presence here."

With those words, he snapped a salute, which Markham quickly returned and Violet found that they were on the road, yet again.

Chapter Seventeen
DANIEL

Daniel finished his dinner and dressed warmly before leaving his rooms. The cells were the coldest part of the castle at that time of year.

Unlike most prison cells, the ones in the Aquilegian castle had large windows, with widely spaced bars, the better for the captives to see the Realm displayed before them. They were located in the top of one of the highest towers of the royal family's residence in the capital. When the castle had been built, King Raymond had specified that those in the cells should still be able to see the world from their prison. They should be able to feel the beautiful, fresh spring air and the clear, cold spring nights. Those who thought that this was only a mild punishment were reminded that prisoners were also exposed to the first winter snows and sweltering summer days.

The first King had been a cunning man.

Daniel knew that when the spring bulbs were beginning to flower, evenings in the cells were bitterly cold, so he layered on thick trousers and a warm cloak. He passed the guards on the way up to the tower and removed his weapons at their station on the entry to the cells. As Crown Prince, this was not his normal practice but he knew enough of Loucius that he didn't want to allow the villain any opportunity to bring him harm. However, he did remove a staff from the rack at the guard station as he didn't want to go in completely unprotected.

The guard on duty led him down a corridor, lined with several cells doors that were flung wide and a few others that were tightly closed. The other members of Loucius's party had also been transferred to the castle and were being kept in separate cells. They had been afforded a bit more luxury than their ringleader, as they at least had a hessian bed frame and a couple of blankets. Loucius's cell had been stripped before he entered and he had had his own clothes and boots removed and searched for any hidden pockets before he had been allowed to redress, minus his boots.

Loucius was sitting by the window when Daniel entered the cell.

"Ah, Prince Daniel," he drawled. "how kind of you to join me in my quarters. I would offer you a seat, but, alas, I haven't any to spare."

"Never mind, Loucius, I'm sure I can manage to stand. I'll admit to having a few too many bruises to make sitting entirely comfortable at this point in time, all thanks to you and yours."

"I'm always happy to oblige," Loucius said with a nod of his head in Daniel's direction.

"I'm terribly sorry to have thwarted your plan to undermine the stability of our Kingdom, although I must admit that I am happy to see you on the other side of captivity. Now, is there anything that you would like to tell me that might encourage me to give you a few more... comforts?"

"I can't imagine what you think I might be able to tell you," said the criminal. "I was acting under duress, my family is being held by the Aramalian Sha'a and I was simply acting on her orders to keep them safe."

He said the last with a wry smile, and Daniel couldn't tell whether he was being truthful. His instinct said no, but his integrity told him to always listen to both sides of the story.

"Do you know if there were any other plans made in case

you failed in your mission?" Daniel asked.

"I'm afraid not," said the Aramalian. "I was always of the opinion that I would succeed."

Ego. Man's greatest downfall.

"Did you have means of communicating whether everything was going to plan with my capture?"

Loucius watched Daniel for a moment, calculating, before answering.

"Each nightly checkpoint we were aiming for has a cache of birds. We were to send a bird back to the Sha'a each morning before setting off."

Daniel quickly devised a plan.

"If you will write notes for me and detail the whereabouts of each of your stop points, I will see to it that you have some more comforts in this tower. When we have finished our task in Aramalia, I may allow you a choice between a cell and joining the monks at Oakville, but this offer will only be made when I am sure that your missives and your information were sound and my family has returned safely to the Realm of the Lilies."

Loucius looked out the window. His cell looked to the east and the mountains that blocked any view of his homeland. He placed a hand on one of the bars before turning back to Daniel.

"And what of my family?" Loucius asked.

Daniel considered this for a few minutes.

"If we continue the missives from your checkpoints, your family should be safe until we reach Aramalia and I show myself. Your ruler should have no reason to harm them. If they truly are captive, I will ensure that they are given the chance to leave your home country and I will see them safe. Whether you see them again depends on your cooperation."

Loucius nodded, thought another moment and then agreed with Daniel's plan.

Daniel pushed away from the wall and asked the guard

without to open the door. "See that Loucius gets some extra sacking to lay on, but no bed, I don't trust him enough for that yet." He turned to a page who was waiting nearby. "Please ask for a scribe to come up here with plenty of paper and a pen. Ensure that the scribe who comes is able to read Aramalian script and if the messages that Loucius writes are coded, he is to get a copy of the code scribed as well."

Loucius looked momentarily crestfallen at the last part, but held himself tall again after a moment.

"Loucius, I shall see you in the morning, before I leave to join my family," Daniel finished

Loucius nodded towards the Prince as he turned and left the cell, ensuring that the guard locked the door firmly behind him.

Chapter Eighteen
DANIEL

Daniel rose slowly from his bed. As he had predicted, it had gotten very cold outside overnight and the air in his room was chilly, although not so cold that he could see the air puff out of his lungs as he sometimes could in the depths of winter.

He walked over to his windows and threw the curtains open, letting the early morning sunlight stream in to puddle at his feet and slowly warm his toes and the flagstones beneath them. His bedroom looked to the south over a distant forest, with a view to the foothills climbing up to the mountains in the east.

He dressed quickly in thick trousers and sturdy boots that did not advertise his role. There was the unpleasant possibility that the Aramalian Sha'a had more spies in his land and did not want to risk exposing that the role of captor and captive had been reversed.

Once dressed, Daniel moved through his suite to his study and found a collection of papers waiting for him. Sir Whittington had placed another missive from his parents on the desk, which stated they would leave Wynbourne for Aquilegia that day, stopping at their usual boarding house overnight. Another stack of papers were the letters from Loucius to his ruler, in the order they should be released, the top page showing the cipher for the messages.

Daniel rang a bell on the wall next to his desk and waited

for a servant to come.

"Please send word down to the main guardhouse asking them to send Lieutenant Leo Lis to me," Daniel asked. "I have a job for him. I would also like some supplies to be prepared for a day's travel and a horse readied, I will be leaving Aquilegia in a few hours."

The page nodded and left the room as Daniel drew some fresh sheets of paper from a drawer on his desk and began writing out instructions for the young lieutenant.

Daniel was roused from his work by a knock on the door about an hour later. He called for the newcomer to enter, then gestured for the young soldier to select some bread and spread from the platter that was still at his elbow. The kitchen staff had sent up so much food that it looked as though Daniel had barely touched it, despite his ravenous feasting.

"My apologies for keeping you waiting, Your Highness," said the soldier from the gate the previous day.

"Lieutenant Lis," Daniel said. "Please, don't concern yourself about the wait, and you may call me Prince Daniel."

The lieutenant nodded and awaited further instruction.

"I am setting you a special task," Daniel began. "As you know, I was recently at the forced hospitality of an Aramalian man. I suspect that my capture was meant to undermine the summit in Aramalia to cement Mellanastia as a nation. Loucius is now working with me to convince his leaders that I am still their prisoner. He has given me information on his camp sites and penned letters to send each night.

"I would like you to travel to the places Loucius has

detailed, in the schedule he has outlined—although you will now be a day later than the original plan—and send off his messages. You may select men to accompany you along the way, I estimate that you will need about twenty as you may face other armed men along the way. Do you feel as though you can achieve this?"

"Yes, sir," said Lis. "Thank you, sir."

They spent an hour running through the plan in detail. The soldier's rank only just qualified him for a mission of this nature, but Daniel trusted his abilities, especially since he had been instrumental in releasing Daniel from captivity.

Once the two had finished their briefing, the Lieutenant left with a smart salute and instructions to be on the road within the next two hours. He was aiming to be at Loucius's next stop point before sunset so they'd have plenty of light on their side if it came to an attack.

It was nearing midday when Daniel returned to his chambers to prepare for the ride to Oakville, so he called for a quick lunch to be sent to the stables. He wasn't planning to rush his ride, but wanted to avoid stopping as much as possible, so he judged a quick meal to be wise. The message from his parents said Violet would be stopping in Leeside the previous night and heading to Ivywood that day. He had a little further to travel than she to reach that same stopping point tonight and less time to do it in, but he could travel faster than Violet and the escort he hoped his parents had given her.

He was wearing brown trousers, soft leather boots and a white, open necked shirt, unknowingly echoing the clothes Violet had changed into when she had entered his realm. He returned to his study and stuffed his copy of the plan for Lis's travels into his satchel.

Daniel found a beef roll for him in the stables, along with the customary saddle bags with supplies. He kept his satchel over his shoulder and slung a small pack with spare clothes behind the saddle before mounting.

The castle chief had come out to farewell him and Daniel left him with some parting instructions. "Please continue with preparations for my parent's arrival tomorrow and keep my stay here as quiet as you possibly can. I shall return with my parents and with another guest tomorrow. Please have one of my guest chambers prepared for a lady visitor."

Sir Whittington nodded his acquiescence and stepped back to allow Daniel to leave the mounting yard.

Daniel's progress through Aquilegia was slow as the streets were busy with people returning home from the bi-weekly markets. The streets were packed with carts and wagons filled with freshly purchased produce. Although he used a few of his shortcuts, it still took nearly an hour–almost twice as long as usual–to cross his home city.

Once he hit the open road, Daniel had no choice but to travel quickly, he had only five hours of daylight left and the ride from Aquilegia to Ivywood took eight and a half hours at a moderate pace. The scenery flew by as he alternated between a gallop and a steady canter to keep his horse from tiring too quickly. He stopped only a couple of times at streams beside the road to allow himself and his horse to drink.

Despite these efforts, the sun was setting when he approached the turn off to Ivywood. The last rays of the sun were turning the sky a brilliant peach colour, with a few clouds brightening to red, when Daniel left the road to Port Town for the one to Ivywood and Oakville

It was several hours past dinner time and Daniel's stomach had long passed the rumbling phase when he finally reached Ivywood. Daniel headed straight towards the manor where the royal family usually resided for the summer months. He had no doubt that word of Violet's arrival would have been sent ahead to the manor and rooms would have been prepared for her there.

Daniel rode straight around to the stables, handing the reins to a stable hand before striding through the servant's entrance into the manor itself.

The manor here was much less regal than the one in Wynbourne, lacking the grand entryway of the other home. Instead, the main doors led into a square vestibule with a staircase on the left hand that wound its way up to the second story. Daniel rang a bell in the entry way, rousing the butler from his nook.

The tall, skinny man was shocked to find the Prince standing before him and stammered an apology for keeping him waiting.

"Don't worry about that, please have a meal prepared for me in my study and have someone escort me to Lady Violet's rooms."

The butler nodded and a maid quickly arrived to lead him up the stairs to the guest chambers at the far end of the building. The maid told him that the lady had arrived about an hour before dinner, eaten alone in her rooms and not asked for much except bathing water and solitude.

The maid knocked on the door and called out, "My lady, you have a visitor."

"Please, give them my regards, but I do not wish to be seen until the morning."

Daniel thought something in her voice sounded strange and called out himself. "Violet. Please. It's me, Daniel."

There was a sound in the room as if something had been dropped and a little squeak of surprise.

"P-Prince Daniel?" she squeaked.

"Of course."

"Please, give me a moment."

Daniel agreed and told the maid to return to her duties. She looked a bit disgruntled to be giving up her role of chaperone, but did not argue. Daniel sat on a seat in the hall until he heard a voice call out to him.

He entered the room slightly anxious, he did not know what sort of reception he'd receive. *Given I left out a few details of my life, had her follow me into my world and then got kidnapped... it's probably not going to be all hugs and 'oh how I've missed you.'*

When he entered, she was standing by the window, facing the thick brocade curtains that were already drawn against the night's chill. The soft glow of the lamp next to her picked up all the golden highlights in her red hair and set the ribbon detail on her dress to shimmer.

"Violet," he started as she turned around, his heart thumping in his chest, "I am so glad—"

But his sentence was cut short as the redhead by the window turned and he realised that it was not Violet who stood before him.

"Sarah?"

Chapter Nineteen
VIOLET

Violet desperately tried to conceal how heavily she was breathing as they moved further up the mountain towards Dragonhome. She had not considered herself unfit, but a short way into their walk she'd gotten short of breath.

They had been on the road long enough to witness a startling moonrise. The great white orb had risen before them and cast a clear, white light across their path. The way was smooth and not particularly steep, but the climb was steady and her legs were starting to ache. She had started an inner monologue of very harsh words for Daniel when she finally found him. So far his world had given her aching muscles and very little sleep.

Violet's inner tirade was getting fairly heated when Markham called out that they were due for a rest break and their guide directed them to a circle of benches in a clear, flat area. Violet had fallen behind even the ponies as she struggled to continue up the slope, so she was last to sit. Markham brought her a glass bottle of water and some sweet bread to snack on.

The lieutenant sat next to Violet and waited for her breathing to calm before trying to speak to her.

"These last few days have not been what you expected, have they?" he asked.

"I didn't really expect anything. I've been beyond expectations since I walked up to that stupid tree. I don't quite wish that I hadn't come to this world, yet, but I am certainly not the happiest camper right now."

Markham looked a bit puzzled at her peculiar saying, but her meaning was quite clear. He couldn't think of a way to help her, so he simply left the refreshments on the bench beside her and wandered off to admire the view of the land laid out before them.

Violet sat in silence while she drank the fresh, cool water, then came to a decision. She had set out with Markham to find Daniel. *Once the dirty rat of a... Daniel. Once Daniel is safe, I'll decide what to do.*

She resigned herself to being out in the wilderness, hiking up a mountain to see Dragons.

Probably still less insane than working in the ED on a full moon.

Suddenly, she remembered the magic of her necklace. She carefully undid the clasp and pulled the delicate chain away from her neck. She cupped the pendant in her hands and thought of Daniel, then began to gently shake the charm. This time, the heat in her hands started slowly, spreading through her fingertips and slowly retracting into the pendant.

She opened her palms and was surprised to find that instead of pointing up the mountain range to her right, the pendant pointed nearly directly in front of her. She looked at it for a moment, puzzled, then stood. She wound her way between the other benches and past the ponies, trying not to twist the direction of the pendant in her hands.

She approached the edge of the cliff face adjacent to their picnic area carefully and looked from her palm to the realm, trying to work out what where it was pointing.

Markham approached her. "Is something wrong?"

Violet wasn't quite sure how to explain, so she simply pointed ahead and asked, "What's out there?"

"Well," he said. "Our path curved a little, so Millswood is

down there and a little to our left. You can see the towers of Aquilegia off to our right and out that way, ahead of us, is Ivywood, then Oakville."

"Oh," said Violet. "I must have done it wrong. The king said I would be able to find Daniel with this necklace and I thought it worked before, but I guess I did it wrong and I've found the monks instead."

"Unfortunately, I can't be any help with mysticism," Markham said, ruefully.

Violet shrugged and went back to her bench to rest her muscles until the break was over.

After about fifteen minutes, the guide grouped the ponies together again and prepared them for the second leg of their journey. Violet's abusive inner monologue had waned and she switched to a positive one for herself to keep up her spirits as they walked up the last part of the mountain.

The image that helped her rally the most was that of the soft, warm bed that Markham had promised was at the end of this part of the journey.

Duck down pillows and thick, fluffy blankets and maybe some really soft pyjamas. She, well, it would normally be daydreamed, but it was night time.

"You are a strong young lady," Markham said as they set off.

Her daydream-in-darkness shattered, it took her a moment to comprehend his words.

"Thank you," Violet said, a smile flitting across her flushed face. "I have had to be, at times. I lost my parents when I was only a teenager and I have been by myself for a long time."

"That must have been hard," the soldier said, his voice soft.

She smiled.

"It was. Really hard at times. But I kept getting up and

going every morning with the help of a little saying I made up."

She paused and caught her breath before continuing.

"I choose to live for those who don't have a choice," she said. "Too many people, my parents included, have their lives cut much shorter than they wanted them to be. They leave the world with so many things unsaid and so many achievements unreached. I feel that it would be a waste if I did not keep trying on their behalf."

She gave a little shrug and a smile as she said the last part, feeling a bit foolish, but the moonlight showed on a pensive expression on Markham's face. After a time, he spoke.

"That is true on this world too, Lady Violet. I have seen many things in my relatively few years and have been fortunate enough to live in peaceful times. I know a bit about your world from tales Prince Daniel has told me and I know that you have a greater ability to keep people alive, but you also have greater dangers. I think I can understand your views."

They walked in comfortable silence for a time, Markham offering his arm to steady Violet when her legs started to get too tired to hold her. Fortunately, as the moon was heading towards its zenith, the ground began to level out and the guide paused and pointed.

"That is the entrance to Dragonhome," he said, gesturing to a great, dark cave before them. "At the moment, it will be stiflingly hot in there from the breath of nearly eighty sleeping dragons, but come morning, it will be safe for you to enter. The boarding house is this way."

They followed the rock wall to the left of the cave where the pine trees that had been lining the path thinned out. Sheltered on the far left were the stables and ahead was a long, ranch style building. Their guide let out a high-pitched whistle, drawing a stable hand and soldier from the boarding house. The guide took the ponies and Markham turned towards the soldier and saluted.

"Kindest greetings," said Markham, after introducing himself and Violet. "We are hoping to take some of your comforts and ask for your help."

"Of course," the young soldier replied. "I am Lieutenant Daniel Aurekio. What can we do for you?"

Violet leant against a verandah post while the two soldiers talked and lamented that all of the masseuse's hard work had probably been undone. She was also worried that there would be more muscles adding themselves to the list of complainants in the morning.

After a few minutes of talking, Lieutenant Aurekio noticed Violet's difficulties and interrupted the planning to ask for her to be shown to a room.

"Violet," Markham said gently. "Follow this man to your room and rest for tonight. Someone will alert the dragons to our need and they will wait for us. You may sleep long and late."

Violet nodded dozily before following the other man to a room. She was too tired to take in much detail of the room, only noticing the split-log walls before spotting the bed. It lived up to her dream of being large, plush and covered in blankets that she was almost certain would be too warm for comfort.

She struggled out of her laces and layers and managed to get into a light cotton shift after rubbing herself with the masseuse's salve. She fell into the bed where she contrarily woke up because the sheets were too cold and her muscles were too sore for sleep. She sighed at the irony and turned to thinking about Daniel.

She considered trying the necklace again, but knew it would be no good, as her sense of direction had been completely turned around in the last part of the journey when the path had started to switch back on itself. She was sure she had done the spell exactly the same as before and hoped she hadn't been wrong the first time too, as the king and queen had acted on her guidance.

She lay in bed worrying for a while until the blankets got warm enough to help her sore muscles relax and gently lull her to sleep.

Chapter Twenty
DANIEL

It was past midnight when Daniel returned to the road that would lead him straight to Leeside.

He had allowed himself a short rest break to eat a light dinner before asking for another horse so he could continue riding into the night. Since leaving Ivywood, he had only stopped once to allow the horse to drink and catch its breath. The moon was now high overhead and the midnight shadows of the trees were puddled at the base of their trunks like discarded petticoats as Daniel raced to beat the morning to Leeside.

His mind, however, was racing in circles. Where was Violet? What were his parents doing? Was he heading in the right direction? *Where could Violet be?*

Each question had several possible solutions and he knew that most of them would be answered in a few hours when he reached Leeside, but his nerves were chafing at the time it would take to reach them. He had to refrain from urging his horse to run as fast as it could, knowing that it would only be a short gain and ultimately he was better off maintaining a steady pace.

At some point during the ride, he felt the prickling, squeezing sensation that he had felt previously and realised Violet was trying to locate him again. He didn't know a way to reverse the magic and find her, if that was even possible, so he turned his mind back to trying to work out where his parents might have sent her.

All Sarah Courts had been able to tell him was that Violet and Markham had been sent to search for him, but she did not know where they had headed when they left Leeside in the middle of the night. Eventually, Daniel decided to stop speculating and focused solely on the road ahead of him, all the options were making his head spin and it was pointless to worry before seeing his parents.

As Violet would say, those worries are future Daniel's problem.

It was a few hours before dawn when he saw the shadowy shapes of houses flanking the road ahead and he slowed his pace to quieten his passage between the houses. He rode to Mrs Goodwin's boarding house in the centre of town and skirted the building to head straight to the stables. He didn't expect to find anyone there at such an early hour, but a teenage boy came sleepily out of the stables when he heard Daniel arrive.

Daniel dismounted and asked the boy to care for the needs of his horse and then headed towards the back door of the boarding house and knocked. Unfortunately, those inside the house were not as attentive as the boy in the stable and Daniel had to walk around to the main door of the house. He considered trying to climb the balcony, but didn't think it would reflect well on him, so he knocked again and waited a few more minutes for the door to be opened.

"What is it?" asked the gruff voice of the burly man who opened the door.

"I need to speak to the king immediately," Daniel said. "Please let me in."

Daniel tried to slip through the door into the boarding house, but the man blocked him with the bulk of his body and asked him where he thought he was going. Daniel reached out, grabbed the man by his wrist and spun him around, twisting his arm up behind his back using a martial arts move he had learnt on Violet's world.

"Please," Daniel repeated. "Let me in."

The man was breathing heavily from the pain in his wrist and shoulder as he tried to shuffle away from the doorway and allow the prince to enter. Daniel then asked the man for the directions to the room his parents were staying in before releasing his wrist and heading towards the stairs ahead of him.

Daniel climbed the stairs as quickly and quietly as he could, still being considerate of the other sleeping patrons. He turned down the corridor, dimly lit by broadly spaced candles, saw a pair of soldiers guarding his parent's room and headed down the corridor towards them. As they were members of the family guard, they immediately recognised Prince Daniel and welcomed him warmly. They had not known about his apparent kidnapping, but they all had a deep respect for the young Prince that only partly stemmed from the fact that he would one day be King.

"Let me pass," Daniel said. "I must speak with my parents."

The two soldiers nodded, and parted, allowing him clear access to the door.

His parents' chamber was almost completely dark compared to the corridor, and Daniel had to think about the layout of the room from his previous visits. While he thought, his eyes adjusted to the darkness and he made out the shape of the curtained bed in front of him. He approached the left-hand side of the bed, where his father usually slept, and pulled back the curtain quietly so as not to bother his mother. He was startled, but not surprised when he found himself face-to-blade with his father's dagger.

"Daniel," Cameron said, putting his knife down. "Astrid, wake up, Daniel is here!"

Daniel tried to stop his father from interrupting the queen's sleep, but Cameron wanted to ease the worry that his wife had felt for their son in the last few days.

When the queen woke, she flung herself onto her son and told him how happy she was to see him safe. She embraced him for a few minutes before letting him go and demanding, "What happened?"

"I will tell you, but you are still in bed. Why don't you dress more warmly and join me by the fire?"

While Daniel added fuel and stoked the fire, Cameron and Astrid a few layers over their nightclothes before sitting in the armchairs by the fire. Daniel quickly filled them in on what had happened to him in the previous days. Finally, Daniel had finished his story and was able to ask his parents about Violet.

"Violet!" the queen said. "Oh, what shall we do?"

Daniel looked between the two of them with his eyebrows raised, asking for more

The king explained "When we worked out that you had been intercepted, we counted on the fact that you would be taken prisoner rather than killed offhand. I asked Violet to use the magic of the locket to try to find you."

"I felt it," Daniel said in the pause that his father left for him. "I think she tried to find me again tonight, a few hours after sunset."

"Once we saw that you were headed in the direction of Aquilegia, we thought, correctly, that your captors would take you through the Eastern Pass to the lands beyond. I decided to ask for help from the only beings that I thought would be able to locate you. I asked Markham to take Violet to Dragonhome."

King Cameron choked out the last words, a guilty admission that he had sent his son's girlfriend to appeal to dragons to help rescue him. An appeal which was complete pointless, because Daniel had saved himself.

The colour drained from Daniel's face when he heard where his father had sent Violet, horror twisted his stomach as he melted back into his chair.

I don't know whether to shout at them for sending her into such a situation or commiserate with them for feeling it was necessary.

Daniel leant forwards and rubbed his face with his hands before looking up at his father again.

"Where were they going from here?" Daniel asked.

"They were here two days ago and left in the night. They should have reached Millswood yesterday afternoon and I imagine that they would be heading to Dragonhome soon," the King said, sadness in his voice.

"I have no way of getting to her then," Daniel said, sounding defeated. "Will Jessica be there?"

It was Astrid who finally spoke to answer his question.

"As far as we know, yes, your sister will be there."

Chapter Twenty-one
VIOLET

Violet was awakened by sunlight sneaking through a gap in the curtains to shine in her eyes. The light was strong and bright and she thought it must be about midmorning. Her mouth was dry and she searched around for the bottle of water that she usually kept by the bed before realising that she still wasn't in her own bed.

Dragonhome, she remembered as she rolled over, sat up and stretched her arms above her head. Surprisingly, she could move without too many muscles protesting, despite her worries of the night before. She had some pain in her buttocks and the front of her thighs felt tight, so she did some quick yoga poses before dressing for the day.

She searched through her bag and found a pair of thin cotton pants which she slipped on under a thicker pair of woollen pants. She wore her corset with a white shirt and a fitted vest and set her necklace in the dimple in her throat. She found a leather thong in her bag and used it to loosely bind her hair at the nape of her neck.

When she felt adequately dressed, Violet stuffed everything back into her bag and checked the room to make sure she hadn't left anything. She noticed a table by the window that held a box with a note on top. Violet knitted her brow, puzzled, when she saw her name written in broad cursive script.

She opened the note and read:

Violet,

I look forward to meeting you. Please take this small gift I have had prepared for you and meet me in the communal hall for breakfast as soon as you are ready.

See you soon, Jessica.

Violet crinkled her brow, wondering who Jessica was as she lifted the long, slender box off the table. She lifted the lid to find a layer of white fabric. She gently unfolded the fabric to reveal a knife in a leather holster that was attached to a brown leather belt patterned with delicately worked violets.

She pulled the knife from the holster, revealing a light, shiny blade with a leather-bound handle. Violet did not know what to make of the gift, so she simply placed the belt around her hips and made her way out of the room she had slept in.

Violet vaguely remembered the way back through the wood-panelled corridors to the common area of the building. She saw Markham sitting at a table with another person, who was looking out the window opposite Violet. Markham's companion had a slight build, narrow shoulders and close-cropped brown hair. It wasn't until she turned her head that Violet determined Markham's companion was a young woman.

Violet didn't want to interrupt Markham's conversation, so she crossed the room to a buffet table and prepared herself a jam sandwich and a glass of fresh orange juice. The jam was apricot with a hint of lemon peel and rosemary, giving it a tart flavour that was delicious on the soft bread.

Markham stayed deep in conversation with the woman, and Violet had finished her breakfast before he noticed her and waved for her to join them. The brown-haired woman turned when she saw Markham beckoning and gave Violet a tentative smile.

She stood and Violet saw that she was wearing a leather vest that accentuated her tiny waist and small bust. Her face was small and dominated by large brown eyes the same deep-brown as her hair.

"Hello," said the brown-haired lady. "My name is Jessica, it is lovely to meet you."

Violet returned the introduction, then asked, "Did you leave me a gift?"

"Yes," said Jessica, broadening her smile. "I hope you like it, the belt fits you well. Now, it is time to go to the den, we mustn't waste any more time in the hunt for Prince Daniel."

Violet looked at Markham questioningly.

"Don't worry," Markham said. "She knows everything, including where you come from."

Violet could only nod. There were too many other people around to ask further questions and Jessica had already started moving purposefully towards the door. Violet hurried to catch up, dodging the occupants of the other tables along the way. They reached the door and Jessica continued to lead the way across the open yard towards the path leading back to Dragonhome. They paused to allow Jessica to strap a sword to the wide belt hanging across her hips and then her sturdy boots led the way down the path.

"I went in early this morning and asked for a dragon to wait to hear your plea," Jessica explained. "They took me quite seriously, as one of the Elders has waited for you, her name is Pragmoon. Try not to be too nervous, she will be able to sense it. She will sense many things about you.

"Dragons can scry you to see your future. That's how I knew you would be coming here, but I didn't know when or why. Pragmoon just told me to expect a visit from a flower and the only thing I could decipher from that was that you would be coming."

143

The brunette smiled broadly and shrugged, as if implying that all you could do was trust what they said.

"Who are you?" Violet asked.

"I am an envoy between The Realm of the Lilies and Dragonhome. I ensure that the people of the realm are adequately remunerated for any stock that the dragons take and I make sure that the dragons are happy with the treaty."

Violet didn't know what to say. It seemed a lot of responsibility for a woman who appeared to only be in her mid-twenties.

Within minutes, they were back at the cavernous entrance to Dragonhome and Jessica was leading them out of the sunlight and into the dimness of the caves.

There were flaming torches mounted on the walls, giving off a smoky, fluttering light that did little more than stop the newcomers from bumping into the larger rocks jutting into their path. Jessica looked as though she could have navigated her way through without the torches, on a night with no moon and with her eyes shut, and she nearly danced towards the dangers ahead.

The air was warm and dry, despite the altitude and the coldness of the air outside. There was also a tang to the air, a mixture of the smell of a freshly struck match and a snake cage.

They had been walking for nearly fifteen minutes and Violet's hair and clothes were starting to get sticky with sweat when the cave ahead began to lighten and Violet felt fresh, cool air blowing on her face. As they got closer she saw that the cave opened into a vast dale between the peaks of the surrounding mountains.

The ground of the dale was bare soil and rock, the only relief from the unrelenting brown-grey being thin blades of grass at the base of a few boulders. Nothing else could grow in the hard-packed ground where the great winged beasts beat their paths to the hollows in the rock walls that led to their homes.

Jessica led them to a cave directly across the open dale from where they were standing. They dodged piles of slag from melted rocks and great furrows in the ground.

"These are made by young dragons. They fight to build their strength, ensuring that they are can to fly over the mountains, catch game and return without issues when they go on their first hunting expeditions. There aren't many young at any given time and their parents bring food for them until they are big enough to go for themselves. It can take up to twelve moons for them to make their first hunting trips, so their parents can lose a bit of weight from sharing their food for so long, but the young ones return the favour when their elders get too old to fly."

"You know a lot about the dragons," Violet said, grimacing as she scraped her leg on a jutting piece of rock. "How did you come to be the envoy?"

"I was born to be the envoy," Jessica said, wryly.

When it seemed as though Jessica wasn't going to give any more information, Markham answered for her.

"She's the princess."

Violet stopped for a second, thinking about what Markham had just said.

"That would make you... Daniel's sister?" Violet asked.

"Yes," said Jessica. "Younger by two years. Born to be the envoy to the dragons, like the other younger siblings for the two generations of royal families before mine. The nursery rhymes sung to me as a child were about dragons and I have been reading books on dragon lore since I learnt my letters. To me, they are not beasts to cause fear, but intelligences to match wits with."

"Although she was always willing to make up fearsome tales about dragons to scare other children, in every village she's ever stayed in," Markham said, smiling.

Violet sensed a camaraderie between the pair and

realised that Jessica must have joined Markham and Daniel in their childhood games.

They reached the mouth of a cave and Jessica explained that each opening led to a few dragon dens, with some entrances leading straight back into the mountain, some climbing and some dropping down. These paths were not as well lit, but they were wide and clear, pathways worn smooth by the passage of many dragons over time.

They passed the entrances to a few other dragon chambers as they wound deep into the mountain, spotting the glitter of light on gold and gems as they passed the empty quarters. Finally, Jessica stopped outside a chamber that echoed with deep, rumbling breathing and emanated warmth into the tunnel.

"Here we are," Jessica said. "The chambers of Pragmoon."

Chapter Twenty-two
VIOLET

"Before we go in, there are some important things I should tell you," Jessica said, looking at Markham and Violet in turn. "Markham, you know some of this, but Violet, there will be a lot for you to take in. Our treaty with the dragons provides protection for the lives of both species. Within our realm, dragons are free to hunt, as long as they pay for their food, as all other residents do. On our side, our people cannot hunt them. Occasionally, someone will try to set up an elaborate dragon trap and our treaty says that if they are caught, the dragons will be able to mete out justice as they see fit. It is usually fiery.

"We also offer the dragons some level of protection outside of Realm and we send out emissaries to negotiate similar terms with other nations. It is not common knowledge, but we are currently helping dragonkind reach an agreement with the Aramalian ruler and we have already brokered one with the Mellanastians. Our relationship with the dragons at the moment is tenuous as we have not been able to reach an agreement with the Aramalians that is to the dragons' satisfaction."

Jessica paused and Violet and Markham nodded their understanding.

"Pragmoon is one of the dragon elders. Although she is generally quite accepting of humans, some other dragons of her generation fondly recall the taste of us and she sometimes has trouble keeping them in check. Be wary of your words and actions."

Violet shuddered as the younger girl turned away, adjusted her vest and strode into the dragon's den. Markham followed, looking confident and Violet tried to stop her fingers from shaking and her heart from racing.

They walked a short way down the wide passage that led to the den and Violet gasped as the great space opened up before her. There were torches mounted at intervals around the great room, lighting the little nooks and shelves that held bits of treasure all the way up the walls. Violet could dimly make out the roof high above, but thought that a nine-story office building would quite easily fit within the chamber. The floor was smooth and flat and the whole place looked as though it had been shaped by the great beast that was hunkered down in the centre of the room.

Pragmoon was lying in the centre of the room like a cat, legs and chin flat on the floor, shimmering tail curled around her. Her scales were about the size of Violet's hands and were an iridescent white in colour, flashing purple or pink depending on where the light caught them. She had a double row of deep purple fins running from the ridges above her eyes, down either side of her spine to the tip of her tail.

Violet realised that Jessica and Markham had moved ahead when she had stopped and saw that the princess stood eye-to-eye with the enormous beast, the dragon looking down her long nose to the woman standing before her. Pragmoon's body extended and rose behind her head to a height of about six metres at the top of her tallest fins.

"Pragmoon," Jessica said. "I have brought the visitors I mentioned this morning. They have asked for an audience so they can appeal for your help."

The dragon opened her enormous blue eyes and lifted her head to look down on her visitors. Violet hurried to join the other two as Markham started talking to the dragon.

"I would like to ask for help from the dragons," he said, after introducing himself. "It appears as though Prince Daniel has been kidnapped in an effort to sabotage the upcoming summit in Aramalia regarding the Mellanastian nation. We believe Prince Daniel is to be taken through the mountain pass to the north of Dragonhome and would like to ask a dragon to help us locate them and secure his freedom."

Pragmoon looked down at the group for a minute, considering their request, before she turned to Violet.

"You are not of this world, child," she said, in a voice that sounded like tinkling glass to Violet's ears. "I have seen many things, and I see you in a world with a bluer sky than ours, where the shiny beasts that fly through the sky are not dragons and humans build themselves tall towers to work and live in."

"This is true," Violet said. "We have tall buildings in our cities and aeroplanes that fly through the sky to carry passengers all over the world."

The dragon nodded.

"I think it is many years since dragons have flown on your air currents," Pragmoon said, in the voice that did not seem to match the size of her.

"Dragons are a myth on my world, at least they are now. There have never been any properly documented sightings."

"I sense that you speak true." Pragmoon turned her attention back to Markham before speaking again. "I will help you with your task and then I will accompany you to Aramalia. It is time I stopped relying on humans to negotiate for us. It will make the agreement more binding for all in Dragonhome and should put an end to complaints against the treaties."

Jessica thought about this quickly.

"You would like to negotiate your own terms for the treaty with Aramalia?" the young woman asked.

"Yes," answered the great dragon. "The concessions that you have been able to obtain have not been to our satisfaction. We feel that it is time to become directly involved."

"Will this affect the treaty with the Realm?" Jessica asked, looking crestfallen.

Pragmoon made a light huffling noise in her throat and Violet thought it sounded like she was laughing as she leant in and nudged Jessica in the chest with her nose.

"Don't worry, little Jess," Pragmoon said. "You are doing your job excellently."

For the first time, Violet saw the young princess smile unreservedly, and the gentle upturning of her lips transformed her from pretty to stunning. Jessica reached out and stroked the bridge of Pragmoon's nose and the dragon huffed warm breath in her face, drawing a giggle from the young woman.

"Our best chances of finding the Prince and his kidnappers would be in the evening, once the group has stopped for the day," Markham said after a few minutes. "They will need to light a fire for their camp, Pragmoon would you be able to scent that?"

"Of course," replied the dragon.

Markham nodded and started discussing plans with Pragmoon. After a short time, it was decided that the humans would return to the barracks for the day, while Pragmoon would go hunting. In the evening, Pragmoon would meet them at their lodgings and they would fly over the mountains to find the camp. Pragmoon had said that she would easily be able to carry the three of them and still be able to carry Daniel when they found him.

When this was all agreed, the group made their way back out of the cave. This time the dragon brought up the rear and the torchlight on her scales created sparkling spots of light around them, like multi-faceted diamonds catching the sunlight.

When they did get out in the sun, the light off the dragon's scales was dazzling and Violet found herself wishing for her sunglasses in the glare.

"My apologies," Pragmoon said, noticing their discomfort.

She paused for a moment and the glare reduced when her scales deepened to a shade of purple to match her spinal fins, reducing the reflections. Violet cocked her head, confused.

Jessica chucked. "Dragons usually have three colours in their scales, their base colour and two others. They can change their colour to any of these three, or a blend of them, as they wish."

With a quick farewell, Pragmoon took to the sky, standing on her back legs and launching herself like a dart into the air before unfurling her wings like sails about her and catching the wind off the mountains. The trio watched her until she disappeared beyond the peaks of the mountains surrounding Dragonhome.

Chapter Twenty-three
DANIEL

Daniel chafed at the slow travelling pace. After some early morning discussion, Daniel and his parents had been forced to accept that the only option they had was to proceed with the plan to travel to Aramalia with Daniel's presence on the trip kept a secret. Daniel was irked that this meant he had to travel in the enclosed carriage with his mother.

"Oh, Daniel," Queen Astrid chided. "You needn't look so surly. We did what we thought we had to do to get you back. You understand that don't you?"

"Of course I do," Daniel replied. "I just don't like that I can't go to her. I let her watch me enter the Realm with the hope that we would be able to be together, I am at fault if anything happens to her."

Daniel looked away from his mother to watch the countryside pass through the window. He imagined their pace was slow enough that he could count the leaves on each tree they passed.

"I know you hold this young woman in high regard, Daniel, but I feel that your worries are misplaced. You are the prince and the safety of the people of this realm is your responsibility. You have already been captured due to the distraction she provides, which put your father and me in a very awkward situation.

"I don't want to discount what you feel for each other,

but really, you need to accept your role. Your sister will keep Violet safe. It's time for you to focus on the trip to Aramalia and the politics we will face when we get there."

Daniel suppressed anger at his mother's inference that he was not embracing his role as Prince of the Realm as he continued to stare out the window. However, after a time, he was forced to accept that she was right. He had spent too much time with Violet late and shirked his responsibilities to the Realm. If he had not been distracted by thoughts of Violet, he never would have been captured, and if he had not been sulking about leaving her behind, he would have taken an escort with him when he left the thicket.

He sighed. "You are right, Mother."

"Of course I am," the Queen said. "I have had many years of practice at it. I had to learn a lot in a hurry when I married your father. I had only ten years to prepare to be Queen, where your father had thirty to prepare for his Kingship. Your wife, whoever she may be, will have less than two years. This will be a hard task for anyone, but it would be even harder for this woman from another world if you chose her."

Astrid reached out and grasped on of Daniel's hands where it rested on his knee.

"Some might think that all a queen does is sit quietly and look pretty, but that is not the case. Each season, I prepare the household to be moved between counties, I arrange your father's schedule for the people he must meet in each town and I keep track of all of the relationships between businesses and traders across the nation."

Daniel flipped his hand over and squeezed his mother's palm back, studying their fingers for a moment before meeting her gaze. "I know, mother. I have watched you since I was a child. I know you hoped that I would choose someone every time we moved for the last eight years or more, but you know that the only one I was ever interested in has already been claimed."

"You always could have chosen Mary instead. She is a lovely young girl," Astrid said obliquely.

"I really don't want to have this argument again, not when the woman I do love is currently courting danger with dragons."

Daniel's outburst effectively ended conversation for a time, both passengers in the carriage ignoring each other. Daniel studiously watched the scenery and Astrid used the travel time to look over the journal she had kept in the few weeks they had been in Wynbourne.

Gradually, Astrid was able to bring Daniel back to himself by drawing him into her musing about the business happenings in the Wynbourne area. Of particular interest to them both was the transport agreement between the wool merchants and the grain growers. Mother and son spent a good part of the day discussing this and whether similar practices could be put into place in other Counties of the Realm.

It was nearing sunset when the convoy finally reached the gates of Aquilegia. Daniel was still anxious about Violet, but had managed to turn his mind to their work and the pair had devised some strategies to try out in different areas of the realm.

The note of the horses hooves on the road changed as they entered the city and the sound began to echo off the walls of surrounding buildings. Daniel sat back in his seat while his mother leant forwards to wave to the people in the streets who looked in at their beloved Queen.

When they reached the castle, Daniel went to his quarters to wash and prepare for the evening. There were a few notes waiting on the desk in his study for him, a couple from Lieutenant Lis and one from the guards in the tower.

The one from the tower was simple. Loucius had requested an audience with him. The other two were missives from the team carrying out the charade of Daniel's continued capture.

The first had been sent the previous night to say that they had reached the place that Loucius had said he was due to stop on Daniel's second night of captivity. Lis and his team had successfully contained the checkpoint and were camping the night before heading on and he had sent the message back to Aramalia at the same time as they sent the one to Daniel.

The second note was from that morning, detailing that a rider had arrived in the early hours wondering where Loucius was. They had swiftly apprehended the woman and sent her back to Aquilegia with the others they had captured the night before.

Daniel quickly skimmed over the messages before preparing for dinner in his parents' quarters.

He smelled roast lamb as he headed down the corridor and felt his stomach rumble, they hadn't eaten much on the road during the day and Daniel hadn't realised how hungry he was.

King Cameron looked tired when he let Daniel into the room.

"Hard ride today, Father?" Daniel asked.

"Not too bad, there have been a few things keeping me awake at night lately though."

Daniel apologised to his father for the trouble that his capture had caused. His mother's words during the day had shown him that he had been reckless and he was sorry, but he would take it as a lesson to help him become a better King when he took the throne.

After a quick meal, King and Prince went to see the Aramalian kidnapper while Astrid called Sir Whittington to finalise the plans and provisions for their trip to the countries beyond the mountains.

Loucius was sitting in much the same place when father

and son entered the cell as when Daniel had visited him previously, watching the world outside dim.

"Your Highness," Loucius said, giving a bow from where he sat. "So lovely to meet you."

"Lovely is not the word I would use," King Cameron commented. "Although, I have to say, I am glad that my son managed to escape your clutches."

Cameron looked at the felon as though he was a cockroach and he had a very strong urge to squash him.

"It is fortunate that my son has already made an arrangement with you that may spare your life," Cameron said. "I fear that, if I had been here in his place, I would not have shown as much mercy."

Loucius nodded.

"Then I am very fortunate indeed," he said.

"You wanted to see me?" Daniel asked.

"Only to ask how your charade is playing out."

"So far they have been successful, arriving at the first stop a day late. A messenger from the next camp arrived this morning though, is this unusual?"

"I'm not sure," Loucius said, shrugging. "I've never missed a check-in before to know what they would do."

Loucius managed to endure the scrutiny of the two men while they tried to determine if he was being truthful.

Finally, Cameron nodded.

"We leave for Aramalia tomorrow," he said. "I expect we will be away for a couple of weeks. We will endeavour to find your family as my son promised. If we find that the situation is not as you described, these will be the last weeks of your life."

Cameron turned and left the cell, and Daniel eyed the prisoner for a few moments longer before joining his father as he walked back through the castle.

They were just crossing a courtyard between the prison tower and their own quarters when they heard a faint flapping, cracking sound.

Cameron and Daniel looked at each other.

"Quickly," said the king. "To the north wall."

They both turned and ran towards a broad section of the wall, climbing the stairs as quickly as they could as the distant sound grew louder and closer.

King and Prince had just enough time to catch their breath and compose themselves before they were buffeted by the wind off the wings of a dragon as it landed on the wall before them.

Chapter Twenty-four
VIOLET

Violet spent most of the day talking with Princess Jessica while they waited for Pragmoon to collect them.

The young woman was open and friendly when it came to talking about her favourite places in the realm and tales of childhood fun with her brother.

"Well," Jessica said. "Daniel is a couple of years older than me, so he had already learnt how to make trouble long before I arrived, but I have never been one to step down from a challenge, so I always tried to do whatever he did."

Jessica smiled impishly as she told Violet about how she and Daniel had made their way through a raspberry patch just outside Ivywood, where the family usually spent their summers.

"I think it was just over fifteen years ago, Daniel told me that he could pick more raspberries than me, because he was much older and bigger than I was. Of course he was, but he was also a boy and guileless, so he had no idea that I might try to cheat him," Jessica laughed. "Daniel set about trying to climb the brambles without getting stuck so he could collect the fattest berries from the top of the bushes. I had a different method, I knew that the birds would have had their pick of the berries from the top of the bush, but there were loads of berries near the ground, in the middle of the patch.

"Being smaller and skinnier than my brother, I wound

my way around the long stalks of the bushes, getting deeper and deeper and filling my basket as I went. Every now and then I would also find Daniel's basket and help myself to a few, not enough to make a dent, but still enough to make a difference.

"Eventually, we found that our baskets were nearly full, but we had worked ourselves so deep into the raspberry bushes that we had no hope of escaping and we had to sit there and call out until someone heard us. It took nearly an hour to get us out and Mother became quite frantic about the heat and our poor little heads. You can imagine her horror when we finally came out of the bushes, red from nose to navel with the juice from the two baskets of berries we had dared each other to eat before the rescuers reached us."

Violet laughed hard and long at her tales. Jessica was a wonderful storyteller, her eyes lit up, her smile glowed and her hands waved all over the place, aiding the descriptions of the trouble she and her brother had caused before they had grown into their responsibilities.

Jessica grew more serious when Violet asked for tales of the dragons.

"There is so much to tell," said Jessica. "They live in family groups, with those who are able to hunt caring for young and old alike. There have been times when food has been scarce or the dragon population too high and they have been quite violent towards each other.

"At the moment, there are seventy or eighty Dragons living in Dragonhome. This is a very large number for them, usually their dens hold fewer than fifty and it is extremely rare for a group of more than sixty dragons to get along together. I think Pragmoon is so intent on making an agreement with Aramalia because she would like to split the group. I think she might also use the trip to find a place for the new den to live."

"How will she decide how to split the den?" Violet asked.

"There are six family groups in Dragonhome. It would make sense to send three of these to the new den. I think she will keep the more troublesome dragons here and send one senior and two of the less fiery families there."

Violet nodded and the pair fell silent for a little while, watching little birds flitting through the trees opposite the porch they were sitting on. They sat back and enjoyed the crisp, cool air and the bright sunshine while Aurekio took Markham on a tour of the barracks and training yards.

Just after midday the kitchen hands rang a bell to call everyone in for lunch. Markham waved to the women as he came over from the barracks and disappeared inside to collect a tray of lunch to share. He returned with sandwiches, sliced fruit and fresh juice and they ate well, filling their bellies ahead of their evening mission.

"Now," Jessica said when they had satisfied themselves, "Markham brought me a letter from my parents detailing your arrival here and they told me you'd used the necklace Daniel had made for you. Have you used it again since then?"

Violet was a bit surprised by the question, but told Jessica about using the necklace the night before.

"But I must have done it wrong, because it pointed to Oakville, not the mountains as it should have."

"That's strange," Jessica said, frowning. "It sounds as though you did it right, I learnt a lot about my great-grandmother's necklace from my grandfather and I have seen it many times."

"Should I try it again?" Violet asked.

"No, it's okay," Jessica said.

Jessica gazed unseeingly at the mountains before them for a moment, chewing her lip, and then turned her gaze squarely back to the woman in front of her.

"I think it would be wise to go to Aquilegia and see if my

parents have gained any more information on the whereabouts of my brother before we start scouring the lands beyond for him."

Violet spent the remainder of the afternoon anxiously awaiting Pragmoon's arrival. Markham had disappeared back to the barracks after lunch and Jessica had left a short time later, worry still carving fine furrows in her forehead. They had left Violet sitting on the verandah in the afternoon sunlight, watching the comings and goings of the soldiers between barracks and training yard.

As the sun was dropping towards the peaks of the surrounding mountains, Jessica came searching for Violet and told her to prepare for the journey.

"Pragmoon will be here soon. You should collect your things and be ready."

Violet nodded and rose, eyeing the Princess as she did so. The younger woman had changed from the loose trousers of the morning into a pair of leather-panelled jodhpurs paired with knee high boots, a loose-sleeved shirt and a different leather vest, this one with a lily motif set in gold filigree. She also had a tight, gold circlet on her head and several gold rings upon her fingers. This was the biggest show of jewels Violet had seen since arriving in the Realm of the Lilies and she wondered who Jessica thought she might need to convince of her status as Princess of the Realm.

Violet returned to her room to collect her bag, leaving out her cloak to wear for the journey back over the mountains. Violet hadn't quite come to terms with what they were about to do. Seeing the dragon today was one thing, but planning to ride on the back of the majestic–*and terrifying*–creature was something completely different.

She walked back through the boarding house as strange sounds rose outside, a mixture of cracking sails and screeching car brakes. She didn't realise that it was the dragons returning to Dragonhome for the night until she joined Jessica on the verandah again.

"Aren't they amazing?" Jessica asked.

That's one word for it, Violet that as she looked up to see the great beasts dancing across the sky, screeching in joy as they wove their flights together, touching wings here and there. Welcoming each other home for the evening.

"More like petrifying," Violet said, her heart rate increasing as she thought of sitting on Pragmoon's back while the dragon did a barrel roll.

"I felt that way about them once, too," Jessica admitted. "But I have come to love their evening song and dance."

"Have you ever ridden a dragon while they were doing it?"

"No," Jessica said, laughing, before turning serious again. "In truth, I don't fly as often as you would expect, they generally only allow it when the need is great and if it will benefit human and dragon alike."

Violet was surprised to hear this, she had thought Jessica, as envoy, would fly frequently. *I don't know if that's comforting or makes this idea even scarier,* she thought.

When the evening flight was beginning to wane, Markham returned to the verandah, this time with his pack slung over his shoulder.

"Well, ladies," the soldier said brightly. "Are we ready to take to the skies?"

Violet simply smiled wanly in response, feeling the blood drain from her face as she did so. She had never been particularly keen on flying in an aircraft, which was fully enclosed and had seatbelts. She had no idea how she would feel when she climbed onto the back of a dragon.

Jessica's response was to raise her arm to the sky and point to the iridescent pink and purple dragon that had flung her wings wide and was using them like parachutes to slow her descent towards the open area in front of the boarding house.

"Well then," Pragmoon said in her musical voice, as she touched down in front of them. "Shall we prepare to leave?"

Chapter Twenty-five
VIOLET

"I think we need to change our flight plan," Jessica said as Pragmoon lowered her head to listen.

Jessica explained about the necklace the Monks had made for her great-grandmother and the replica Daniel had made for Violet. She went on to explain that Violet had used it on the day that she arrived in the Realm and again the night before, but the results from the second night did not fit with the predicted path of the kidnappers.

"Hmm," hummed Pragmoon. "I don't know much about the Monks as their magic works differently to ours, but I think it is usually reliable. Jessica, I think you are right, we should make our way to the capital, but we should take a route along the mountain range, just in case."

Markham nodded his agreement and Pragmoon went through her pre-flight information, telling the humans how to mount and where to sit.

Jessica, as Princess and envoy, climbed up first, nestling herself between a pair of fins at the dragon's shoulders.

"After you, Lady Violet," Markham said, holding a hand out towards the dragon.

Nothing to see here, just getting on a dragon.

Violet took a deep breath in and stepped towards the dragon's front foot. Pragmoon had flattened her belly and legs to the ground so that her body was not too steep to climb up and it was just like walking up a steep driveway.

Violet was surprised to feel warmth coming from the dragon's skin when she reached out her hands to touch the fins and steady herself.

Violet looked at Jessica, and saw her sitting cross-legged between two fins, with her knees pressed out to brace herself. Violet copied her and nestled her bag in her lap, adjusting the strap as she did so. As she settled in, she was hit by a sudden wave of panic.

Her heart began pounding in her chest, her breathing became rapid and she felt as though she had to squeeze each breath in past a metal band around her chest. She could only begin to calm herself when she felt Markham's hand squeezing her shoulder. She used the pressure of his hand as a focus point to slow down her breathing and calm her heart rate.

When he felt the tension in her shoulders abate, Markham leant down to speak to her.

"You are doing amazingly," he said. "I am your protector, you will be safe."

Violet took another deep breath and nodded in response, she didn't feel as though she had calmed enough to talk yet.

Violet became aware of a vibration through her sit bones that matched the rumble of Pragmoon's breathing, which was almost loud enough to rule out conversation from where she was sitting. She also realised that the heat was not only coming from the dragon's fins, but emanated from the skin of the dragon as well, now she understood why Jessica had chosen not to wear thick clothing for the flight. *She's like a giant space heater*.

"Are you ready?" Pragmoon asked.

All three passengers called out that they were seated and secure, each grabbing hold of the edges of the fins and bracing their knees tighter as Pragmoon took to the sky.

Pragmoon was unable to take off in her usual manner of springing straight up for fear of dislodging the humans on her back. Instead she could only leap a little higher than the boarding house before she had to start flapping her wings. Each time she raised her wings there was a slight compression between the fins along her spine and her passengers felt pinched into place and then scarily free when the dragon beat her great wings downwards.

After a short time, the three passengers got used to the compression cycle of the fins and were able to match it by relaxing their legs. Violet lamented that this was probably going to result in her being aware of a completely different set of muscles the next day.

Within minutes, they were above the mountain range and could see the sun dipping down towards the horizon, casting long shadows across the parts of the Realm of the Lilies that they could see below. Pragmoon turned away from the Realm and kept climbing so that she was far above the highest peaks.

"It will take us a little while to reach the Eastern Pass," Pragmoon sang to them. "I suggest you enjoy the sights, there are few on this world who have had the privilege."

The others took this in as silently as Violet. They were all busy with their own thoughts.

Violet had calmed her heart before they had taken to the sky, but now she found that it pounded with excitement. She would not have called herself an adrenaline junkie before now, but she found herself shrieking with delight when Pragmoon banked steeply to follow a small trail through the mountains.

The warmth of the dragon's scales stopped her fingers and toes from getting cold, but her cheeks were pink from the chill air rushing past them. Her legs were now getting a break as Pragmoon had reached a height where she could glide and Violet found that she need only apply a gentle pressure to the fins to stay where she was. Occasionally, she heard her companions calling out, but she couldn't work out if they were trying to talk or exclaiming with fear, excitement or both.

Eventually, the dragon crossed over the peaks of the mountains to the east, leaving the day behind them to view the lands beyond the Realm. The sun had set and the moon was only just rising, so Violet couldn't see much of the lands beyond the mountains, but she had only a few seconds to think about this before Pragmoon pointed her nose towards the ground and arrowed into a dive.

This time, Violet's shriek definitely carried more fear than excitement as she saw the ground rushing towards her and felt as though she would slide from her seat into Jessica at any moment, sending them both hurtling to their end. Of course, Pragmoon levelled her flight in time to cruise over the tops of the bushes at the base of the mountains before banking steeply and heading towards the start of a trail that Violet could now see a short way ahead of them.

"The Eastern Pass," Jessica yelled out. "Although I guess it's the Western Pass from this direction."

Violet smiled, unseen by her companions, as she again braced herself in time with the flapping of the dragon's wings. They flew low to the ground, only twenty or so metres above the trail, as they followed its wobbly ascension of the mountain.

It took a little under an hour for them to reach the crest of the mountain again, each member of the party scouring the trail and ground surrounding it for a trace of the kidnapping party. So far, they had only seen one other group of travellers, a couple with a cart who were travelling towards Mellanastia, transporting fibres.

On the other side of the mountain range, the path became harder for them to follow as it passed through deep, rocky crevices. Pragmoon assured them that if there was a camp, she would smell the smoke.

"Are you sure they would light a fire?" Violet asked, not

expecting anyone to hear or answer, but the wind of their flight carried her voice back to Markham.

"It would be very unwise to camp in this part of the mountain without a campfire to scare off the wild cats that live in the rocks," the soldier called to her. "They come out to hunt at night and soldiers who have put down their weapons for an evening meal can easily become a creature's supper."

They spent another hour scouring the pass on the Western side of the mountains and came across two more groups of campers. One was a group of traders with a few wagons and the other seemed to be a group of off-duty soldiers, singing bawdy songs and playing with fire.

As they levelled out again, Jessica started to fidget and suddenly let go with her right hand to point in front of them.

"Look," the princess shouted. "Aquilegia!"

Violet craned her neck so that she could see around the other girl and managed to make out the dull glow of the city before them. The shapes of the walls were darker smears in the evening gloom, rising several stories above the ground and marked with the dim flames of torches on every third crenel.

As they got closer, Violet saw soldiers on the walls, who all snapped respectful salutes to the dragon that passed almost within arm's reach above their heads. Shadows appeared on the curtains of the two-story houses they passed over as they traversed the maze of streets, covering a distance she estimated would take half an hour on foot in mere minutes.

Suddenly, Pragmoon lifted higher up into the air and climbed over the towers of the castle before turning to the right, heading north. She banked steadily, turning to again face the castle. Finally, the dragon slowed her pace as she approached the wall surrounding the castle again, before landing in front of a collection of people awaiting her arrival.

"Welcome, great dragon, to the Castle of Aquilegia," Violet heard a voice, maybe the king's, call out.

"Thank you for your welcome, King Cameron. My name is Pragmoon, I come to seek counsel for myself and to bring some others to see you."

Pragmoon dipped her head and extended a leg to allow her passengers to alight on the wall.

Violet found that the stiffness she had expected to feel in her legs was not there, probably thanks to the heat the dragon had been infusing them with while they flew. She was, however, still a bit unsteady thanks to the excitement of the flight and Markham had to help her climb down.

She stood looking at her feet for a moment, allowing her body to adjust to being on solid ground again and reminding her legs that they did not need to keep up their cycle of tensing and relaxing. She didn't look up from her feet until she heard a quick tapping of heels coming towards them and found Queen Astrid hurrying to join the welcoming party.

When Violet looked up, she saw a man standing a few feet in front of her, he must have walked very quietly as she had not heard him approach.

He looked familiar, and yet different. The clothes were strange to her, but she knew the piercing brown eyes anywhere.

"Prince Daniel," Violet said, the only words that seemed sensible when there were so many others clamouring to be said.

"Violet," Daniel said. "I…"

"Please, Daniel," Queen Astrid quickly interrupted. "Save your reunion for a more appropriate time. We have many other things to discuss with the elder of the dragons, and time enough later for courtesies."

"Of course," Daniel said, but he had taken a tight grasp of Violet's hand and she had the feeling that very few things in either of their worlds could convince him to let her go.

Chapter Twenty-six
VIOLET

"Open the counsel hall," the king called out.

Violet watched on in silence as a group of men moved off to two great doors embedded in the stonework where the wall rose higher. It took two men to move each of the doors, revealing a great chamber beyond. Cameron and his party moved through first and Violet saw stylised dragons carved into the stone doorframe as she passed though.

The room was large and sparsely furnished, with only a few armchairs in front of a large fireplace laid with dusty logs. They walked to the rear of the room and sat, Daniel keeping Violet close by drawing her to a twin chair with him.

Pragmoon followed them into the hall and asked the king if he would like her to light the fire.

"No, thank you," Cameron said. "I think we will be warm enough with you in the room tonight."

Pragmoon nodded. The warmth emanating from the dragon's scales was already taking the chill from the room and Violet found that her cheeks were starting to warm up again and she began to doze in the warmth and low hum of conversation she could not follow.

The group were discussing plans for the trip to Aramalia. Whether King and Queen should still leave the next day, what role the dragon would play, how Daniel would travel. *This is not an area I can help in, so I guess I'll just try not to snore.*

When it seemed as though the group had come to a decision about their plans and were only organising the finer details, Daniel asked if he may be excused to escort Violet to his guest quarters.

Violet walked wearily alongside Daniel as he led her silently down from the wall and across the courtyard to the tower where his quarters were. She had spent the last four days chasing this man across another world and when she'd finally found him, it had been a complete anticlimax.

She hadn't even had a chance to say hello to him.

He led her up a couple of flights of stairs and opened a door to a guest suite and then led her up the passageway to show her where his study was.

"You'll be able to find me in here when you wake in the morning," he said. "We can talk then, or now, if you like."

"Just tell me one thing," Violet said. "How did you escape?"

"I signalled a guard when the cart they had me hidden in entered the city," he said. "Listen, I'm sorry. I never..."

He trailed off as she put a finger to his lips.

"I'm much too tired and a little bit confused," she said. "I'll talk to you in the morning."

She leant forwards and kissed him on the cheek, before returning to her room for a well-deserved, worry-free sleep.

Violet woke dazed again and it took a moment to run through the previous day and work out where she was. As she scoured her memory, she remembered.

Daniel was free!

She had been far too tired and wrung out to be excited when she saw him the night before, but a full night of sleep had allowed the stress and anxiety of the last few days to fade away. Now she could accept that she had been transported to another world, one with beasts of legend, magic and mystery. Now that Daniel was safe, she could begin to enjoy herself.

She climbed out of bed and carefully stepped onto the thick, woven mat next to it. She could feel the cold coming from the stonework and did not want to set her bare toes on them. One of the dresses the queen had made for her in Millswood was hanging from a clothes stand near the heavily curtained window and her undergarments were set on a bench next to it.

Violet leapfrogged from one mat to the next to reach her clothing without getting cold feet and hastily drew on her layers. Once she was respectably attired, she opened the curtains to look out at the world. Her room was on the third story of the tower, so she could only just see above the wall surrounding the castle and mainly saw the roofs of houses and the brilliant blue sky above. She could see the stables in the yard below though and noticed there was surprisingly little activity. It took her a moment to remember that Cameron and Astrid had planned to begin their journey to Aramalia that day and were probably hours gone by now.

She hurried out of her room towards Daniel's study and stood outside for a moment, not sure what formalities were required. In the end, she simply knocked and entered when he called out to her.

"Did you bring up the missives from Lieutenant Lis?" he asked without looking up from his paperwork.

Violet cleared her throat, and he looked up.

"Violet," Daniel said, rising from his chair. "I—sorry—good morning."

"Good morning," Violet smiled as she crossed the room to sit in the arm chair in front of his desk. "I feel like we should introduce ourselves again. Hello, I'm Violet, I'm twenty-seven. I'm a nurse. I live alone. I lost my parents a long time ago, and I like cats."

"Nice to meet you, Violet," Daniel said, also smiling. "My name is Daniel, I am the Crown Prince of the Realm of the Lilies, I am twenty-eight, and in two years I will be the king. I am a foolish man who has told many lies to a young lady I hold in high regard and I am so thankful that she is here with me now so that I might make amends."

Violet smiled. "I think I understand. I'm still hurt that you lied, but I probably wouldn't have believed the truth until I came here anyway. Your home is lovely and I am glad that I followed you."

Daniel's smile dropped as his expression became serious. "I am so grateful that you followed me too. Without you, my disappearance may have gone unnoticed for another day and the message for extra vigilance to the guards at the gate may have come through too late."

Daniel stood and walked around his desk to stand next to her chair. He reached out a hand and drew her up to stand before him. She was only a few centimetres shorter than him and he did not have to bend down far to kiss her. The kiss contained all of the passion that he had held back with the truth of his life and had Violet forgetting both of their worlds for a few moments.

They were interrupted by a knock on the door, which had to be repeated before Daniel would allow the interloper to draw him away from Violet.

"My apologies," the young soldier said. "I bring the latest message from Lieutenant Lis."

"Never mind the interruption, thank you," Daniel said. "You may go."

The soldier hurried from the room, pretending not to notice the deep red of Violet's cheeks.

"Well," said Violet. "I probably shouldn't distract you anymore. I'll go back to my room for a while."

"No," Daniel pleaded, as he gently guided her back to her chair. "I would like to talk to you about the trip to Aramalia and your plans."

Violet nodded and Daniel rang a bell to ask for a brunch tray to be brought up for the pair of them, before opening the letter from Lieutenant Lis. He gave Violet a more detailed description of his captivity and release, and the plan with Lis, before telling her of the contents of the letter.

"He says that they reached the third night's camping ground last night. There was a man who had camped out in a cave waiting for them. They had some trouble luring him out of the cave, but they did get him eventually and settled in to camp along the trail in the mountains last night."

"Wait," Violet said. "I think we saw them, we flew over a group of soldiers with a campfire on this side of the mountain range. You should ask your sister, or Markham."

"I can bring Teddy up here later, but Jessica has already left. My parents wanted her well out of harm's way, so they sent her to Ivywood. She can retreat to the Monastery if there looks to be any trouble brewing and Pragmoon will assign a Dragon to keep watch over her. As you can imagine, she was not very happy with that plan."

Violet could imagine that the fiery, independent young woman would not be happy with that. Regardless of her insecurity about keeping the relationship with the dragons strong, she would not be happy with being swept to safety.

"Teddy?" She asked, confused by the apparent pet name.

"Lieutenant Markham's first name is Teddy. Didn't he tell you?" A small, sly smile came across Daniel's features.

"Hmm," Violet said. "Somehow it never came up."

Daniel laughed, he was not surprised, Teddy Markham had been a bit self-conscious about his first name for as long as Daniel could remember knowing him.

"Now, my Lady Violet," Daniel said. "I'm afraid we are nearing a time when you may have to make a choice.

Tonight, I shall head off by dragon for the first stage of my plan. You may come with me, stay in the Realm and wait for me to return, or you can simply return to your world and forget about me."

He said the last with a joking smile, trying to hide the pain she made out in the crinkles in his eyes as he suggested it.

"I don't think it would ever be easy to simply forget you," Violet said. She reached out to the desk and took his hand. "These last few days have been such a whirl and I haven't even seen you! I think it is too soon to decide if I should stay here with you, but I would like to see more of the Realm and your world."

"Well then, would you like to join me on my journey to Aramalia tonight?"

Chapter Twenty-seven
VIOLET

Violet, Daniel and Markham spent a few hours closeted in Daniel's study making plans before taking a break for lunch on the terrace.

They were still on the third story, but the terrace was on the other side of the tower from Violet's room and they had a view of the marshalling yard and entry gates of the castle. There was a wooden outdoor setting in the middle of the terrace and a few planters with brightly coloured flowers catching the spring sunlight.

The air was still cool, but the sunshine on their backs as they ate was warm and they grew hot as they finished their lunch. They had been planning their trip all morning, so Violet turned the conversation to lighter matters.

"Markham," Violet said. "Have you made any wedding plans yet?"

The soldier went a bit pink in the cheeks and Daniel suddenly had a deep interest in the flowers closest to the table.

"Did I say something wrong?" Violet asked.

"No," Markham answered, plastering on a smile. "Plans have just been a bit tricky with my postings. We think we may want to get married towards the end of spring, we just need to know when I will be home for long enough to hold the ceremony."

Violet smiled and was about to ask if Sarah had

everything she needed when Daniel took over the conversation.

"Only a few more hours until we leave now, I suggest we take a break from our planning and prepare for the evening's travel." His tone indicated that it was an order, not a suggestion.

Markham stood and snapped a sharp salute to Daniel before heading inside. Daniel's sudden switch in mood was confusing, and he had moved away from the table to looking towards the courtyard. His pose did not exactly invite conversation.

"I guess I'll go too, then," Violet said, walking towards the door.

"Wait," Daniel said with a sigh and beckoned her to join him. "I'm sorry, it's complicated. Sarah is not a person Teddy and I tend to talk about together. We were childhood playmates, every spring I would join them in their games. Naturally, as we grew, our affection for Sarah grew too, but it took some time for Sarah to decide who she wanted to give her affection to.

"A few years ago, it finally became clear that Teddy was the one who had won her heart, but, despite meeting you, it has still been hard to talk about them. In truth, they have been engaged for much longer than people usually are here. Teddy has been waiting for me to give my blessing and until now, I haven't been ready."

He smiled ruefully at her as he finished his tale of unrequited love. Violet didn't know what to say, so she said nothing, but placed her hand on his on the terrace wall.

"Well then," Daniel said. "We have a few hours before we leave. What would you like to do?"

"I would like to spend some time getting to know Daniel the Prince a bit better," Violet said. She put her arms around his neck and pulled herself up on her toes to kiss him. "While taking a solid nap. I haven't had a solid night of sleep since I got here and I don't see one in our immediate future either."

"Very well, my lady. Allow me to escort you to your chambers."

He placed his hands on her cinched waist and drew her close to him, matching the curves of their bodies to each other. Then he growled at her playfully and hauled her, shrieking, into his arms, she playfully beat at his shoulders as he carried her inside and to her bedroom.

Her threw her gently onto the bed and climbed on next to her.

"You can't sleep in all these layers, let me help you with that gown."

He undid the laces of her dress, then sat her up to pull her outer dress up over her head.

"You're better at that than I am," she joked.

"I've had more practice," he said, then paused. "That didn't sound as good as I thought it would."

She laughed and attacked his shirt buttons. He wore only one layer and removing the shirt revealed a torso sculpted and bronzed by hours of shirtless sword practice. Although they had been dating for nearly three months, this was the first time she had been treated to the sight of his bare chest. She winced when she noticed the purple bruises on his side, but didn't get long to sympathise, he had turned his attention to the laces of her corset and was swiftly pulling them out.

"Hey," she said. "Don't pull them all of the way out, do you know how long these things take to do up?"

"Sorry," he said, sheepishly, taking his hands away. "I'm usually only involved in this part."

She mock-glared at him as she loosened the laces and waved him over when she was ready for him to pull it up over her head. This time when he pulled her close, there was only one layer of fabric between his chest and hers and the liberation from the corset was extra sweet.

"Violet Truman," he said. "I love you."

"Daniel Reyne," she said. "I love you, too. Although, I have questioned my judgement a few times in the past few days."

Daniel drew back and studied her face. "I'm sorry. I'm sorry I couldn't tell you the truth about my home or my family and I'm sorry that you got thrown straight into the deep end of visiting royalty and riding dragons without my support when you got here."

She stayed quiet, letting his words soothe her. She had questioned her ability to judge people when she had arrived in the Realm. She'd thought he was a genuine person, but he had kept so much of himself back from her.

"I understand why you did, and you being kidnapped wasn't your fault. But it will take a while for me to trust you again."

A brief look of sadness passed over his face, but then he smiled softly.

"That seems fair." He kissed her gently, then laid down beside her and pulled her close, her back to his chest. "You said you wanted to know Prince Daniel better. What do you want to know?"

"Well, I already know you like raspberries." She giggled.

He pulled back and rolled so he could see her face, then groaned. "Jessica."

"Tell me some more stories. Your favourite places, time of year, the seasons in this world. Tell me everything.

He spent the next hour teaching her of his world, until the quiet hum of his voice sent her to sleep.

***

A few hours later, Daniel roused himself from their

sleepy nest.

"We should get ready," he said. "I will go back to my quarters to prepare and send a maid to fill a bath for you."

He hurriedly dressed and pressed his lips to hers before leaving her in the tangled bedclothes. She sighed, not wanting to move.

She stayed in the warmth of the bed a little while longer, planning to wait for the maid. But her bladder had a different plan. She rose, collected a robe and headed through to the bathroom.

A few minutes later, the poor maid was horrified to find that Violet had started running the bath herself and hastily raced to make amends by laying out fresh underclothes and asking what clothing she would like prepared.

Violet thought for a few minutes before asking for a pair of trousers, a shirt and a vest, figuring there wouldn't be many people to judge her for her clothing while they were on the back of the dragon. She enjoyed a long soak in the bath, scrubbing her skin and teasing the tangles from her hair.

The water was starting to chill when she climbed from the bath with fingers wrinkly as prunes and goose bumps immediately rising on her arms. The maid quickly wrapped her in a plush bathrobe. As Violet still wasn't quite used to open nudity, she was grateful for the cover up.

The maid had laid a small fire to ward off the early evening chill in the air and Violet's clothes were set out next to it. She thanked the maid for her help and sent her away so she could dress.

She stood in front of the fire, warming her fingers and toes before dressing and heading out to find Daniel.

Daniel and Markham were deep in conversation when Violet let herself into the study.

"Violet," Daniel said, smiling, when he noticed her crossing the room. "We were just going over our final plans, come over and I will fill you in."

Violet moved around the desk to stand next to him and look at the map he had spread out before him, this one had the Realm of the Lilies marked on it, but it also spread further, covering the narrow stretch of land that would be Mellanastia and reaching out to the hotter lands of Aramalia.

"The Aramalian capital, Terisha, sits atop tall cliffs at the centre of a broad bay. Access to the water is by thousands of steps for people, or massive cranes for cargo.

"It will take my parents four days to reach Terisha," Daniel said. "When they stop today, they will have just made it through the pass and will be on the edge of Mellanastia. As yet, they do not have a capital, only a few small villages, but where they stop will be the site of the new city.

Violet nodded. They had covered all of this earlier in the afternoon. In detail.

"Tonight, Pragmoon will fly over to Aramalia, following the same path as my parent. Except it will take us a little less than a night to fly it. We will stop to make camp near morning. During the day tomorrow, we will help Pragmoon scout for places for a new den and in the evening we will fly back to Terisha."

Markham took up the tale.

"I have spoken with Loucius today and he has detailed where we can find his family in the Terishan Palace. We will find them and free them, if need be."

"After that, we retreat to the new den until my parents arrive for the Summit and then find the right time to make a grand entrance with Pragmoon, showing that I do support the move and the dragons are keen to be involved in the treaty too."

Violet nodded her understanding. "Let's just hope that everything goes as planned."

"Of course it will," Daniel said. "With you by my side, how could anything go wrong?"

Chapter Twenty-eight
DANIEL

Daniel raced to his room to collect the last of the things he needed for the trip. Formal clothing for all members of his small party had been sent with his parents, so he needed little more than the clothes he was wearing. He had instructed Violet and Markham to also travel light, a few fresh clothes and their weapons would be all they would need.

The tailors had been called in to fashion a couple of large bags that could be secured between the pairs of fins on Pragmoon's back and these had been packed with everything else the humans would need for their expedition. Daniel had watched pages load and fasten these bags when Pragmoon had arrived earlier and had left the other two with the dragon while he rushed off.

He hustled to collect his sword and crown from his bedroom and a satchel that contained more detailed maps of Mellanastia and Aramalia to help with the search for a new den. He fastened his sword around his waist, tucked his crown into the satchel with his maps headed back to the north wall.

He dodged pages returning horses to their stables for the evening in the courtyard, and raced up the stairs to find the stunning Violet waiting for him, looking more attractive in the loose trousers and tight vest than she had in the dress she had worn earlier.

He went up to her, planted a kiss on her lips, took her hand and turned to speak to the captain of the guard.

"I trust everything will be in order in our absence," he said. "Continue as you would during our seasonal absences, but with a little extra vigilance."

"Yes, my lord," the captain said, bowing.

"You can expect the Royal Family to return in a fortnight," Daniel said, then turned to the Sir Whittington. "Please have everything in order for a week's stay here before we travel back to Wynbourne."

The castle chief nodded.

"Right," Daniel said. "Let's be off."

He turned to Violet.

"Now, how do I ride one of these?" he whispered in her ear.

"You haven't been on a dragon before?" Violet asked him, just as quietly.

"Don't let any of them know," he said, gesturing to the castle staff who were watching on. "I'm meant to know everything about the realm, but dragons are Jessica's speciality and this is the first dragon I've ever ridden."

"Don't worry," Violet smiled. "I've got you covered, just follow me."

Violet led the way confidently up Pragmoon's leg, stroking the dragon's scaly ribcage as she climbed. Markham stepped up to Daniel's side to watch the young woman settle herself in between the dragon's shoulder blades.

"To look at her now, one would think she had been riding that dragon for years," Markham observed. "What did you say to her?"

"Just that this is the first dragon I've ridden," Daniel said, smiling.

"You are a rogue."

"How dare you dirty the name of your prince with such

a slur?" Daniel joked, walking towards Pragmoon.

He made sure that he climbed slowly, steadying himself more than he needed to for Violet's benefit, and settled into the nook between the pair of fins behind Violet. He tucked his satchel into his lap, ensuring it was tightly closed, then reached forwards to squeeze Violet's shoulder and give her a stiff smile. She reached up and squeezed his hand, looking confident, much better than Markham said she had been the night before.

Markham knocked Daniel's back as he climbed up and Daniel interpreted it as a deliberate show of disapproval for his lie, but it had made Violet more comfortable, so he didn't feel guilty. Markham called out when he was settled and Pragmoon bellowed a warning to those still remaining on the wall. The spectators hurried to shelter in the great doorway of the hall before Pragmoon turned to face away from the castle keep, unfurled her broad wings and sprang into the air.

Daniel looked out to the west and saw the sun slip below the horizon, pulling the brilliant sunset colours of orange and yellow with it. The moon was still a few hours from rising and when they turned towards the mountains all they could make out were misty smears of shadow against the dark sky.

Daniel thought about the previous times he had flown on a dragon. He had told Violet a half-lie, Pragmoon was the first dragon he had flown on, but today was not his first flight. His position with regard to the dragons was not as important as that of his sister, but it was vastly different. Where Jessica ensured that the relationship between the Realm and Dragonhome remained healthy, Daniel was the one who occasionally called on the dragons for help.

Daniel had appealed for help twice. The first time to help locate a small child who had wandered off from a village near Millswood when Daniel had been training there. As it was mid-autumn and the sun was near to setting, Daniel had raced up the mountain to appeal to the dragons for help. Pragmoon had come to his aid, having a soft spot for young of all species. She had flown him down over the mountains and they'd scoured the hills and valleys for the child until they finally found her huddled under a tree at the edge of a copse. The family had been so grateful to the dragon for finding the toddler that they renamed her Praese, after one of Pragmoon's own children.

The second time Daniel had appealed for help was when a section of road near the southern pass was being plagued by a group of brigands. Being so close to the thicket, the king was particularly wary of the group of criminals and sent Daniel to ask for help to find their hiding place. It took several days of scouring a broad area in southern Milton County and up into the foothills of the southern ranges before they found them. The group had found a tunnel that led through one of the smaller mountains to an open dell, surrounded by steep, rocky walls. All Daniel had to do was sit outside with Pragmoon and wait for the criminals to come out of their hiding place so they could be taken into custody.

The one other time Daniel had flown, it had not been with Pragmoon. It was again autumn and he was staying at their home in Eremion, in Thomas County, when he was approached by a great black dragon who asked him for help. The dragon had been out hunting for a fat sheep to feed himself and a youngling when he had felt a tickling on his belly and turned to find that someone had been hailing him with stones using a slingshot. Daniel was immediately concerned, it was within the treaty that this dragon could demand the culprit's death and the prince was horrified. The dragon, named Arabod, asked for Daniel's help to find the person responsible and he accepted with a heavy heart.

Arabod swiftly flew back to the place where he had been

hit and Daniel was dismayed to see another hail of stones coming towards them as they flew over a pile of tumbledown rocks on a small slope. Daniel bid the Dragon to land, confident that the slingshot fodder wouldn't cause them any harm, and dismounted to call out to the hidden person in the rocks.

"Come out from there for the Prince of the Realm," Daniel had cried.

"Ha, the dragon cannot defend himself so he has to have someone masquerade to do it for him," came the taunting reply.

"This dragon has brought me here to witness the breaking of our treaty and administer the necessary justice. Step out now, or I will be forced to haul you out on the tip of my sword for failing to listen to your future king."

"Neither king nor dragon has ever served me well enough that I wish to obey them now," came the voice.

Daniel was confused.

"If you have a complaint to make, please tell me," Daniel appealed. "You will not be harmed if you come out now and state your case."

There was a rattling in the rocks and a man in his early twenties came out from his hiding place. He looked both dragon and prince over from head to toe and nodded, then began to talk.

"My flocks have all been scoured by this one without payment and when I appealed to the King. I was told that all stock taken had been accounted for. I have been left with neither payment nor stock, because of that wretched treaty."

The man spat on the ground to show his distaste for the situation.

"Arabod, what do you say to these claims?"

"It is true, I have been taking sheep from this area, but I have been presenting my catches in town and paying my debts. The ledgers will reflect this."

"Sir, would you travel with us to Eremion to settle this matter?"

The man nodded, reluctantly, and Daniel asked Arabod to carry them both back to town to view the ledgers.

"Well, yes," the keeper of the ledgers said. "I have records of Arabod collecting a sheep here every couple of days, I asked the owner of the farm for one myself assuming that it was good meat. Can't say I saw the appeal in it though, it was a bit tough for my taste."

Daniel checked the name in the ledger for payment, when he said it out loud, the man he had collected from the rocks shouted.

"That thief!" he yelled. "He told me that he changed the town records, but he's been stealing from me all this time!"

Daniel calmed the man and asked him to explain the situation.

"Father left us his farm when he passed. He always ignored Andras's greed, so he didn't say how the farm should be split. That—" the man cut his sentence short and eyed the prince. "—schemer, took all the pasture land and left me the half with the rocky terrain and poor soil."

He took a moment to calm himself before continuing. "I didn't even have a shelter or material to build one. All through summer I camped near the creek bed, watching as it slowly dried up."

Daniel exchanged a glance with the man hovering over the ledgers, then met Arabod's eyes through the window behind him.

"I raised sheep. They fattened up well on the grass that grows between the rocks that make it impossible for me to plant crops. Then that one—" He gestured at Arabod. "—started taking my sheep and I didn't receive any payment. I didn't have any other choice..."

Daniel and Arabod exchanged a glance.

"Come," said Arabod through the open window. "Let us visit your brother."

The two men climbed back onto the dragon and the farmer directed them to what had previously been his family home. The yard had been neglected and the fields had not been prepared for the next crop to be planted. The few lingering livestock did not look well cared for and there was a fearful-looking dog sitting by the door of the house.

The dragon bellowed for the man when they landed and they waited a few minutes for him to present himself. He came to the door, wiping his hands on a soiled tea towel and stood in the doorway, eyeing the visitors suspiciously.

"What do you want?" he asked.

"I am Prince Daniel and this is Arabod. We are here to investigate some payments that should have come to your brother, but appear to have come to you."

"I don't know what you're talking about," the man replied.

"I'm sure you do," Daniel said. "The keeper of the ledgers told us that he had even come to you for a sheep because the dragon had been coming so often and paying so well."

"By taking the payments meant for this man, you have brought my actions into question and put the treaty under threat," Arabod said. "I ask Prince Daniel to bear witness as I call for dragon justice."

"I will bear witness," Daniel said. "Please, step out here into the yard and stand with your brother."

"Your actions caused this man, your brother, to cast stones at me as he thought I had violated the treaty," Arabod said. The elder brother smiled unpleasantly.

"I forgive him for his actions as I understand they came from desperation.

"Your actions, however, stemmed from greed. Dragonkind treat their family with respect and care for each other as much as they care for themselves. I find your actions against your brother to be against nature and your actions against me to be a violation of the treaty. I sentence you to death by fire."

The man took in the words and a look of fear crossed his face. He turned to run back into the house, but Daniel was blocking the door. With few other options, he started running across the open yard, away from the dragon. The dragon did not need to move. He simply blasted the fleeing man with flame, reducing him to a pile of ashes on the ground and the scent of burning in the air.

"I am sorry for the loss of your father and your mistreatment at the hands of your brother," Arabod said to the young man. "Prince Daniel, I will await your readiness."

Daniel approached the young man. "By Arabod's actions, you are now the sole owner of this land."

The man turned to him with tears running down his face. "What have I done?"

"Nothing I wouldn't have done."

Having nothing else to say to the grieving man, Daniel returned to Arabod, who flew him back to his autumnal home.

Chapter Twenty-nine
DANIEL

"Sir," Markham called, bringing Daniel back from his recollections. "I think I see something up ahead."

They had been flying for nearly two hours and had reached the peaks of the mountains about half an hour earlier. Pragmoon kept a steady height of about five hundred metres above the ground, where she could see earthbound happenings well enough, but was immune to any threat from below. Daniel looked to where Markham was pointing and saw flickering lights in the middle distance.

"That must be where my parents and the Mellanastian leaders are staying tonight," Daniel said. "Pragmoon, will we be able to stop there?"

"Yes," the dragon said. "I expected you would want to seek counsel with your parents, we will stop there soon."

Daniel looked to the form of Violet in front of him. She had adjusted well to the rhythm of Pragmoon's wing beats and he watched her relax on the upbeat and stretch out her legs to match the down. He was in awe of how well she seemed to be adjusting to changes between his world and her own and had to respect how she was handling the situation she had been put into when she followed him through the fig tree.

When asked to rescue the man she loved after discovering all of the lies he had told her, she had jumped straight in. When asked to ride a dragon to find him, she had jumped straight on. He had found himself a very special lady and planned to hold on to her as tightly as he could.

He was just finishing his appraisal of the young woman when he felt Pragmoon dive. He tensed his muscles just in time as Pragmoon pulled her wings in tight, broadening the space between her spinal fins.

She touched down gently just outside the ring of wagons that had been assembled around the campfires and allowed her passengers to dismount.

"I will hunt," she said. "You will hear me when I return."

Daniel thanked her and turned towards the wagons, making his way between the two nearest ones. He found his way blocked by crossed swords when he reached the edge of the wagons nearest the firelight and he announced himself and his companions.

His parents were sitting near a large fire alongside a couple of Mellanastian elders, eating the remnants of a stew prepared by the locals.

"Daniel!" Astrid said as she noticed her son walking around the fire to greet them. "Daniel, you know the Mellanastian elders, Spiridon Honrik and Elisa Mytal?"

Daniel nodded and introduced Violet and Markham to the Mellanastians.

"Lovely to meet you," Violet said, bobbing a curtsey. "I have heard much of your land and I hope that one day I will get the opportunity to see it in the daylight."

"I am sure that you will, my dear," Elisa said. "Not too soon, but there will be days to come where you will be able to explore at length."

"Thank you, Elisa," Spiridon said, dryly. "My cousin is gifted with a small amount of foresight. Sometimes she can see things as they may, eventually, happen."

Daniel saw Violet smile awkwardly, but he also saw his

mother's slight nod of approval at the way the young woman had handled herself. Elisa offered the newcomers some stew which they gratefully accepted as they had only eaten a light supper before leaving Aquilegia.

Astrid called Violet over to sit with her and Elisa, and the two gave Violet a lesson in Mellanastian history. Daniel walked over to share a bench seat with his father, who had finished his dinner and was quietly drinking a goblet of wine while watching the three women.

"Well, Daniel," he said. "I think you have been fortunate with that young lady. If you are exceptionally lucky, you may be able to entice her to stay by your side."

Daniel looked at the rosy flush in Violet's cheeks and the gleam in her eyes as she listened intently to a tale his mother was telling her and had to agree with his father. He would count himself lucky if she chose to stay with him.

"The tasks we were gifted through our birth are not always easy," King Cameron said to his son with a sigh. "Sometimes the hardest thing we have to do on a given day is decide where a fence should be built, other days we have the fate of nations on our hands.

"It is a tough path to walk, Daniel, and the only advice I would give you with regard to love is to make sure you can be strong enough. You will have days where all you want to do is throw her into your bed, but there will also be days where you want to throw each other out of a window. Passion, understanding and forgiveness are all needed in a relationship, and there are few other people in the realm who will need a supportive partner as much as you."

Daniel took this in silently.

"Did I ever tell you how your mother and I met?" Cameron asked, turning to his son.

"I don't think I ever heard the full story. I know she lived on the farm near Leeside, but I don't know much more than that."

"We were still teenagers when we met. It was autumn and I was undergoing sword training at different barracks, refining my technique. I was travelling from Ivywood to Millswood when I saw her."

A soft smile crossed Cameron's face and his eyes lit up at the reminiscence as much as the firelight.

"You remember that your grandparents' farmhouse is quite close to the road. As I was passing it that day, a young woman came out of the henhouse, swearing at the chickens that were trying to trip her up as she carried her haul of eggs inside. She tells me that she was usually quite able to get around the wretched things, but it happened that, as I watched, she slipped in a particularly muddy patch in the yard and fell hard onto her behind.

"Eggs went flying, up in the air and then down, all around her. As I had been taught to always be kind to anyone in a sticky situation, I took it upon myself to help the young maiden. So I crossed the yard and reached out to help her. Imagine my surprise when this gorgeous young woman, covered in muck, mud and egg yolk, decided that my intentions were less than chivalrous. She waited until I was close enough and then kicked me behind my knee, knocking me down into the mud with her."

Father and son laughed together for a moment.

"I knew then that your mother had the inner strength and fire I needed in a wife and that I would do whatever I could to get the girl to marry me. I don't think you have quite uncovered all of her depths, but I think that Violet may be the woman for you, as your mother has been to me for all of these years."

Daniel smiled and thanked his father for his support of Violet, he did not wish to disappoint his family any more than he already had in his pursuit of her. His father's support felt like forgiveness for his lapses in his duties in the past months.

Cameron put a hand on Daniel's shoulder and squeezed tightly, then removed it and patted him on the back.

"I love you," Daniel said.

"And I love you, son," King Cameron said.

Spiridon approached them after they had sat for a few minutes in silence, watching the women they loved across the bonfire, talking to each other with the worry lines of the past few days wiped from their faces.

"Excuse me, sirs," the Mellanastian elder said. "Might I interrupt you for a few minutes."

"Of course you can, Spiridon," Cameron said. "There will be many other nights that my son and I can spend mooning over how fair our ladies look by firelight."

His comment drew a laugh from the others.

"We have had word from one of the other camps that there has been a skirmish of swordsmen further along the road. Two small groups of men, about a half a day's ride from here have clashed. It appears as though one group were camping and the other happened upon them and brought them to their mercy."

Daniel and Cameron exchanged glances, trying to decide who would be best to answer the question through eye gaze only.

"That is probably my fault," Daniel said. "I managed to capture a spy and conspirator of the Sha'a and he gave me information on a route that he was meant to follow and notes he was to send to the Aramalian leader to give information of his whereabouts. I sent a group of soldiers to take up his route and send messages in his place."

"In all honesty, Daniel was a captive for a short time before he became this man's captor," Cameron said. "He is sending on information that gives the impression he is still being held against his will.

"Another lesson you should learn, my son, is when you are with friends and how much of the truth you should tell your allies. Also—never lie, lest you forget the web you have spun and accidentally get caught on your own sticky strands."

Daniel nodded and bowed to his father's wisdom, the Mellanastian man smiled at the exchange.

"Your father is a very clever and canny man, Prince Daniel. I hope that you have learnt well from him."

"I have certainly always tried to take his lessons to heart and will continue to do so," Daniel said, bowing his head to Spiridon.

"Daniel," Violet's voice called out from over the fire.

He looked up to see her standing and pointing up. He followed her gesture to see firelight reflecting off of Pragmoon's scales as she flew overhead, sending strands of smoke twirling.

"Father, Master Spiridon, I think my ride is here. All faring well, I shall see you all in Terisha," Daniel said, bowing to the Mellanastian and embracing his father.

"Fare you well on your mission," Spiridon said, placing both hands over his heart in the Mellanastian fashion.

Daniel walked around the fire to Violet and Astrid.

"Travel safely," Astrid said, pulling Daniel into a tight hug.

"Mother, we will be fine." Daniel smiled and kissed his mother on the cheek.

"We will see you in a few days," Violet said, catching his mother in a hug too.

Daniel saw his mother smile and kiss the young woman, before Violet whisked around to the other side of the fireplace to give Cameron a quick hug before their departure.

"She is a lovely young woman, Daniel," Astrid said. "Keep her safe."

"I will," he said, before hailing Markham and leading the three of them through the gap in caravans to where

Pragmoon waited for them.

The Dragon's musical voice came through the darkness to them.

"Shall we fly?"

Chapter Thirty
VIOLET

The moon had risen while they were having their dinner at the Mellanastian campsite and Pragmoon's scales sparkled white in the moonlight as Violet, Daniel and Markham approached her.

They climbed up onto Pragmoon's back in silence, Daniel deftly helping Violet up, putting his claimed lack of experience into question.

"Daniel," Violet asked suspiciously. "Were you leaving out some portions of the truth in regard to your flying experience when we left Aquilegia?"

Although she could only see his face by moonlight, she still saw the faint flush that rose up on his cheeks.

"Well," he answered, seeming to consider his words. "Pragmoon is the first dragon I flew on."

He tried to flash Violet a winning smile, but she was standing higher on Pragmoon's back than he was and made a formidable form before him.

"Okay," he admitted. "This is the third time I have ridden Pragmoon and I have ridden another dragon as well."

Violet shook her head at him and turned away, nestling herself into her spot between Pragmoon's fins.

I shouldn't be surprised. This isn't the first lie he's told me.

Still, she'd thought he might stop now that she knew about his home. It was only a white lie in comparison to all the others he had told her, but still. It hurt.

"Violet," he pleaded. "I'm sorry, I was just trying to make you feel more comfortable."

She didn't answer him, she couldn't think of anything to say that wouldn't make her feel petty. She heard Markham's voice behind them.

"I told you it was a bad idea."

Violet simply shook her head again. She was embarrassed that his simple comment, had given her so much more confidence and even more embarrassed that Markham had witnessed the change Daniel's lie had wrought in her. She'd always thought she was a strong woman and that she could instil herself with the confidence to do anything she wanted to, but his offhand lie had shaken that belief.

Violet felt a purr in Pragmoon's chest beneath her and heard the tinkling voice, but it seemed as though the words were only heard by her this time.

"Be calm, Lady Violet," came Pragmoon's private message. "Soon all of your strengths will be revealed. You are about to enter a trying time, but hold out. You will be more than you are now once it has passed."

Violet snorted. *Because the things I've faced since I arrived on this world so far haven't been trying?*

"All troubles are different and require different strengths, Violet," Pragmoon chided, answering Violet's inner thought. "You will see."

Violet sat for a moment with her mouth gaping, shocked that the dragon had heard her thoughts. She barely had a moment to get herself together and probe the dragon before Daniel called out that the men were settled and ready to go.

Violet braced herself for Pragmoon's jump into the air, and kept her seat when they took flight.

"Violet!" Daniel yelled against the wind a short time later.

She remained stiff backed and facing forwards, she knew her anger would be short-lived, but she wasn't ready to be placated.

"Violet!" he yelled again, more insistently.

"What!" she yelled back to him, without looking back.

"Look to your left!" he called.

She did as he suggested and realised they'd risen high enough that she could now see the ocean to the north. It presented a spectacular panorama of waves highlighted with moonlight, presenting rolling points of white in the darkness. There was one area though, where the wave broke in different directions. *I wonder what's causing that.*

"One of my water-bound cousins," Pragmoon answered her question. "A draegira. They are our equals in size, but plunge to the depths of the oceans instead of the heights of the skies, they generally live alone in caves along the cliffs on the shore."

Pragmoon responded to Violet's mental request to fly a little closer to the ocean so that they could see the draegira a little better, but turned down the dragon's offer to hail the beast and ask it to swim to shore.

"How are you suddenly able to communicate with me without us speaking?" Violet tried to think the question to Pragmoon, but felt she still had to say it aloud, although she spoke quietly so Daniel couldn't hear.

"It is something that dragons are able to do." Pragmoon's answer tinkled into Violet's ears. "It is also easier when I am carrying someone, but few humans know of this ability. I have decided that I trust you enough to share my skills with you."

Violet thanked the dragon for her trust and wondered if any dragons had spoken to Daniel in such a way.

"No," Pragmoon said. "Such communication always leaves a mark in a person's mind and he bears no such marks. Any dragon you meet now will know that I have placed my trust in you and be inclined to do the same."

"Thank you," Violet said. Then fell into a musing silence.

After a time, Violet realised her irritation with Daniel had faded and she looked back at him while the dragon was coasting and smiled. He looked relieved when he smiled back at her and reached forwards to squeeze her shoulder, but he nearly tumbled from his seat when Pragmoon suddenly and unexpectedly turned away from the ocean again.

Violet laughed, she had felt the movement rippling through the dragon's muscles beneath her and barely moved while Daniel tipped violently into one of Pragmoon's fins.

They spent the next few hours flying over terrain that was largely unremarkable, dominated by patches of bare scrub and rocky land that was unsuitable for farming. The land seem largely uninhabited aside from a few gatherings marked by small campfires close to the road that followed the cliffs.

All the better for the Aramalians to move in, Violet thought.

A distant smear of light appeared on the horizon as they neared Terisha, the seat of the Aramalian Sha'a. Violet did not know much about the woman, other than her name. Yesmin.

She began to feel some pity for the woman, there would be a very awkward situation when Daniel suddenly appeared at the banquet in a few nights time. The move to formally recognise Mellanastia as a nation would carry a lot more weight with the Crown Prince there, as the Sha'a well knew.

Just as the shapes of the buildings in Terisha, including the great, domed palace of the Sha'a, became visible, Pragmoon turned towards the mountain range to the east. The sky behind the mountains was still dark, but a faint band of lighter sky a little to the south was appearing. Their goal was to find a quiet spot in the mountains to camp within an hour's flight of Terisha.

In the end, Violet estimated that it only took them forty minutes to fly from the city to a small plateau that extended from a deep cave within the mountain to a grassy platform with sheer sides all around. Violet almost instantly became bitterly cold after leaving her seat between Pragmoon's fins. She hadn't realised how much she had been relying on the dragon's warmth while they were flying.

Daniel and Markham quickly set about removing the bags and pulling out things to make camp. Daniel pulled a thick blanket out and draped it over Violet's shoulders, rubbing them to warm her up.

"We'll make camp quickly," he said, planting a quick kiss on her lips, before turning back to Markham.

They've either done this before, or their army has a really good training program, Violet thought as she watched Daniel and Markham work. They removed a thick ground cover from the bag, quickly pegging out the corners and sides, and then spread out a large tent across it. They hitched poles up in opposite corners and then both walked around the tent in a clockwise direction, hoisting up the sides with tall poles as they went. To Violet's eye, the thick canvas was heavy and should have been awkward to manage, but the men had it up within minutes.

Violet walked around to the cliff side of the tent, where the men had faced the opening, and followed them inside. Daniel was hooking an extra length of canvas up inside, partitioning off one end of the tent.

"Your sleeping quarters, mi'lady," he said, smiling. "I'm afraid you won't find all the comforts of either of our homes here, but hopefully you will get some rest."

Markham returned from another trip to the bag of supplies with a few more blankets and ducked through the screen to spread them out on the ground for her to sleep on. Violet watched for a moment, but turned when she heard Daniel re-enter, huffing and grunting with effort as he carried in a round brazier made of thick steel. Violet was thankful at the thought of a fire to warm the chill air in the tent, but not without worry.

"Won't we need to worry about that setting the tent on fire?" she asked.

"No," Daniel reassured her. "You'll see."

Just then, Pragmoon stuck her head in through the opening of the tent and pushed her nostrils up close to the steel orb. She breathed air out through her nose that, while not fiery, was hot enough to make the steel glow orange and begin to remove the chill from the air.

"Oh, that's so nice," Violet said, stretching out her fingers as she approached the orb.

"Whoa, there," Daniel said, catching Violet as she tripped over a cushion on the floor.

Her fingers were centimetres away from the hot metal when he halted her progress.

Violet blushed. "Thanks. And thank you for the warmth, Pragmoon."

The dragon nodded her great head and withdrew from the tent and Violet settled down on the cushion she'd tripped over.

One of the men had set a pot of water on the flat top of the orb and this was starting to steam when Daniel joined Violet on the floor. Markham entered again and secured the tent flap behind him, signalling that they were ready to settle in for a rest.

Tea was brewed from the water and toast was prepared. There was little talk over their early breakfast and the three quickly decided to catch some sleep while they could. Violet could barely keep her eyes open over the hot tea in front of her.

"Are you coming?" she asked Daniel as she stood to head towards her nest of blankets.

"I wasn't sure if you would want me too," he said, uncertainty in his voice.

"Of course I do. It's freezing in there and I don't have a hot water bottle!"

Markham laughed. "In that case, sir, you had better go with her, I don't want to be called up for that duty. It would get me into too much trouble."

Daniel playfully cuffed his friend around the ear and followed Violet behind the curtain.

Violet hastily removed her cloak, shirt and corset, leaving on her shift, trousers and socks before picking up her pre-warmed blanket and diving into the others on the floor. Daniel did the same and burrowed into the blankets next to her.

She snuggled up to him, her head on his chest. He pulled his arm tight around her back and they quickly fell asleep, warm and comfortable in each other's arms.

Chapter Thirty-one
VIOLET

When Violet woke, the air in the tent had become hot and clammy. The heat of the sun was radiating through the canvas of the tent and her skin was sticky with sweat. She wriggled herself free of Daniel's sweaty embrace and out of their blanket nest.

She threw her cloak on over her underclothes and ducked around the flap partitioning the tent. She saw Markham deeply asleep in the corner of the tent and tried to slip out without letting too much light in and waking him.

Pragmoon was sunning herself on the plateau, covering almost the entire grassed area with her wings. The dragon raised her purple-scaled head when she heard the tent opening behind her.

"Good morning, Lady Violet," the dragon purred, aloud.

"Good morning, Pragmoon," Violet replied, squinting and raising an arm against the brightness of the sunlight.

It was cooler outside than in the tent. The air was still cold enough that clouds of condensation puffed from her mouth when she breathed, but the sunshine was deliciously warm. Violet guessed that it was late morning, as the sun was high but not quite directly overhead, meaning she had slept for five or six hours. It was enough to refresh her, but she felt sticky and had a headache from how stifling it had become in the tent.

"Pragmoon, do you know if there is any water nearby

where I can wash?" Violet asked.

The Dragon nodded and directed her through the cave at the back of the cliff.

"I think it will be quite dark, but I can hear bubbling water echoing, so it must open up within."

Violet thanked the dragon and returned to the tent quietly to collect a robe, towel and fresh underclothes, which she stuffed into a small bag that she slung over her shoulder. She had been loath to re-enter and risk waking the men from their sleep, so she tiptoed back out again.

Back in the sunshine, she turned away from the view of the land beyond the spreadeagled dragon and headed towards the broad cave entrance behind the tent. The path within was wide and smooth and Violet wondered how it had been created. It was almost as broad as a highway tunnel and so high she couldn't make out the top in the shadows. It became narrower a short way in and while two dragons would have fit abreast at the start of the tunnel, Pragmoon would have to start squeezing if she were to follow Violet this far.

After about ten minutes of walking, Violet heard the tinkling water Pragmoon had mentioned and marvelled at the range of the Dragon's hearing. The pitch darkness of the tunnel also began to lift and she could make out the shapes of boulders protruded from the walls and floor.

The light became patchy and it looked like there was a mouldering curtain hanging across the passageway. Violet approached the patchy section and was surprised to find the curtain was actually a plant. The vine had broad, thick leaves a rich emerald in colour that overlapped each other, giving the patchy effect to the light seeping back into the tunnel. The leaves were slightly sticky when Violet reached out to move them aside.

She gasped when she saw what the vine had been hiding. A rich green oasis that was open to the sky high above, with tall trees and thick vines growing up to the opening. The source of the tinkling water was a waterfall that spouted from a crack in the wall and fell to a place she couldn't see behind the foliage.

The ground was thickly covered with bushes, trees and grasses, that grew rampantly in the little tropical Eden. Beads of water dripped from the leaves of a tree in front of her and Violet realised her hair was now plastered to her head with humidity as well as sweat.

She made her way through the maze of foliage to where she thought she would find the base of the waterfall. She came across a little outlet stream first, bubbling and steaming as it passed in front of her, Violet could not guess where it might leave the cave, but she was very interested in finding the source.

She turned left and headed towards the waterfall. After pushing her way through some thick tree branches, she reached the edge of a brilliantly clear lake, with boulders and greenery framing the water falling from high above. The water must have been coming from a hot spring as the top of the waterfall was almost obscured with steam, but the fall cooled it, so it was delightfully warm when she dipped her fingers into the lake.

She stood on one of the tall rocks alongside the lake and looked slowly around the wall of the cave. She could barely tell where she had entered from, but couldn't make out any other entrances to the cave either. She judged that it would be safe to bathe and pulled her towel and fresh underwear from her bag, hanging them on a tree branch, before removing her soiled and sticky clothes and tossing them on the ground.

She walked to the water's edge, stepping carefully on the slippery rocks. When she entered the water, she found it warm enough to turn her skin pink, but not enough to burn and she dunked herself under and swam over to where the waterfall landed. She was conscious of her nudity and started to feel a bit anxious when she realised that the magnificently clear water of the lake left her body magnificently exposed.

"It's okay, Violet," she said to calm herself. "There is no-one here, no-one to see anything."

She took a few deep breaths as she floated on her back towards the waterfall until she felt a gentle mist on her face. The sound of the falls had also started to thump in her ears, about ten times louder than the tap in the bathtub when she was a kid. She found that there was a sandy beach at the back of the falls and she rose out of the lake to stand in the streaming water.

She stood for a long time with the warm water massaging her sore shoulders and scalp, her eyes closed against the water running into her eyes and ears. Suddenly, the note of the falling water changed. Violet cocked her head to make sense of the sound.

She stepped backwards, out of the stream of water, and bumped into someone. Her heart started thumping in her chest and the person behind her moved as she turned around and opened her eyes.

"Daniel!" She gasped. "You scared the life out of me!"

"I called out to you when I got here, but you couldn't hear me over the waterfall," He smiled. "My only option was to swim out and join you."

Violet suddenly realised that she wasn't the only one who was naked and blushed.

"How did you find me?"

"I woke up alone and I was worried. Pragmoon told me where you had headed, so I brought us a picnic, but I think that can wait."

Daniel reached out and pulled Violet close, kissing her hotly as his hands roamed over her naked body. All thoughts of their stunning surroundings were forgotten as they sank to the sandy beach, water from the falls raining on them and their wet bodies pressed against each other.

When they once again expanded their attention to the world beyond the space their bodies were in, Violet winced. The sandy shore beneath the waterfall had pressed against her skin and she felt... well exfoliated. Daniel had suffered similarly.

"It is fortunate that I plan to wear long sleeves to the meetings in Terisha," he said, smiling.

"Very," said Violet.

They rose to stand at the edge of the falling water together, this time sharing kisses as gentle as the mist that was falling on them.

"Are you ready for that picnic now?" Violet asked.

He nodded and smiled as he swept a lock of soaked hair back from her face, tucking it behind her ear.

"Come on," he said, taking her hand as he headed back towards the pool. "I left the food with your clothes, would you like to swim back, or walk along the shore?"

Violet opted for swimming. *Walking naked on a beach next to someone is a whole different thing to... ahem... bathing with them.*

They splashed about in the water playfully, swimming under and around each other, Violet occasionally managing to dunk Daniel and shrieking and swimming away if he tried to do the same. They had laughed their way across most of the lake and were quite near to where Violet had left her clothes before the water became shallow enough to stand in.

Violet was startled when she bumped against Daniel, standing rigidly stiff and tall, in the chest-deep water. She stood and saw him staring towards the shore, his right hand at his left hip, instinctively reaching to unsheathe an absent blade. She turned her head to see what had caught his attention and held back a shriek when she saw a group of three men standing on the shore in front of them, all with long swords at their hips.

"Welcome to the grotto," said the man at the front of the group, his arms crossed over his chest. "I see that you have been spending your time here as couples usually do, but I'm afraid that you have broken our laws and must come with me to speak your case before our elders."

"I'm terribly sorry, sir," Daniel said. "We did not know there was anyone living up this high in the mountains. We did not realise that there were any laws to break."

"Yes," smiled the man. "Those will be the next questions for you. How and why you have come to our mountains."

"Of course, I can explain that to your leaders and we shall be quickly on our way, we never intended to stay long up here."

"I'm afraid that may not be possible, my friend. The reason not many know of us, is because any who come here are very rarely allowed to leave."

The three men on the shore drew their blades and pointed them directly at the couple in the water.

Chapter Thirty-two
DANIEL

Daniel reached a hand out to Violet and felt her grasp it tightly, she had pressed herself close against his back, using him as a shield against the glances of the men on the shore.

"Okay," Daniel said. "We'll come with you, you don't need to use your swords to convince us. Please, can you give us a little privacy while we dress?"

The man onshore nodded and directed his companions to position themselves around where Violet had placed her fresh clothes, facing away from where the couple would come out of the water.

"I'll go out first and hold up a towel for you, don't worry, we'll be okay," Daniel said, squeezing Violet's hand.

Daniel led the way to the shore, standing tall and confident, despite apparently being a captive again. Truthfully, he was worried, he had never heard about any people living in the mountains beyond Aramalia. He did not think the men were Aramalian as their clothing was plain, where Aramalian soldiers wore rich fabrics and were highly ornamented. The hands that held the swords were callused and rough, but more from hard work in rough conditions than hours of drilling. Adding to that, their swords were dull and looked like they weren't used very often.

Daniel thought he would probably be able to fight them and win, or at least let Violet get away to seek help from Markham, but he was intrigued by these people. How could there be a community up here with their own laws and rituals, when the heart of the Aramalian Empire was less than half a day's ride away?

Daniel reached the shore and thought quickly about whether he should attempt to escape or continue to comply with their demands. He decided to play along for now, his decision helped along when he remembered he had not brought any weapons with him. Like Violet, he'd thought they were alone in the mountains and had not thought there would be any danger to find them.

He picked up a towel for Violet and beckoned her up out of the water, meeting her at knee depth to wrap her up and not minding his own continued nakedness in front of the strangers. He rubbed her shoulders as he drew her to the shore, whispering as he went.

"It won't take long for Markham to come and look for us because we're due to leave the plateau within the next couple of hours. He'll work out what has happened and ask Pragmoon to help find us. Just play along for now though. Do as they ask and I'll make sure no-one hurts you."

"But I can—" Violet whispered back before Daniel cut her off.

"Shhhh," he said. "We're too close now, they might hear you."

Violet looked at him with pinched eyebrows and pursed lips, her annoyance at being interrupted evident. He rubbed her shoulders through the towel, trying to calm her, although he preferred her to be cranky at him than scared of the men surrounding them. She moved over to the bushes where she had set out her underclothes and he took the towel off of her shoulders and held it up to screen her from the other men while she dressed.

When she was finished, Daniel fetched his own clothes, dressing in the light trousers and open necked shirt he had worn into the grotto. He took a step back to stand next to

Violet and squeezed her hand before speaking to the mountain men.

"We're ready," he said. "Allow us to introduce ourselves, my name is Daniel and this is Violet, we are travellers and apologise for trespassing on your lands."

"I am Carlt," said the leader of the three men. "These are Trey and Gam. We are mountain men and your apologies are best saved for our leader."

"Who is your leader?" Daniel asked as they started walking. Carlt took the lead, Violet and Daniel together in the middle, and Trey and Gam behind them.

"The Mountain Man is our leader and he will be very interested in what you have to say. It has been almost a year since anyone from outside stumbled across our settlement, and those who know about us are few."

"You usually find travellers more regularly than that?" Daniel asked.

"Trespassers," Carlt corrected. "We sometimes saw them as often as every three months, but they have waned recently."

The group crossed the little outlet stream from the lake and trekked around the edge, almost to the base of the waterfall, and turned onto a narrow path that cut through the lush greenery. The path was visible, but not completely free of vegetation, so Daniel assumed it was not heavily used.

Carlt led them a short way along the path before the trees thinned out and they saw a different tunnel opening up before them. The entrance to this tunnel had been cleared of foliage and carved with images that clearly showed how couples usually spent their time in the grotto. Daniel looked at Violet and raised his eyebrows at the lewd carvings. Violet flushed and dropped her gaze from his.

"Quite imaginative craftsmen you have up here," Daniel commented to Carlt as they entered the cave.

"Sculpted from life, of course," Carlt commented, drawing a flush to Daniel's cheeks.

The tunnel they had entered was short and lit from the other end, and it didn't take them long to emerge into bright sunlight. Daniel shielded his eyes and scanned the scenery.

They were in an open, grassed area between the high peaks of the mountains and there were huts set out in small groups before them. The path meandered through the settlement to a square with a large, rock-edged firepit in the middle and rows of benches surrounding it. To their right was a large hall, built with raw timber and rocks.

"This way," Carlt said, leading them around the firepit to some steps which climbed to a paved patio in front of the building.

A man stood guard outside the door. He looked over the barely dressed prisoners in front of him, before nodding to Carlt and opening the door to the hall. Daniel noticed Violet scanning the sky overhead as they were led inside and wondered what she was hoping to see.

The builders had used stretched hide rather than glass, so it was dim inside despite the closely-spaced windows along the walls behind them and to either side. The wall opposite the entryway had only one door set in it and Carlt walked over to the door while Trey and Gam led Violet and Daniel to sit on a pile of cushions at one end of the building.

Daniel searched the room with his eyes while they waited, looking for clues of who these people were, what they might need and any possible lever he could use to secure their freedom. The room was sparsely furnished, with only a few piles of cushions and long shelves flanking the internal door. The shelves were filled with seemingly unrelated objects, a large conch shell, a bull's skull and a few books. Daniel recognised some books from Aramalia and some from the Realm, but others had writing on the sides that he could not read.

He had resorted to tracing the pattern embroidered on the cushion he was sitting on when Carlt finally re-entered. The young man was leading a stern, grey-haired man back into the room. The new man's face was chiselled and worn, and he held himself as though he carried a great weight.

"Intruders," he said, approaching the young couple. "What are you doing in my lands?"

Daniel slipped into his most diplomatic mode, bowing from his seated position in deference to the newcomer.

"Please accept our apologies. We did not know that the lands in these high mountains were claimed. We were simply seeking a peaceful place to spend a few days."

"It's a long way to come for a bit of peace and quiet," Carlt said, but the newcomer hushed him.

"There is something you aren't telling me," he said, eyeing the two carefully. "But we will get to the bottom of it. I am Foran, the leader of the people who live here. We call ourselves the Men of the Mountain."

"We are both surprised and pleased to meet you, I am Daniel and this is my fiancée, Violet."

Violet let out a small grunt at his claim, but otherwise stayed silent.

"Your fiancée?" Foran asked. "Well, perhaps you will be able to use the marriage grotto without breaking the law someday. Traditionally, only newly joined couples may enter the glade, otherwise there would never be any peace in there... probably not a lot of work done out here either, now I think of it. I think we can forgive that transgression, you should not be punished for breaking a law you knew nothing about."

"Thank you, Sir Foran," Daniel said. "We appreciate your kindness. May I ask, could you please tell us what this settlement is? Are you an Aramalian settlement, or from another country that I have not heard of?"

The man looked as if he had sucked on a lemon when

Daniel mentioned Aramalia.

"Pah, Aramalia," Foran said. "We are not associated with that witch! Most of the people here, myself included, have escaped from the clutches of the Sha'a. Whether they were sometime prisoners of Yesmin, or left before she had a chance to wreak revenge on them for something. The people here are refugees.

"I found the valley here nearly fifteen years ago, I didn't have quite so many scars then and my back was stronger. Yesmin had tried to capture my whole village because the town leader had said he thought she was corrupting the country. I, and a few others, escaped the round up, but we didn't dare move to another village, lest she decide to condemn any who had harboured us, so we travelled to the high mountains. We found this valley and here we sit today."

Foran smiled and shrugged.

"It doesn't quite have all the luxuries of my former home, but it has become a place where we can feel safe. Not everyone is from Aramalia here either. There are others who have come from the lands on the other side of the mountains.

"Now, Master Daniel, I would appreciate it if you would elaborate on your own identity?"

Daniel opened his mouth to answer honestly, but his words were drowned out by the great shriek of a dragon from the square outside the hall.

Chapter Thirty-three
VIOLET

"Violet," came Pragmoon's voice in Violet's mind. "I'm outside."

"I never would have guessed," Violet though back drily, a small smile creeping onto her lips as she reassured the dragon of their safety.

Daniel looked at her, alarmed, and she turned her smile into a reassuring one, reaching over to squeeze his leg.

The guards surrounding them had leapt up from their seats when they heard the dragon roar, and now stood with hands by their sides and fear on their faces. Foran remained seated and merely studied the couple in front of him more intently than he had before.

"Would that be a friend of yours outside?" he asked.

"Yes," Violet said. "Pragmoon, Elder of Dragonhome, is without, waiting for us to join her and begin our work for the day."

"Work?" Foran knitted his eyebrows. "What work do you do that requires the assistance of the beasts of the sky?"

"Please," Daniel said. "Come outside with us, I might have a proposal for you."

Foran nodded slightly and rose to his feet, waving his hand to indicate that his prisoners should do the same thing. The mountain leader led the way to the door, standing tall and proud as he opened it and stepped out to find himself eye-to-enormous-eye with the dragon.

Violet quickly communicated with Pragmoon that Daniel had a plan and told the dragon that there was no immediate danger to anyone. he did not need to be their fierce protector, yet.

"Greetings, Mountain Man," Pragmoon said aloud. "I have come to find my friends."

"They are here," Foran said, bowing sketchily.

Violet looked around at the houses surrounding the great firepit. Doors and windows were being cracked open so that those within could see the great beast. The faces that Violet could see though the crack-like openings were thin and fearful. They were terrified.

"Foran," Violet said, reaching out to touch the man on the shoulder. "Please, tell your people that they have nothing to fear. Pragmoon will not hurt them as long you do not harm us."

Daniel and Pragmoon both nodded their agreement with Violet's statement.

Foran stepped to the front of the paved area outside the hall and called out in a voice that carried through the small collection of huts.

"My people, we have been joined by strangers, two people from off the mountain, and their friend here. They tell me we have nothing to fear from their presence and I believe them. Please, go about you duties while I speak with them. When I have anything to report, I will call for assembly. Go safely, Men of the Mountain."

He stepped back and spoke quietly to one of the guards, then asked Violet and Daniel to join him on the benches around the firepit.

"I have asked for cushions and breakfast to be brought for us," Foran said.

Violet's stomach growled loudly at the mention of food. She gave a sheepish smile and apologised. "Sorry, we haven't eaten yet today. Oh, there will also be another person joining us."

Pragmoon unfolded a wing and allowed Markham to

slide down and join them. Daniel introduced him to the mountain leader after looking incredulously at Violet for a moment.

They were joined by a couple of Foran's advisors, rounding out the breakfast party to six people and one dragon, sitting around the empty firepit and tucking into a meal of apples, oats and warm milk. When they were all sitting comfortably and their bellies were full, Daniel cradled a cup of warm milk and began their tale.

"Thank you for the meal," he began, drawing a gracious nod from their host. "Allow me to introduce us properly, I am Daniel Reyne, Crown Prince of the Realm of the Lilies, this is my friend and confidante, Violet Truman and this is my guard and friend, Theodore Markham."

Foran gave a nod, but his demeanour did not change after learning Danial was a prince.

"We are en route to Terisha for a summit regarding the formation of a new nation, Mellanastia, between my own country and Aramalian lands. The Sha'a does not support the move and is trying to undermine the summit."

Daniel went on to outline the details of his capture, the plan to reappear in Aramalia on the night of the summit and their attempts to recognise the new nation without a bloody war breaking out.

Foran listened quietly, leaning forwards with his chin resting on his hand. He sat thinking for a long while and finally asked why the dragons were interested.

"Allow me to speak on behalf of my kind," Pragmoon said. "We have an agreement with Daniel's realm, where we hunt animals and pay for our kills. In return, neither dragon nor human hunt one another.

"However, our numbers have grown, there are now too many of us to live comfortably in our mountain home. We have been trying to make an agreement with the Aramalian leader, but, so far, nothing has been achieved. I have travelled here with Prince Daniel, both as a favour to the country we already have a treaty with and to push our ambition to treat with Aramalia."

"It seems that a treaty with dragonkind would be of benefit to the Sha'a. Why has she not yet agreed to it?"

"So far, it is us who have not agreed," Pragmoon explained. "The Sha'a asks more of us than we would give. She asks for protection of her borders and assistance in times of trouble. I fear that her ambition would see us used to expand her empire and worry that those who come to Aramalia would be forced to battle those who stay in the Realm."

"That is a reasonable concern, given the history of the Sha'a," Foran said, he turned back to Daniel. "Prince Daniel, you said you had a proposal, I think I might now know what this is."

"Quite possibly," Daniel said with a smile. "One of our tasks while we are over here is to find a place for the dragons to live when acceptable terms can be agreed on with the Sha'a. I was wondering, are there many other caves and tunnels around this area that are like the one you found us in?"

"Yes," said Foran. "There is another dell a little higher up the mountain with more great tunnels and caves. We have not yet found any others with plant life such as the one you were swimming in, but there may still be others."

"Then perhaps we can to treat with you instead," said the dragon.

Foran and Pragmoon began discussing options. The dragons might help with building in the village, humans could share their livestock and both parties could share knowledge that might lead to a peaceful settlement for dragons and humans alike.

Violet and Daniel took a stroll around the settlement while the others spoke. Violet noticed that people had emerged from their homes and started moving about again, some hanging wet washing on lines strung up between trees and others tending gardens. The children were running around the firepit and looking at the dragon with awe. The older kids had started daring each other to run up and touch her tail. Pragmoon noticed their game and started twitching it away as they approached, making them work harder.

Soon, the children had realised that she meant them no harm and started to touch her, gingerly at first, then admiringly as they felt how smooth and warm her scales were. While Pragmoon was still intent on the conversation with Foran and his advisors, she also played with the children, changing the colour of her scales and occasionally poking the shyest ones with her tail, drawing giggles from the group.

Violet leant against Daniel and smiled as she watched them playing.

"I wonder how Pragmoon knew that we needed her," Daniel asked, curiously.

Violet shrugged and tried to not give away her secret. When they'd been caught, she had made contact with Pragmoon in her mind. She was going to tell Daniel about it at the time, but he'd shushed her. Now that she was no longer so fearful of their situation, she felt it was something that should be kept a secret, especially as Pragmoon had said not many humans knew about that skill.

"Maybe she foresaw it."

"Hmm," said Daniel. "It would have been nice if she had seen it before we got caught."

"Ahh, but then we would have missed out on our time together before the capture," she said cheekily. "Would you have preferred to miss out on that as well?"

"You minx," he said, turning to kiss her.

He looked at her and sighed, lines of concern appear

around his eyes.

"What is it?" Violet asked.

"Come with me," he said, taking her hand and leading her away from the houses. He propped her against a tree. "Wait here a minute."

He walked back to the village and disappeared behind the houses. He returned a few minutes later, smiling broadly, and almost bounced his way back to where Violet was sitting.

"Violet, things have not gone as I would have planned for you since you entered my world, you've travelled half of my country on horseback, flown across two other countries on dragon and been captured in your undergarments. I'm amazed and astonished at what you have done since you arrived here."

"Thank you?" Violet said quizzically.

"This is not how I would have planned to ask you this question. It is not the romantic scene that I imagined and that you deserve, but I feel that every time I introduce you as my friend or companion, I am doing you an injustice.

"And so, Violet Truman," he said, popping open a polished wooden box that had been hidden in his hand and dropping down to one knee. "Would you do me the honour of becoming my wife?"

Violet looked at the man, the ring and their surroundings, her heart pounding and mind swirling with thoughts.

"What? Now?" she asked eventually, incredulously.

Daniel laughed.

"No, not right now, maybe in a few months. I'll give you time to be sure of your decision, but I would like to be able to introduce you to people as my fiancée. So they know that if anyone should try to claim you or harm you, I will be there to defend you."

"Wow, gosh. I... I never imagined that I would need

defending," Violet stuttered. "Sorry, what am I saying, of course, yes!"

He took the ring out of the box. It held a large square diamond, surrounded by gold filigree and flanked on either side by sparkling square emeralds. Violet held out her hand and he slipped the shining ring onto her finger. It was a little snug sliding over her knuckle, but otherwise it fitted perfectly.

"Now, can I kiss my future bride?" Daniel asked rising to his feet.

In answer, Violet held her arms out and squeezed him close as they kissed.

Chapter Thirty-four
VIOLET

"Isn't it lucky that it fits so well," Violet said, rolling her hand so that the ring could catch the sunlight.

Daniel looked a bit sheepish.

"Some might call it luck, others might call the memory of your lost heart ring to mind. I borrowed it."

He removed the lining of the box and pulled out another ring, this one was merely a thin band of silver with a small heart stuck on it.

"Oh," Violet exclaimed. "I'm so glad, I thought that was gone forever. My mother gave it to me."

"Yes, I didn't realise when I took it. I'm sorry."

She slipped the heart ring onto the ring finger of her right hand, relieved to have it back, she felt like she had let her mother down when she'd realised it was missing.

"Come on," he said. "Let's see if they have managed to agree to anything in our absence."

"Um, do you think that maybe we could go back to our camp and get some clothes first?" Violet asked, looking down at her thin undergarments.

"Oh, didn't he tell you?" Daniel asked, wickedly, "Markham packed up some things for us and brought them with him, that's how I got the ring, it was in my satchel."

"What?" Violet screeched, playfully punching his shoulder. "So I didn't need to be getting about in my underclothes all this time? I think I take back my acceptance."

"Ha, you are a funny lady."

They walked back to the camp, hand-in-jewel-bedecked-hand, greeting the others with grins on their faces.

"About time you joined us again," Markham said. "Why the boyish grin?"

"Allow me to introduce Violet Truman, my fiancée," Daniel said with a smile.

Markham let out a whoop, frightening the children who were still playing with Pragmoon, and leapt up, catching his friend in an enormous hug.

"Congratulations, you are a lucky man," Markham said to his friend. "Violet, you are an amazing young woman and you will be such a wonderful Queen."

"Queen?" She asked, stunned.

"Hopefully not for many years," Daniel said, squeezing her shoulder.

Violet stood silent for a moment, she had not thought that far ahead when she had accepted Daniel's proposal. Pragmoon's voice trilled into her mind.

"Don't worry," the dragon said privately. "You'll be fine."

"Easy enough for you to say," Violet thought back.

"Just breathe," the dragon instructed.

Daniel disappeared behind Pragmoon's wing for a moment and reappeared with a small bag. He handed it to Violet as he planted a kiss on her lips. Foran waved over a young woman from one of the nearby houses and asked her to show Violet to a place where she could dress in privacy.

Violet thanked the man and followed the young woman to a house on the outside of the square, leaving Daniel with Markham, Foran and the dragon. Violet had barely stepped into the house when she heard a rumble from Pragmoon, followed a few seconds later by the crack of her wings unfolding. She was momentarily worried, and her heart rate spiked.

"Don't worry," Pragmoon said in Violet's mind. "We're not leaving without you. I'm going to scout."

Violet waited until she heard the door of her borrowed bedroom close before diving into the bag Markham had hurriedly stuffed with clothes for her. Normally, she chose fresh clothes before showering and had them laid out and ready to put on after. Unfortunately, she had not done so that morning. Consequently, Markham had simply selected a few things from her larger bag to stuff into the smaller one.

She searched the bag, mentally cataloguing what was there, and then dressed in loose, dark brown trousers, a camel-coloured shirt and a brown vest. Her boots were in the bag too and she swapped the light shoes she had worn into the cave for the hardier footwear.

There was as knock on the door of the cottage and Violet heard the villager's feet pad on the packed dirt floor to the door. Muffled voices came through the door of the room she was in. She couldn't hear the words, but she recognised Daniel's voice. Violet hurriedly stuffed her belongings back in her bag and left her borrowed dressing room.

She emerged from the room, her hair still a tangled mop as Markham had not packed a hairbrush, and found Daniel waiting for her by the door.

"There you are," he said. "Foran has invited us on a tour of the settlement. Would you like to come?"

Violet thought for a minute, she was still tired from all of the hurried journeys she had made in the last week, but she didn't really want to be separated from Daniel in this camp of strangers.

"Will it take long?" She asked.

"An hour or so," he said. "Then we can head back to our campsite to rest up and prepare for tonight's travel."

Violet nodded her agreement and they walked hand in hand back to the square. Pragmoon had left a pile of their belongings near the firepit and Violet placed her bag with it.

Foran greeted her with a large smile.

"You look much refreshed, Lady Violet," he said. "Those colours suit your skin and hair and make your eyes look even more wondrous."

Violet thanked him for the compliment, but Daniel joked with the man.

"Excuse me, but the engagement ring on her finger has been there for barely an hour," he kidded. "I would appreciate it if you would leave it a little longer before trying to convince her to change her mind with your honeyed words."

"My apologies, Prince Daniel," Foran said with a smile and a shallow bow.

The trio laughed and Violet playfully hit Daniel on the shoulder.

"Do you really thinks I could be so easily swayed?" she asked.

They set off on their tour of the valley. Foran started by explaining that the square was the heart of the settlement, most people only had to travel a few minutes on foot to join the evening festivities around the firepit. Meals were cooked on racks over the flames and some put bread dough in cast iron pots that they placed on coals a few hours before dinner.

Violet marvelled at the sense of community in the place, often families would share their meals: one family preparing the meat for the day, another the bread, while a third would prepare vegetables before all families converged with their plates in the evening to eat their fill.

The tour moved on through a gap in the houses to the pegged-out beds of vegetables planted beyond. Foran explained that they grew most of their vegetables and fruit in the valley as he led them through the paddocks to the orchard. They had small herds of livestock, free-range chickens and some dairy cows, but they didn't often have a lot of meat to go around.

Foran had a few contacts in the villages around the feet of the mountains in Aramalia, most of whom were people whose family members he had helped escape from the Sha'a. Through them, the mountain community was able to trade some of their goods for flour, livestock and other items they were unable to produce in their hideaway.

They walked past the stables which housed only a half a dozen horses as the animals were too rarely used and too expensive to feed to warrant having more. Violet reached out to pat a brown horse on the nose, the feeling of the horse's coat under her fingers sending a sharp stab of longing into her heart as she thought of Star.

Adjoining the stables was a small smithy, servicing the horses and the settlement. The blacksmith uncurled from his stance over the anvil when he saw the trio walk past and waved an ash covered hand before returning to the work before him.

Violet smiled, marvelling that all of the people in the settlement seemed to work so well together. She had seen people with dirt-encrusted fingernails planting new crops in the paddocks, children playing games together while their mothers tended sprouting crops and whole families working together to collect water. This was all in addition to the families working together on their meals. Violet didn't know of any communities on her own world that worked so closely together.

Their last stop was the warehouses. These were located in a group of caves close to the grotto where they had been found, but the entrances had been closed off and thick doors barred their progress. Foran asked Daniel to help him push the door of the central warehouse aside, then they stepped into the cool, dark storage area.

Violet was amazed by the amount of produce stored on the neat shelves and the crates stacked down the middle of the cave. It might only be a small settlement, but it was definitely a productive, and well-organised, one.

Foran wrapped up the tour by guiding them back to where they had been captured. Their bags had been placed by the entrance of the cave and they picked them up before Foran led them back to the waterfall.

"I do not wish to go on and view the land that used to be my home, there are too many bitter memories sleeping there," Foran confessed. "I do not envy your mission, the Sha'a is a hard opponent to face, but I wish you luck and safe travel. I find it hard to believe that we will meet again, but stranger things have happened. Farewell."

"Thank you, Foran," Daniel said. "I hope that your good fortune in the mountains continues and that one day I may be able to help ease your isolation. May your negotiations with the dragons prove to be fruitful for you all."

Violet did not feel she had anything to add to the formal exchange so she simply nodded a farewell to the mountain man and they turned to make their way back to the camp.

DANIEL

They walked in silence for a while, navigating their way back through the lush greenery to the dark tunnel and their campsite beyond. The walk seemed shorter on the return trip—knowing the path ahead always makes it seem so—and they emerged on the plateau in bright sunshine after a few minutes.

They walked to the edge of the plateau and looked down over the country beyond. A span of fertile land was spread at the feet of the mountains like a plush green picnic rug that wasn't quite laid out flat, the places where the rug bunched forming little hills and waterways. The green swathe only lasted a few kilometres before giving way to sandy desert beyond.

Daniel cast his eye back to the fertile land before him and studied the roads, not many people travelled along them and the few there looked like ants returning to their nests, which were the small settlements scattered across the swathe. He couldn't make out any movement of soldiers or heralds, no-one waving the flag of the Empire as they travelled along. The Sha'a seemed to currently be focussed on Terisha.

The capital was only visible as a blur against the horizon, just before the darker smear of ocean melded with the blue of the sky. Daniel narrowed his eyes as he thought of the possible threats that lurked there. The Sha'a's plots, and the meeting with Loucius's wife and any number of people with swords who would happily do anything to please the woman in charge of the country.

He sighed.

"Are you okay?" Violet asked.

He turned to her and smiled, trying to ease away the lines of worry he could see on her face.

"My heart is heavy with my duties as prince, but having you beside me helps to ease them."

She smiled back and he admired the green flecks that sparkled in her eyes and the way the afternoon sunlight gilded her hair. He reached out to stroke her face and kissed her gently, trying to pour all of his love and appreciation for her into it. He pulled away before the kiss could light any deeper desires and rested his forehead against hers.

"I love you," he breathed.

"And I you," she said, standing up on her toes and wrapping her arms around his neck.

Daniel should have felt completely safe and comfortable in her embrace, but he had a heavy, nagging feeling in his gut that there was something wrong. He knew it was probably just caused by worry for his family and the peace meetings in the days ahead, but he couldn't shake the feeling that there would be bad news before long. He didn't want to worry Violet though, he had already put her through so much since she had entered his world and he didn't want to burden her with more. He tried to ease the tension he was carrying between his eyes and shoulders while they stood, embracing each other on the edge of a cliff with a land of dangers only a few hundred metres below.

They were pulled from their silent reverie by the screech of a hawk as it dove through the air, down to the grass at the foot of the cliff far below.

Violet gently lowered her heels and released him first, turning her gaze towards Terisha.

"I guess we head that way soon," she said.

"All too soon," Daniel replied. "But not yet, we must wait until the sun sets and darkness gives us cover. I don't want to let the Sha'a know of our presence ahead of time."

Violet nodded and pulled her arms tight against her sides to ward off a sudden shiver. Daniel didn't know if it was from cold or fear, but he went into the tent and returned with a cloak, wrapping it tightly around her shoulders.

She turned and smiled again, but he thought that this time her smile looked a little more distant and the light worry lines around her eyes were a little deeper than they had been a moment before.

"It will be okay, I'm sure everything in Terisha will work out fine and we will be back in Aquilegia and planning our wedding before you know it," Daniel said, smiling at his fiancée. "If you are worried about tonight, you could always stay in the mountains, I'm sure Foran would allow you to stay up here for a few days."

"Do you really think that I would let you travel without me after all I've done in the last few days?" she asked jokingly, but the worry lines returned again, along with a look of uncertainty when she continued. "No, it is not the immediate future I am worried about, but further along. When I accepted your proposal, I forgot for a moment that you weren't just the clumsy guy I met in my ED, you are a Prince in this world. When we are married, I will be a princess and eventually...."

"A queen," Daniel finished for her when she trailed off.

Daniel looked into Violet's eyes, trying to see into her mind and learn what he needed to say to comfort her.

"A queen," She repeated. "I don't know how to be a Queen! If you have a wound that needs dressing or a concussion to treat, I'm your lady. But when it comes to running kingdoms, I haven't the faintest clue. I only know of one queen in my own world and all she ever seems to do is open hospital wings and wave at her adoring public."

Daniel laughed and was forced to hold his hands in front of him in defence as she turned murderous eyes on him.

"I'm sorry," he sputtered out quickly. "You are leaping too far, too fast." He reached forwards and cupped her face in his hands. "All of the big decisions about the Kingdom will be my responsibility, not yours. The queen generally knows everything, organises everything and makes sure we get everywhere when we need to. You will have my mother to help you for a few years at least. My parents will step down from their roles, not leave the country."

"Now it sounds as though I'm just a secretary with a fancy hat!"

Daniel dropped his hands from her face, spun away from her and threw them in the air. When he turned back she was standing with her spine straight and her face held in a stern expression.

"I am wise enough to know that there are some arguments you cannot win," Daniel said as he stepped back to her, this time placing his hands around her waist and pulling her gently towards him. "I know you are worried and scared, but I think you will be fine, if you don't want to organise, then you may set up medical clinics wherever we go and tend to scrapes and concussions."

"Could I really?" Violet asked with hope in her eyes.

"Of course you could, you would be the queen!" he smiled as he said it. "So, what do you say? Will you at least agree to spending some time with my mother, learning what she does before deciding whether you can marry me?"

"Hmm," she said, a wry smile curling the corner of her mouth. "I guess so. You had better be on your best behaviour though. I want to make sure that you are worth changing my whole life for."

"Prince's honour," He leant down and kissed her, squeezing her tight as he did.

"Come along then," she said, pulling away after a moment. "We have work to do."

He sighed as they turned away from the land of his enemy to look at the camp they had to pack away. Markham had only had time to throw a few bags together when Pragmoon had summoned him that morning, so the tent remained standing with an assortment of belongings inside.

They set to work piling up cushions, folding blankets and packing all of their clothes neatly away. Daniel hauled the brazier from the tent, then stretched out the kinks in his back and wiped sweat from his forehead. Violet stepped from the tent as he watched, folded blankets bundled in her arms and sweat plastering wisps of hair to her forehead.

He tortured himself with a fleeting thought of returning to the lake with her to freshen up, but shook his head. He didn't want to be captured by Foran's men twice in one day.

"What are you shaking your head about?" Violet asked as walked back to the tent.

"I was just thinking about throwing you back in that lake to cool down," he said.

"I think you might have been thinking about more than just a swim though, am I right?"

He grinned in reply and she shook her head, laughing as she walked back into the tent for the next load.

If we hadn't already packed all the cushions, he thought.

He shook his shoulders and returned to the task at hand, wondering if her presence would be a distraction in the next few days. He immediately pushed these thoughts to the back of his mind. Now that he had her, he wouldn't be without her for all the riches in either of their worlds.

Once they had emptied the tent, they set about collapsing it. With Violet's inexperience, it took them much longer than usual as Daniel had to call out instructions and she was not expecting it to weigh so much. When she lifted her first pole, it skewed sideways, pulling the canvas with it. Eventually though, they had the tent parcelled up, the groundsheet wrapped around it and everything ready for Markham and Pragmoon's return.

It was nearing evening and there was not much shade left on the plateau so they grabbed a couple of cushions from the pile and retreated to the opening of one of the caves for a light supper of bread and cheese. They had barely settled back onto their cushions when they heard the flapping of wings and watched Pragmoon land lightly a few metres from their feet.

"Please don't tell me I have to get up again," Violet groaned from her pile of cushions to his right.

He told her not to worry, they had earned their rest for the evening and could stay there to finish their meal.

"Besides, Markham has been sitting down all day, he will surely have enough energy to load the dragon by himself,"

Daniel said as Markham approached them.

The soldier shot a dirty glance at his Prince, threw a cushion to the ground and plonked down on it himself.

"I assure you, the sitting down I did was not relaxing, most of the time I found that my seat was almost vertical with a great distance between myself and the ground below me. The few times when I wasn't soaring to dizzying heights, I was hiking across steep and wretchedly rocky areas of the hills or walking within tunnels deep inside the mountains themselves. Not my idea of a good day off."

Daniel laughed and apologised for his friend's discomfort.

"Just a few more days and we can return home for a well-earned rest, but first, we go to Terisha."

"We shall fly very soon," Pragmoon chimed in.

Daniel looked to the walled city away in the distance, trying to squash the feeling of foreboding in the pit of his stomach.

"Yes," he agreed, almost to himself. "And I am beginning to fear what we are flying to."

Chapter Thirty-five
DANIEL

Shortly after the sun had set, the trio of humans stowed all of their belongings on the back of the dragon and prepared to leave the plateau. Daniel glanced around one last time before waving to the other two that it was okay to climb onto Pragmoon's back.

Daniel admired the way Violet climbed with confidence to her place between the dragon's shoulders and settled herself down for the flight. He climbed up and settled in behind her and Markham sat with his back to the large bag that held their supplies.

Markham called out when he was securely tucked between fins and Pragmoon took a few great steps towards the edge of the plateau and leapt straight off, throwing her wings wide and catching the current almost silently. The moon had not yet risen, so she did not cast a shadow on the ground as she flew swiftly towards Terisha, gliding on the air currents high above the ground.

They reached Terisha too quickly for Daniel, he wanted more time to collect his thoughts and iron out his plan before starting his search for Loucius's family. He had to shake his other concerns from his mind to direct Pragmoon across the city when they flew over the walls.

Loucius had given Daniel a description of a walled garden that made up part of his family's quarters within the palace grounds and Daniel scoured the darkness for the landmarks he had detailed. There he saw a yard with a large tree, but no flower beds. That garden had both, but the flowers were not laid out correctly. There, Daniel saw it. It had a tree in the northern corner of the garden and a flower bed in the shape of a serpent flowing around the northern and western walls.

He pointed it out to the dragon, then braced for the dive. Pragmoon had explained that she would need to fly quite high to avoid the keen eyes of the guards, so they needed to drop quickly and steeply into Loucius's yard. Daniel's head span as they suddenly plummeted to the ground, the momentum of their descent throwing Violet's body backwards into his. He tensed all of the muscles in his body and clasped the forward edges of the fins he was pinched between, trying desperately to stay on the dragon's back.

It felt like they spent minutes diving to the ground, but in reality, it only took Pragmoon a few seconds to land gently in the garden after Daniel pointed it out to her.

Despite the silence of their approach, a woman stood before them in the garden when they dismounted. She held a large sword in her softly shaking hands, held straight out from her body.

"Greetings," Daniel said quietly. "We mean you no harm."

The woman swore at them and threatened to call the guards.

"I don't think you will," Daniel said. "If you genuinely thought to call the guards you would have done so immediately, not tried to confront the intruders in your enclosed courtyard with a sword borrowed from your husband."

The woman narrowed her eyes and surveyed the intruders suspiciously.

"Who are you and who sent you?" she asked. "You cannot be hers, she does not yet have any dragons on her side, so you must be from the Realm. What do you want from me?"

"I am the Prince of the Realm and your husband sent me."

A mixture of relief, anger and finally hatred flowed across her face.

"He's still alive then," she dropped the point of the sword into the dirt and leant on it, relaxing her tense posture. "Captured in his plot, I guess, and now he sends a prince after me. As if I've not got enough trouble from the last batch of royalty he got me involved with."

"He told me he only got involved in the plot to capture me because the Sha'a has been holding you hostage, is this true?" Daniel asked.

"Try to open the doors and leave my sumptuous prison. The guards out there will kill you before they even look at you if you take a step outside the doors. More, they can enter whenever they please. Should I show you the bruises?"

Daniel heard Violet draw a sharp breath in at the woman's implication.

"I am sorry for your treatment at the hands of your captors," Daniel said. "It might please you to know that your husband is currently residing in one of the towers of my own palace, and it is a far from comfortable home."

The woman shrugged, she had accepted her lot in life. Despite the abuse of her guards, she lived in comfortable quarters, was able to tend to a garden she loved and always had plenty to eat and drink, unlike many in her home country who barely had enough food for their families. There were far worse places she could be forced to live.

"We have come to seek your help and release you from your cell, if you will allow us."

"What would you ask of me?" Her voice was resigned, as if she thought they would take with force what she wasn't willing to surrender freely.

"Tell us everything you know about the plans against my family and help us learn the layout of the palace," Daniel urged.

"I don't know if I will be able to help you, much of what I know is from my husband. If he told you where I am, surely he must have told you all of his plans too."

"Please, just tell us," Violet appealed. "We need to know if there were any other plans against those from the Realm."

"There isn't much really," the woman shrugged. "I knew he and his crew planned to kidnap the Prince, but no details about the travel, or where they meant to keep you. Then there was the plan for the attack on the road, but I don't know when that was meant to happen and that was only in the initial planning phase when Loucius left, I think they had decided not to go ahead with it."

The blood rushed from Daniel's face and the foreboding chill intensified. "What attack?"

"Loucius didn't mention it?" Uncertainty tinged the woman's voice. "I think it was only a secondary plan, in case they didn't find you in time. Loucius told me that the Sha'a planned to have a group of soldiers mount an attack on your convoy. But that was only one of the first options they came across for sabotaging the summit and was dismissed, she didn't think an open attack would help her cause."

Violet stepped forwards, reaching out to grasp the woman's hands. "What do you know about this planned attack?"

"Not a lot," the woman shrugged. "Loucius didn't plan it in detail. He thought of it, the Sha'a said it was too aggressive and he moved on to the next plan, but kept the idea in his mind in case he needed it as a backup."

Daniel conferred with Markham quietly.

"A back up plan?" the prince asked the soldier.

"It makes sense. I always like to have an idea of what to

do if things go wrong," Markham mused.

"Surely we don't need to be concerned, though, Loucius's messages are still going through, there is no need for the Sha'a to think that a backup might be needed. Unless..." Daniel trailed off and turned back to the woman. "The messages that Loucius sends back when he makes camp each night, what information was he to share?"

The woman shuffled her feet and adjusted her weight on the sword.

"I'm not sure. I don't think it is usually much, just a report that they have reached their camp for the night."

The chill in Daniel's blood turned to a fever. The missives Daniel had sent off with Lieutenant Lis had contained detailed information on the road, the landscape, and even health notes on some of the men. He asked a belated question of the woman before them.

"I'm sorry for my rudeness, please tell us your name."

"Zora, my lord."

"Zora, my family may be in danger. Please tell me everything you know about the planned attack."

Zora sensed the urgency in the stranger's voice and drew herself up straight.

"There isn't really much to tell," she said, hastily continuing when she saw the frenzied look in Daniel's eyes. "I think they were planning a night time ambush? Somewhere on the road between where they want to make the new country and the current border of ours. They were to fight without banner or armour so the Sha'a could claim they were among the brigands who attack on that road frequently."

Daniel scanned his mental map of the countries. "Between Mellanastia and Aramalia, that's not a large distance. My parents were in Mellanastia last night and I would expect them to arrive here in two days. One more night on the road between there and here... but they will be well inside Aramalian land by tomorrow night. Oh God," he said, looking up at his companions with fear in his eyes. "That means they will attack tonight."

"We must move swiftly," Markham said.

"Zora," Daniel said, earnestly. "We will return, and if you wish us to take you to safety, we will. But we must leave quickly now. Thank you for your help."

Daniel turned away and started walking quickly back towards the dragon concealed in the shadows of the garden wall. Markham trailed close behind and Violet had to take a few running steps to catch them up.

"You'll leave me here for the Sha'a's guards?" Zora asked shrilly, chasing after them.

Daniel turned on his heel and stood with his chest to hers, looking into her face. This proved to be uncomfortably close for her and she shrank down and away.

"Madam, I see many ways that you could barricade the entrance to your rooms and means of escaping if you wished to," Daniel looked pointedly at the tree growing close to the garden wall. "I would suggest that you explore such options while you await our return."

The woman sagged but did not offer a response and Daniel walked away from her again, joining Violet and Markham on Pragmoon's back. He did not even need to signal that he was ready, the Dragon simply stood on her hind legs and sprang into the air. The swift leap knocked Violet loose and she landed in Daniel's lap again. Her eyes were accusing when they looked up at him.

"What is it?" he asked, anxious about how he many have upset her.

"Are you always so cruel?" she asked.

He was baffled, and thought over the events of the last few minutes to work out how she had labelled him so, but could not fault his actions.

"You left that woman there to be played with by the

guards and possibly killed by the Sha'a. Why?"

"Where could I have taken her?"

She harrumphed in answer, he could tell that she knew there were no other options, but it went against the morals taught on her world. She pulled herself up from his lap and sat, stiff-backed and silent, in front of him.

Daniel sighed, he had not done much to please her since she followed him here. He hoped that one day he would be able to show her enough of the beauty of his world to counteract all the bad she had seen in her first few days.

Pragmoon slowly transitioned her flight trajectory from almost vertical to horizontal and Daniel made out the lights of Terisha winking at them far below. In a few minutes, they had passed over the city completely and were travelling faster than Daniel had ever flown, high above the coast road that led to Mellanastia. Pragmoon had understood the need for haste without Daniel telling her, he was curious about this, but his mind was too full of concern for his parents to allow him to wonder over the dragon.

An attack, he thought, *How could I not have expected that?*

He tried to remember the lay of the coast road and work out where the soldiers might be. Where his parents would have stopped for the night. How long it would take the soldiers to reach them after nightfall. He could think of a few different scenarios, but couldn't decide on any of them.

It was nearing midnight and Daniel expected it would take an hour, even at this speed, to reach the first possible camp ground. He sat restlessly, worrying, fidgeting. Violet turned back to look at him.

"Pragmoon says calm down, she is going as fast as she can and your bouncing doesn't help."

"What? I didn't hear her say anything," Daniel immediately stopped his fussing, puzzled now.

"The wind is too loud," Violet said after a pause. "I only

just heard her."

He watched her as she spoke, her face did not give away a lie, but he sensed there was more. He looked at her questioningly, but she simply turned her face back into the wind and left him wondering. Still, he stopped bouncing.

He did not know how much time had passed before he heard Violet cry out and point over the Dragon's left shoulder.

Before Daniel could turn to look, Pragmoon had banked, allowing all of her passengers to see what Violet had.

A large fire.

The distance meant that Daniel could make out little of the scene, but the space to the right of the fire was inky black, indicating it was near the cliffs. He made out the pale streak of the road a little to the left and a sharp pain stabbed through his heart.

He nearly vomited with fear and worry when he realised that his prediction was correct, the fires were the burning wagons of his parent's entourage. He was too late to warn them.

They had already been attacked.

Chapter Thirty-six
VIOLET

Pragmoon leapt skywards as soon as her passengers dismounted, eager to defend the rulers of the Realm and preserve the treaty. Violet heard her growling at the attackers and watched her flick her wings in fury as she herded the enemy soldiers towards the swords of the human defenders. Violet thought she must be keeping her breath in check so as not to add to the fires already blazing and imagined the dragon would find that frustrating.

Daniel had turned his back on the flames for a moment and looked at Violet, fury carved into his features.

"Stay here," he commanded. "Markham, guard her. I need to know what has happened here."

He swiftly turned on his heel, but Markham shouted for him to return.

"No! Your Highness, you must not." Markham added the epithet to placate the anger that was now directed at him. "Your parents have been attacked, but it is not your duty to defend them now. You must stay here, out of harm's way. If anything has happened to them and you follow their fate, the Realm of the Lilies will be lost."

Daniel swore and threw his dagger down into the soft ground.

"Go," the Prince growled, gesturing towards the sounds of fighting with his sword. "Find my parents and see that they are safe."

Daniel did not look up to watch the soldier leave. Instead, he kicked the dirt with his toes, muttering under his breath. Violet stepped towards him, reaching out her hand to him in appeal, but he turned away from her, placing himself so he could watch the gap in the caravans before them.

"Daniel," Violet pleaded, but she didn't know what more to say.

She walked gingerly towards him and placed her arms around his waist, clenching her hands together over his belly. After a moment, she felt the muscles in his shoulder soften under her cheek as he relaxed them, just a little bit. The smell of smoke, and the sound of shouts and cries carried up the slight rise they were standing on and Violet felt Daniel flinch every time a voice called out to regroup the soldiers of his realm.

He started a few times and his hand moved restlessly to his hip, reaching for the sword he had been forbidden to wield. She felt a battle raging inside him to match the one they were watching, he desperately wanted to join his countrymen and protect his parents, but knew that he needed to stay away.

Finally, they saw the defenders moving forwards in a spearhead, herding the attackers back from their caravan, Markham calling orders at the fore. Pragmoon looped around the back of the attackers, pressing them towards Markham until the soldier called out for them to surrender.

There was some confusion and yelling from the attackers until a man with an authoritative voice called out for his comrades to lay down their weapons. They stepped back from the battle and Violet and Daniel heard the dull thud of their weapons hitting the soil.

Daniel waited only as long as it took for the last man to drop his sword before he pulled out his own and strode towards the former battleground.

Violet followed close behind, taking two steps to each of his strides.

"Markham," he shouted, when he entered the light from the burning caravans. "Report."

Daniel seemed oblivious to the gaze of the soldiers of the realm as he approached Markham, but Violet watched them. Some had looks of sorrow and some of respect bordering on reverence and Violet nearly stopped to question them, but Daniel was unstoppable.

"I do not know all the details, my lord," Markham replied. "It was a bit of a mess when I got down here. I found this group of men and brought them around to harry the attackers from the midst of the caravans. I shall find the highest ranking officer now."

A young soldier stepped forwards.

"Your H-highness," he said, timidly. "If you permit, I will take you to the Queen. Sir Markham can give his report there."

Violet heard a queer note in the soldier's voice, but if Daniel heard it, he said nothing, only nodded curtly and waved his arm for the soldier to lead the way. He led them through the ring of wagons and skirted the central campfire, leading them to the large caravan that belonged to his parents.

They entered the dimness of the caravan without knocking, the smell of blood immediately confronting them. Queen Astrid knelt by a bed and turned, revealing her ashen face in the dim light, to see who had entered. A mixture of emotions crossed her face when she saw her son: fear, worry and sorrow.

"Daniel," she said, sadness tinging her tone.

Violet broke out in goosebumps and her stomach clenched tight as Daniel stepped forwards to where his mother knelt, tears now glinting in her eyes.

"What is it?" he asked, and then he, too, fell to his knees.

Astrid leant over to her son and Violet suddenly saw what had overcome them both.

King Cameron lay on the bed before them, a great, ragged gash across his unmoving chest.

"What happened?" Daniel asked in a whisper.

"I don't know," Astrid said, with a sob. "We were sitting by the campfire and all was well, then a man came up next to your father, pulled out a sword and attacked."

Astrid dissolved into tears as she leant into Daniel's chest.

A man stepped from the shadows past the bed where the King had been laid.

"Your Majesty," he said. "We will not know the truth of it until the morning, but it seems as though the group had been watching us for some time. It may have been that the sentries were slack or they were paid to leave a gap to allow the attacker to enter. Whatever it was, he carried out his plan to murder the King just as the attack began outside the camp. I fear that the murderer may have escaped in the confusion."

Daniel peered at the man in the darkness.

"Master Spiridon, I see that you did not escape unharmed." Daniel observed.

Violet started when she recognised the Mellanastian elder, then she noticed the dark patch of blood spreading from his left shoulder, down his arm.

"It doesn't hurt too much," the little man said, but he showed the lie in his words as he reached up to touch the top of his shoulder with his right hand. "It was the same sword that injured your father, but I was the secondary target and managed to avoid the full attack."

Daniel nodded to the Mellanastian, his face tight with grief as he turned his attention back to his mother and his father's motionless body before him.

The Mellanastian man walked away from them and

beckoned Violet to join him outside the caravan.

"Give them a little time to grieve together," Spiridon said to Violet as he reached to take her hand as she stepped down. "He will be ready for you to help him soon enough."

Violet only nodded in answer, she had suddenly found her corset too restrictive and had been having trouble drawing breath within the caravan. It was as though each breath in did not quite have enough oxygen and she felt like she was being smothered. When she stepped outside, she recognised that she was on the verge of a panic attack and forced herself to slow her breathing, in turn reducing her heart rate and calming her mind.

After a few minutes, she could breathe normally again, although her heart was still racing and her arms still felt a little light. She felt the beginning of the headache that usually came after a panic attack and massaged the trigger points in her neck that usually released the discomfort.

She looked up at the dark patches of sky visible between the skeins of smoke unravelling above her. Most of the fires had been dampened now and the sounds of groaning that had dogged them as they crossed the camp now seemed to be focussed on a single area to the left of the campfire.

Although she was not familiar with treating battlefield wounds, the sound of their groans filling the air drew Violet to help them, despite the troubles she was facing. From experience, she knew that her anxiety would fade, at least for a while, if she busied herself.

She nearly vomited when she saw the first wound. Her years of experience in an emergency room had not prepared her for such gore. One man's hand had almost been severed, only a few bits of determined sinew had kept it attached, and he begged for someone, anyone, to remove it completely. Despite her desire to help, she walked around as if she was part of the smoke herself, seeing, but not absorbing, the horrors around her.

Elisa found her roaming there and drew her back to the main campfire, crooning wordlessly and coaxing her along.

"Come now," she said. "Sit with Elisa, I will prepare you something to help. That Spiridon should not have let you wander."

"I should be used to this," Violet said, dazedly. "I have seen injuries every day. But never so many at once, or... so violent?"

"Violet," Elisa said sternly, turning the younger woman's face towards her. "Come back. You are lost."

Violet felt the command in the other woman's voice and suddenly the fog seemed to clear from her mind. She shook her head as if to clear it.

"Thank you," Violet said, feeling as if she had purpose again. "I should go and help the wounded now."

"Wait," the other woman said, placing a hand on her arm. "Drink this first, it will give you strength."

Violet drank the hot, strong drink, barely even tasting it as she swished it down her throat in her hurry. She thrust the cup back at the woman before turning to the wounded soldiers.

It was a long, hard night, spent working in dim light with meagre supplies. She gave up on bandages at some point in the evening and called Pragmoon to bring her bag of supplies so she could rip her petticoats into strips.

There was one physician in the field, but too many wounded for him to be concerned by the young woman stitching up the minor wounds behind him. He stopped once in that weary night to admire her work and commend her on her ability to stomach the hard task.

Apart from that, her memory of that time was of endless bowls of blood-reddened water, expensive fabric butchered with blunt scissors and the cries of the wounded as they lay either being ministered to or left to breathe their last in peace.

Chapter Thirty-seven
DANIEL

Daniel rubbed his hands over his face, smearing soot and sweat. The campfires had been kept burning through the still night and the sun was just beginning to pierce the thick cloud of smoke still encasing the remaining caravans.

He had spent the night speaking to his soldiers, those left alive and those fading away, thanking them for their loyal service. His chest hurt from the number of guards he had farewelled, twelve of their fifty-strong entourage had lost their lives. Of those remaining, only sixteen were without injury, the same again had minor injuries and the others were injured badly enough that they would need to remain camped for some weeks to recover.

Markham had taken the captive's weapons hours earlier and Pragmoon had made a prison of her body for them. Daniel had given them bandages and supplies so that they could tend to their own injuries, but had not wanted to send in any members of his own party to render aid. He scanned the smoke filled site as the coming daylight started to reveal the mess of the battle.

Markham was rallying the remaining soldiers, getting them prepared to move the caravans. They had lost three in the fires, leaving the two royal caravans, one wagon of supplies and one of Mellanastian wares intended for exhibition.

Daniel looked towards the remains of one of the burnt

out wagons and saw a woman, covered in mud and blood. His sleep-deprived brain took a moment to remember who it was.

"Violet," he said, anguished at having forgotten about her in the night.

She was almost swaying on her feet when she looked over at him, her face expressionless. He skirted around the firepit to her and drew her to sit on one of the logs near the remaining coals.

"Are you okay?" he asked.

She looked at him, dazed.

"There were so many injured," she said. "The wounds were so rough, I stitched some, but others... I just couldn't."

He pulled her close to his chest, he knew about the work she did on her home world and should have known she would try to help the wounded. But the aftermath of battle was far removed from the hospital she had worked in. She was used to seeing people on clean beds and having all the necessary supplies set out in neat, sterilised kits.

He squeezed her tight and then looked up to scan the campsite for help. It was Spiridon who came to his rescue, the Mellanastian man crossing the campsite with a bowl of hot broth for each of them.

"Here," he said, touching Violet on the shoulder. "Drink this."

Daniel nodded his thanks and sipped at the hot brew, it instantly woke him, clearing his mind and giving him strength to face the new day.

"Thank you," Violet said, also sounding awake. "Last night was horrid."

"You worked hard and well, Lady Violet," Spiridon said, inclining his head to her, before moving away from the couple.

"I'm sorry," Daniel said, adding a pang of guilt to the weight of grief in his abdomen. "I shouldn't have left you."

"You didn't," she said, looking up into his face. "I walked out of the caravan, leaving you. It doesn't matter, what must we do now?"

Daniel sighed deeply.

"Too many things," he said. "Come, let us find my mother."

They found Astrid in the same caravan she had been in when they arrived the previous night, but she had not been idle.

King Cameron was now dressed in full formal attire, his face had been bathed, his cares and worries washed away in death. His crown rested atop his head and fresh armour covered the damage done to his chest the previous night. He looked mighty, but hollow. A shrunken version of the man Daniel had counted on for all the years of his life.

The pain in Daniel's chest had abated and he felt empty. He had cried long over the body of his father the previous night and there was no more time for grief.

"Violet!" Astrid exclaimed when she saw the younger woman. "What a mess you are in."

Daniel smiled half-heartedly as his mother started bustling about, calling for her maid to fetch warm water and cloths and forcing Violet to divest herself of her filthy layers. At a loss and out of place, he walked out of the caravan and went looking for Markham.

"Report, please," Daniel said when he found the soldier.

"The situation is not great, Your Majesty," he said. "You know the casualties already and the losses of goods and wagons. We are yet to interview the attackers and decide what to do from here."

Daniel nodded and thought for a few minutes.

"How many soldiers do we have who are able to ride today?"

"Thirty two, sir," Markham replied.

"Split the group," Daniel said. "Fourteen of the uninjured men are to travel with my mother to Terisha, ensure that they have uniforms and armour that is undamaged. Of the remaining, eight should stay here with those who are too injured to move yet and the other ten are to escort my father's body back to Aquilegia.

"Note the names of the other men who were lost last night and send a fast messenger ahead. They are to stop briefly in Mellanastia to pass on word of the attack and then keep travelling to the Realm. I will need notepaper to scribe a message to the castle chief in Aquilegia."

Daniel paused a moment and thought about the other aspects of their travel plans. "Has anything been heard from Leo Lis recently?"

Markham waved over a nearby soldier.

"We lost the communications from Lieutenant Lis last night. One of the caravans that burnt belonged to the officers, but I heard both reports we'd received since you left us in Mellanastia. One arrived shortly after you flew off two nights ago. That night's rendezvous point had been taken successfully and the missive sent through to report to the Aramalian handlers."

The soldier scratched his chin before continuing. "Last night's report was different though. The soldier reported back shortly before we were attacked, it almost seems as though they were waiting for him. When Lieutenant Lis arrived at the appointed place, there was no-one there. The landmarks were right and there were signs that a party had been there in the previous few days, but it was abandoned when they arrived."

Daniel frowned. "I think we can assume the Sha'a knew the kidnapping plot had been unsuccessful. I wonder whether the notes Loucius wrote did give it away," he mused. "But that is a problem for another day. Is that messenger still in the camp?"

"Yes, Your Majesty."

The new title felt like an ill-fitting shirt. Daniel was sure he wasn't ready for it. "Fetch him, I will send a message to Lis as well."

The soldier turned around and trotted off to find the messenger as a page arrived at Daniel's elbow with writing things. Daniel sat down and wrote his messages, then went to check that Astrid approved of his plans.

Astrid and Violet were sitting at the table in the Royal caravan when Daniel entered. Both gave him a strained smile.

Violet looked much refreshed and was cradling a steaming mug in her hands. Astrid had a range of papers and maps in front of her and she beckoned Daniel over to look.

"We are here," she said, pointing to the map. "A short way into the desert lands between Mellanastia and Aramalia. We will need to break camp as soon as possible to reach a safe place to stop tonight."

"Lieutenant Lis is already camped here," Daniel pointed to a place just into the green swathe that marked the start of the Aramalian lands. "I have just prepared a missive telling him to wait there and expect your arrival tonight. You will not reach him until just after nightfall, but the camp will already be set and they can have a meal ready. That will also boost your guard to twenty-four men."

Astrid looked up at her son, calculating.

"You do not intend to travel with me?" she asked.

"No. That way, we can still preserve some element of surprise. The Sha'a knows I am no longer captive, but she may presume I was travelling with you. She may even hope that I was also killed in the attack. If I do not arrive with you, it will keep her questioning."

Daniel went on to outline his plan, his mother nodding approval of each portion. Finally, when he was done, she rose from the table and moved over to where he late husband lay.

She reached out a hand and stroked his hair away from his forehead, tears forming in her eyes.

"Farewell," she whispered as she bent down to place a kiss on his brow.

She rose and withdrew from the caravan, allowing her son some privacy.

Daniel stepped towards the bed, his chest suddenly aching again. He had managed to forget his anguish while planning, but the pain returned when he realised that the time for a final parting had arrived. He dropped to his knees alongside the bed, and rested his arms next to his father's body and his forehead on the still chest.

He breathed in the scent of his father's clothing, changed since the night before, and remembered the man as he had been throughout Daniel's childhood. Always serious while working, but wild on the few occasions he and his sister had torn him away from Kingship for an afternoon. Cameron had always been strong, able to throw them high up in the air until they were nearly half his own height, his shoulder and chest muscles strengthened by an hour of sword practice every morning before breakfast.

Daniel remembered looking out of the window of the Castle in Aquilegia onto the foggy training yards on frosty winter mornings. His hands would leave moist prints on the stone of the windowsill as he tried to make out the shape of his father practicing by the light of flickering torches. When he saw his father preparing to return indoors, he would rush downstairs to meet him, steaming and sweating and loud with exhilaration from the exercise. His father would scoop him up and carry him, over his shoulders or under his arm, while Daniel pretended to try to fight free as he was carted to the dining hall for breakfast.

Then he remembered his teenage years, when his father turned him towards study, learning the ways of the Realm. Guiding him in diplomacy and including him in his morning sword practices. That was when he learnt that the exercise was not only for strength, but also to help gain clarity in the mind.

Daniel felt bile rise up in his throat at the realisation that his father was gone. He was not ready to be without him. He was not ready to rule their Kingdom. He had thought that they would rule side-by-side for many years to come and that they would work together to prepare Daniel's children for their places in the Realm.

Daniel steeled himself. He did not have the time to mourn his father now, there was too much uncertainty for him to waver. The changing of rulers could always cause problems, and never more so than now. The precedent of a King abdicating for the new one to take the throne had been unsettled and that filled Daniel with fear, even without considering the threat of the Sha'a.

"I'm sorry, Father," Daniel said, standing slowly, painfully, like a man who had spent too long in training. He wiped his face with his sleeve as he turned away from his father, feeling as though a part of him had been torn off and left on the bed where Cameron lay.

His eyes met Violet's she still sat quietly at the table, her face echoing his pain. Belatedly, he realised that she had faced the same pain many years earlier, hers compounded by the loss of both of her parents in one night.

She rose slowly, stepped forwards and took his hand, squeezed it with what he imagined was her full strength, and gently walked with him out of the caravan, letting him close the door on his father behind them.

Chapter Thirty-eight
VIOLET

He looks broken, Violet thought as Daniel turned away from the bed where his father lay.

She knew the pain he was feeling, but her own had long since faded to a bittersweet feeling in her heart. She knew she had been robbed of opportunities with her parents, but the thought no longer hurt or made her angry. Not so with Daniel.

His shoulders hunched as he turned and she closed the space between them, taking his hand and hoping to give him the strength he needed to walk out of the caravan.

When they stepped out of the caravan, the soldiers were ranged before them around the firepit that had been set the night before. Slowly, they all bowed to their new king.

She felt Daniel squeeze her hand tightly and saw his posture change out of the corner of her eye. He drew his shoulders back and stood tall and proud. He would not be formally crowned King for some time, but in that moment all there recognised Daniel as their ruler.

A movement to her left made Violet turn and she watched as Astrid, too, bowed, signifying that she was willing to concede to her son. Astrid had told Violet earlier that, although her husband had died, she was still queen. Showing her support for Daniel would help keep the realm stable, and the soldiers who bore witness to this would take this news of her allegiance back to Aquilegia with them.

Violet watched Daniel look around the camp with glistening eyes. He opened his mouth, cleared his throat and then spoke, huskily.

"Thank you. I know that I am not the only person in the realm who will feel the loss of my Father. In time, we will be able to hold a service to recognise what he accomplished while he was King of our Realm. For now, we all have tasks to attend to and must all put our pain aside. Go safely and in peace."

Daniel turned from the crowd and left the circle of caravans, Violet close behind. He kept his strong stance until they were out of sight of the others, then his shoulders bowed again.

"Are you okay?" Violet asked.

"No," he replied. "But I will be, eventually. Right now I want to jump on Pragmoon's back, fly straight to Terisha and roast the Sha'a where she sits."

"I don't think that would be very good for international relations," Violet tried to joke.

"No, and I have to think about that sort of thing now. It's unfortunate."

Violet looked up at him and smiled. "It will pass."

He reached out and pulled her in, holding her tight against his body.

A quiet cough behind them caused Violet to pull away.

Queen Astrid approached.

"My escort is ready," she said. "I will see you in a few days."

"In Terisha," Daniel said.

"In Terisha."

"Travel safely, Mother."

They embraced and Violet felt like she was intruding on their grief. She stepped back, only to bump into Markham.

"Gosh," she exclaimed. "I didn't even hear you come up behind me!"

"Sorry, my lady," Markham smiled. "I came to say farewell and travel safely."

"You aren't coming with us?"

"No. I have been assigned as protector to the Queen," the soldier said with a sigh.

"You don't sound completely happy with that."

"Not exceptionally. I am worried about him," Markham explained. "He is ensuring his mother's safety, but leaving himself unguarded. Be wary."

"Surely we'll be fine with Pragmoon?"

"You should be, but I don't feel as though Daniel will be safe with anything but my own sword at his back."

"I think I understand," Violet said. "Be safe."

She went to hug the soldier, but realised that such familiarity was probably uncommon in the realm and she ended up awkwardly squeezing his upper arms instead.

Daniel called to her and she moved over to where he stood next to Pragmoon. The dragon stretched out, allowing the two humans to sit down on her hind leg and lean back against her body. They sat in silence as they watched the two caravans depart, one taking Daniel's father to rest in state until their return to Aquilegia and the other taking his mother towards further potential danger in Terisha.

The caravans had long since disappeared from sight when Daniel roused himself and walked away from the campsite, towards the cliff. Pragmoon retreated into the woods alongside the road, concealing herself, and Violet followed Daniel towards the edge of the cliff. The sun was high overhead and the glare from the ocean had Violet wishing for sunglasses.

"It wouldn't have happened if it weren't for me," Daniel said, talking out towards the ocean. "If I hadn't been flitting between worlds so much lately... I should have been here."

"You don't know that," Violet turned to face him and placed a hand on the arm across his chest. "You can't blame yourself."

He kept looking stonily out to sea. "If I hadn't been captured by that lout and his gang, I would have been here with my parents when the group attacked..."

"Then you might have been killed as well as, or instead of your father. Then where would your kingdom be?"

"I would have been able to save him. I would have been more alert. If it weren't for..." Daniel finally looked down at Violet, a cold light in his eyes.

"If it weren't for me," she said quietly. "If you hadn't met me, you would have been here to prepare for this meeting. You wouldn't have been distracted on the road and you wouldn't have been captured. If it weren't for me, you wouldn't have been off with Pragmoon in Terisha, you would have been here."

Violet stepped away from him, a sour taste rising in her throat.

I didn't ask for this, her inner voice screamed. *I didn't ask for any of this. He could have just stayed away after that first visit, the first time he met me. He didn't even have to venture into my world in the first place and now this is my fault?*

She bit back all of the venomous responses rising to her lips, then walked away from the cliff edge, trying to find refuge from the mess she now found herself in on this strange world.

Of course there was nowhere for her to storm off to. There was no-one else there and the only landmarks around were trees and the empty road.

"Violet," Pragmoon's voice tinkled in her mind. "Come

to me."

Resigning herself to the fact that she was now only able to do as she was told, she walked into the trees to find the dragon.

"You are upset," Pragmoon stated aloud as Violet approached.

"Apparently, if Daniel hadn't met me, his father would still be alive," Violet explained as she crossed a narrow clearing and climbed onto the dragon's back. She lay down between a pair of fins, her head on Pragmoon's, and looked up to the sky.

The dragon grunted in response. "He wants to blame himself for the king's death and he has chosen to use his relationship with you to do that."

"That sucks," Violet stated.

The dragon huffed a laugh, although the phrase was unknown to her, Violet's meaning came through clearly.

"How can I fix it?" Violet asked.

"I don't know that you can. You need to wait. He will come to different conclusions with time."

"Or he won't. In which case, I'm screwed. Stuck on a different planet with no-one to help me."

"Princess Jessica will help you."

"Unless she agrees with her brother and thinks their father wouldn't have died if it weren't for me."

"Then you can always count on me. While you are in this world, I will always help you and if you wish to return home, I will deliver you to the portal to your realm."

"Thank you."

Violet started thinking silently as she watched small wisps of cloud scud across the sky, then she sat up abruptly.

"Jessica! How will she hear about the loss of the king?"

"A messenger will be sent off when the king's body returns to Aquilegia."

"But that's not very fair, that will take at least two days.

Won't there be preparations to make for the funeral and..."

"Won't it be better for her to live two more days without fear for her mother and brother?"

Violet had to agree with that, but it still felt wrong to let the princess continue on, oblivious to the devastation of the previous night. Suddenly, the horror of the previous night came back and Violet realised that she'd been awake for over a day.

"Sleep," Pragmoon soothed.

Violet didn't need much convincing, the dragon was warm and comfortable, she put her arm over her eyes and drifted off to sleep.

Violet woke with a dry mouth, but didn't feel dank and sweaty as she usually did when she slept during the day. She was laying in the shade with the wind over the cliffs counteracting the heat radiating from the dragon. She slid down and rustled through their supplies for a water flask and swilled a couple of mouthfuls.

"Violet," Daniel's voice was husky.

She looked over to where he stood, leaning against a tree. He looked as though he had been standing there for some time and like he was about to fall asleep where he stood.

"Daniel," she exclaimed. "Come here. Have you slept at all since yesterday?"

She let her nursing instincts kick in as she started bustling around the little clearing. She rummaged through their packs and pulled out a blanket and some cushions and drew him to lie down. She asked Pragmoon to light a fire on some sticks that had been collected by some soldiers before they left and when it was merrily crackling, she put a sooty pot over the coals and boiled some water.

"Here, drink this," she instructed when she had brewed tea using some of the leaves left by the Mellanastians.

Daniel sat up blearily and silently took the cup. When he had drained it, he settled back down on the pillows.

Violet left him be and returned to the dragon's side, placing a pillow under her buttocks and leaning back against the warm scales. She was too highly strung to sleep again–not wanting to leave Daniel so exposed–but Pragmoon spoke again.

"Do not fear for you safety," Pragmoon chimed telepathically. "I will ensure that no harm comes to either of you. I can survive without sleep much better than you humans can, and you must be alert to travel tonight. Rest now."

But Violet still felt guilty and surprisingly wakeful from the small exertion.

"Not yet. Will you tell me a bit about yourself first?" When Pragmoon agreed, Violet asked, "How old are you?"

"I thought it was impolite to ask a lady her age?" the dragon chuckled.

Violet rolled her eyes, *Apparently even dragons are vain now.*

"I am one hundred and thirty-eight years old," Pragmoon answered eventually.

"Is that old by dragon standards?"

"It is not unheard of for a Dragon to live to two hundred years, but one hundred and sixty is more common."

"So you saw the lands before the Reyne family established the Realm of the Lilies then?"

"Yes, I was just entering adulthood when Raymond Reyne was born. Back then, there was no organisation between the regions and dragons had free reign to hunt whatever they willed."

"Do you miss that?" Violet asked when she heard

Pragmoon's wistful tone.

"Not me, particularly, but some other dragons fondly remember how easily a human slides down the throat," Pragmoon chuckled when she felt Violet stiffen. "Don't worry, I prefer my dinner to come without a cover, and cows are generally much cleaner than humans. I like chickens."

"Chickens? Wouldn't one just be a mouthful?"

"About three is a decent meal."

"What about the feathers?"

"They toast right off."

Violet laughed at Pragmoon's irreverent tone.

"Thank you," Violet said, rubbing a hand across the dragon's scales.

She relaxed back against Pragmoon's flank. From where she sat, she could just make out scraps of sea between to the tree trunks and she let her mind and gaze wander. After a short time, she found herself fighting to keep her eyes open and eventually gave in to her body's need to sleep.

Chapter Thirty-nine
DANIEL

Daniel woke with a start, wisps of a dream leaving his heart racing and his palms sweaty.

He had dreamt of his father's death, his mind creating its own version of events. He had been floating above the firepit, watching his father with an indescribable feeling of danger. He saw his own soldiers walk past his parents, the firelight glistening off of their weapons menacingly. The soldiers were laughing and talking amongst each other as they roamed the camp with their meals.

Daniel tensed when he saw one of them flinch and turn towards his father as if he were about to draw his sword, but he had just fumbled his fork and was hastily trying to catch it. Then he saw a man walk through the campsite wearing dark brown clothing. The soldiers paid him no heed, comfortable in the knowledge that others were responsible for their safety.

The weight in his stomach reached a crescendo as the man wove his way through the soldiers towards King Cameron. He tried to shout a warning but no sound escaped his lips and he did not move, regardless of how fiercely he tried to thrash his limbs.

The man in brown came within a few paces of his father. As if sensing the danger, Cameron turned towards the man, but moments too late to see the sword being drawn and slicing towards him. Daniel screamed.

And woke up.

He had rolled away from the pillows and blanket that had served as his bed and was lying on the bare ground. The sheet that had covered him was tangled around his legs and right arm, which explained the restraint he had felt in the dream. He freed himself and looked around, orienting himself back in the real world.

Even when he had worked out where he was and confirmed which parts of the dream translated to reality, his mind still felt hazy. The fire was still alight, but burning low, so he threw a log onto it carelessly, causing hot coals to spring free of the fireplace. He let them be, the area around them was clear, but even if it weren't, he might not have stirred himself to clear them. He was in a destructive mood, especially considering the trees in question were Aramalian.

He was angry. He was angry at the Sha'a for her plotting, at his soldiers for not guarding the camp well enough, at Spiridon for not being the primary target, at Violet for taking him away from his family and then at himself, because he knew that only one of the subjects of his ire was deserving of it.

The Sha'a. He wondered what other plots she had up her sleeve. He had already been victim to two of them, his capture at the hands of Loucius and then his father's murder. What other misery would she cause?

He thought about the upcoming summit to recognise Mellanastia as a nation and wondered idly whether the Realm of the Lilies should still support them. It had already cost his nation so much, he needed to assess whether there were still other risks that he didn't know about—who else had the Sha'a targeted?

He was stirred from his musings by footsteps behind him.

"Hey," Violet said, taking a seat on a log beside him.

He didn't answer.

"You're not yourself right now."

Still he ignored her.

"What happened to your stirring speech last night about not having time to grieve now?"

"That was for them," he muttered. "I don't have to do anything for a few more hours yet."

"You could still try to act like a decent person."

He didn't have an answer for her.

She grunted, got up and walked away.

"We leave at sunset," he called to her.

"Only if you ask nicely," she replied, disdain in her voice.

"What?" He asked, confused.

"I said, only if you ask nicely."

"I heard what you said. I didn't understand your meaning."

"Well," Violet said. "Pragmoon has promised to take me wherever I want to go. If I choose to leave, she will take me to the thicket. It would interfere with your plans for the evening, but I'm sure she would be able to cross both distances over the night and day. You would have to choose whether to come or wait, but I'm sure you'll be fine."

He spun, crossed the distance between them in a bound and raised an arm to strike her. Violet dodged back and Daniel found a burst of flame spouting between them. When he looked, it seemed as though Pragmoon had not moved, but her eyes were open and there was a glittering light in them. Somehow, the dragon looked disdainful.

"Don't you dare," Violet snarled, looking as if she could spit flames herself.

Daniel paused and replayed the last few minutes in his head, then dropped his arm and looked at her, saddened.

"You want to leave?" he asked.

She shrugged. "It's been a big day."

Shame washed over Daniel.

"I'm sorry. It's just..."

"Don't," she interrupted. "Don't try to explain. I know, it's okay. When you are ready to talk, I will be here, but don't shut me out in the meantime."

She reached out a hand to him and he took it, she led them back to their seats by the fire.

"I'm not ready to be King," he confessed.

"I'm not ready to be King's consort."

"King's what?"

"King's consort. Not a term you use here? The lover of the king?"

He considered a joke about whether he would change his mind, but decided his behaviour towards her had already been bad enough for the day.

"Well, I won't be crowned for a few weeks yet. You have some time to get used to it and you could always change your mind."

"True, we'll see how it goes," she smiled, then turned serious again. "How will your sister find out?"

"I think she already knows that you are my lover," he tried to jest.

She rolled her eyes. "Such a man. I meant how will she find out about your father?"

"Someone from the castle will be sent to her in Ivywood. Probably our old nurse, she will be able to comfort her."

"How long will that take?"

"She will probably know late tomorrow. She should recognise the increased danger and retreat to the monastery until we return. The monks will ensure she is safe and she also has a dragon looking out for her."

Pragmoon confirmed this. "I sent word to Dragonhome to send a protector for her. Many dragons respect her, I am sure she will be safe."

"We could send Pragmoon to Dragonhome and ask another dragon to take a message to her," Violet suggested.

"Jessica will be fine," Daniel soothed. "Let her live without worry for us for another day."

Daniel dug some food out of their bag to make supper, finding bread rolls, carrots and dried beef. He placed the last two ingredients in a pot with water to stew and put the rolls near the fire to warm. Violet found a crock of butter, bowls and cutlery and set them out ready.

"Where to next?" she asked.

Daniel sighed. "I will refrain from stopping at my mother's camp tonight, it is sure to be watched. I don't fear any further attacks, they are on Aramalian land now and the Sha'a wouldn't dare an open attack. If she did, it would announce war between our countries. While she is power hungry, I'm sure she would not like the cost of war."

"Which cost?"

"All of her little luxuries, she wouldn't be able to afford them if she had to fund a war."

Violet nodded her understanding. "So, not to the queen's camp then."

"No," Daniel confirmed. "Mother and her guard will arrive in Terisha late tomorrow and I don't want to be far away when that happens."

"Back to the plateau?"

"No, I'm thinking a little closer to hand than that. I think we might pay another visit to Loucius's family."

"You want to stay in the palace in Terisha?"

"Yes. It is the best place to be, I think. The walls are tall enough to ensure privacy and stop anyone climbing in, so no one will think to look in her garden."

"Will you be safe there?"

He noted that she only asked after his safety and not her own before answering. "I think so. I think Zora has genuine feelings for her husband, at the very least she resents the Sha'a for her captivity. I don't think she will report us. Besides, we have a dragon," Daniel said the last part with a grim smile.

They fell into an uncomfortable silence, Daniel imagining the grisly work that he would like to put Pragmoon to in Terisha and Violet lost in her own thoughts.

"I wonder what they will think happened to me," she wondered aloud.

"Hey?" he asked.

"My friends, back at home."

"Do people often disappear on your world?"

"Not these days. Not with all the online social networks and regular surveillance of public places. No-one knew I was going to meet you at the park that day, so they won't be able to narrow it down. I guess they'll just figure I was brutally murdered and my body was hidden somewhere," she said morosely. "It would be kind of awkward if I ever went back. Does time seem to pass at the same rate between worlds? When you were on my world for a day had you only been gone a day here?"

"Not quite, the days here are a little shorter than yours, so sometimes if I left here in the morning and spent a full day and night on your world, I would be returning here the following afternoon," he explained. "Are you thinking about going back?"

"I don't know," she said. "It depends on if you still want me here."

"Of course I still want you here," he answered, too quickly, before he had thought through his words. "I do. I'm sorry I got angry before, everything just went terribly wrong all at once..."

"I understand," she said. "Just try not to blame me for it, okay? It wasn't my fault and it wasn't your fault either. We just have to make the best of a bad situation."

"Okay," he leant in to kiss her, but she turned her face just slightly, only offering her cheek, not her lips.

He accepted the rebuke for his poor behaviour and

hoped that he would be able to make it up to her in time.

"Our dinner is ready," he announced. "Let's eat."

Chapter Forty
VIOLET

After their meal, Violet walked towards the cliffs. She was still tired and overwrought, the emotional outpourings from her fiancé earlier (was he even still her fiancé after the outburst?) and the battlefield healing of the night before had her on the edge of her sanity. She was torn between wanting to scream until her throat burnt or curling up in a ball and crying until her eyes hurt.

The sun was beginning to set, painting brilliant colours across the sky to bid farewell to the day. The sea was relatively calm and reflected the brilliant peach and magenta colouring of the sky. She started when a patch of water was thrown into a flurry, sending the colours shimmering across the surface.

A draegira had broken the surface and was frolicking wildly in the waves it had created. It was small compared to the others Violet now spied. There were half a dozen floating on their backs, gazing up at the sunset. A beautiful whistling music, not unlike whale song, filled the air as they watched the westering sun, completely oblivious of the human watching them.

Violet sat down and curled her legs up to her chest, wrapping her arms around them and hugging herself tight. She watched them as the colours in the sky faded from vibrant to pastel, and deepened through the blues of twilight until night finally fell. She was thankful for the cloak she had thought to grab before leaving the campsite, as the air quickly chilled with the fading of the sunlight.

She heard the buffeting winds of a dragon landing and stood slowly, Pragmoon had returned from her hunt. It was time to fly.

Daniel had packed up their camp, what little there was, in her absence. She had bathed in a little streamlet earlier and changed her clothes, swapping her feminine dress for tight trousers, a shirt and a leather vest. With her knife neatly sheathed and her deep blue cape over all, she felt like a medieval movie character.

They quickly loaded Pragmoon up with their belongings and took to the sky.

The air was even colder at altitude. Violet poked around in a satchel she had obtained from the supply wagons earlier that day and pulled out a felted cap in the same colour blue as her cape. She pulled this down over her ears and let her hair fly free beneath it, hair and face the only part of her visible against the midnight sky.

It wasn't long before they saw the bright campfires of Queen Astrid, the Mellanastians and their soldiers in the distance. Violet's heart leapt into her mouth for a moment at the sight of it, but she remembered that Daniel said they would be ringing the camp with fires tonight.

"Everything seems fine," Daniel called out from behind her. "Let's keep going."

Daniel had told her earlier that those on the ground had been instructed to send out a signal if they needed him to land, but she hadn't been paying close enough attention to what it was. Evidently, it wasn't to be seen.

Soon enough, they had left the haunting fires behind and were speeding towards Terisha. Pragmoon was flying faster than she had before, moving in a series of climbs and falls, working hard to reach high altitudes then freefalling and gliding down, hitting speeds that had Violet's stomach lurching into her mouth. By the time the Aramalian capital was in sight, Violet was well past ready to settle down for the night.

They made their approach to the city the same way they had the night before. Climbing high out of sight and then diving swiftly down into Zora's quarters, at the heart of the Sha'a's domain.

It did not take long for Zora to appear once they set down.

"I did not expect to see you again," the woman said, seeming displeased.

"Madam Zora, I wish to impose on your hospitality. We would like to stay in your garden for a few nights, if it is not too much trouble."

"Too much trouble?" Zora asked languidly. "Would you like me to explain to you the troubles I would be facing at the hands of my leader if she found out that you had visited last night? Why should I harbour the enemy of my leader in my quarters?"

"First, officially, we are not enemies. Therefore you are only offering accommodation, not betraying the Sha'a. Second, need I remind you that your husband is currently residing in my castle. At the moment he is not particularly comfortable, but as you know, comfort is measured on a sliding scale and there are many stops between where he is now and being decidedly uncomfortable."

The woman's face blanched at the mention of her husband.

"What will you offer me in return?" She opened bargaining moves.

"Safety for your family and your choice of what becomes of your husband. I could leave him where he is for a few months to teach him to value his family or I could keep him there forever, whatever you wish."

"How will you get my children out?" She asked,

desperation leaking into her tone.

"Children?" Violet asked.

"Out of where?" Daniel's question seemed more pertinent.

"The Sha'a is keeping them in separate quarters on the other side of the palace. I am allowed to visit them, but I cannot stay there at night. We share our evening meal together and then I am made to leave their rooms."

"Are they safe? Does anybody hurt them?"

"They are kept to themselves, no one is allowed in their quarters except me and their maids."

"How many are there and how old?"

"I have three children. My eldest boy is nine, his sister is six-and-a-half, and the little boy is only two."

Violet's heart ached as the woman told them of her children.

"I will work out a way to get your children free. They are the reason you haven't left, aren't they? I should have asked last night."

"I cannot leave without them, and I dare not lock the door on the soldiers. The only times I have, they have taunted me with threats to visit my daughter instead."

Zora's eyes had taken on a haunted look. Loucius had truly left her and their children in a den of wolves. Violet was angry, she wanted to tear the man the shreds with her fingernails for the horrors he had left his wife to face alone.

"Loucius did speak of you with worry in his voice. He did not expect you to be treated well in his absence, but I don't think he was expecting this. I promise you, we will get your children free."

"Thank you. You may stay in the garden, but I won't be able to give you much in the way of hospitality. I usually take my meals with the children. If servants bring food here, the Sha'a will swiftly become suspicious."

"I understand," Daniel said with a bow. "If you would

allow it, I would like to take some time to rest now, we have barely slept since we saw you last night."

The Aramalian woman nodded and retreated back through her gardens to her rooms in the palace.

Daniel turned to Violet. "Will you sit with me?"

Violet nodded and he led her to where Pragmoon had settled under a rotunda. Her body fitted snugly under the domed roof and her tail was curled around the outside of the little building. They walked to where the Dragon's foreleg met her body. Daniel sat between leg and body and then held out his arms for Violet.

She tucked herself in next to him, half-leaning on his chest, looking out through the sides of the rotunda at the garden and sky.

"The stars are so different here," she said.

"Yes, I was also fascinated by that when I started visiting your world. I bought a book on constellations many months ago. All of the names are old Latin, it is fascinating. Crux, Orion, Sextans. It's amazing that you haven't tried to change them over time."

"We probably have. I'm sure they've all been anglicised, but you are right, I'm surprised that we still have 'Orion the Warrior' and not 'Orion the Smart Phone.'"

"'The Southern Cross' would become the 'Plasma Screen.' Did you know the Pleiades were known as the 'Netted Stars' in Middle Earth?"

Violet laughed. "I never knew that you had read *The Lord of the Rings*."

"Ahhh, confession time. I haven't read the books, I only watched the movies."

"Sacrilege," Violet cried in mock-horror. "You only get the gist of the story, the world-building, in the movie. The books are so much richer, deeper."

"I should have known you would be in that camp, what's wrong with the movies?"

They fell into a mock argument and locked away their earlier disagreement and all of their worries and fears to be thought about later.

"I am sorry about earlier," Daniel said when they reached a comfortable lull in the conversation.

Violet sighed. "I know."

"Do you still love me?" he asked uncertainly.

"Only if you still love me," she said, turning her face towards him and smiling.

He leant forwards and planted a gentle kiss on her lips, "Of course."

"Of course."

They slept, comfortable in each other's arms and confident of their safety in the embrace of the dragon. Both wished they knew what the future held; for themselves, for the Realm, for the rest of the royal family

But for a short time, they resigned themselves to ignorance.

Chapter Forty-one
JESSICA

Jessica settled down to her dinner. Thankfully, it was a quiet meal as there were no guests scheduled. Life as a princess meant a lot of things and one of them was a procession of people coming before the crown. People deserving medals for bravery, others asking for more time to pay their lease, or, the ones Jessica liked the least, the parents parading their eligible bachelors in front of her.

Due to the rushed nature of her travel from Aquilegia, the people of Ivywood hadn't been given enough time to appeal for meetings and she had been left blissfully alone since her arrival. This was a very good thing as she was far too distracted by worry for her family to be able to keep up her demure princess persona. She would have much preferred being out on a dragon with Daniel.

She had just spent a second quiet day in Ivywood, having arrived late in the afternoon two days earlier. She was already getting restless, there was very little to distract her in Ivywood, apart from the collection of books on Dragonlore, which she'd already tried to read, but couldn't stay focussed on.

When she had finished her meal, she retreated to her private study to read the letters she'd received that day, resigned to the fact that her excuses for solitude were running out and she would probably have to see some of the people appealing for an audience the following day.

She started shuffling through the requests. The Ivywood Stitcher's Group wanted to know if she would preside over their supper later in the week, a couple of merchants with unmarried sons suggested a dinner under the guise of discussing the dragon treaty, and a childhood friend asking her to lunch.

She was penning a reply to the last when she heard a knock on the door of her study.

"Come in," she called.

"I beg forgiveness for intruding," a familiar voice called.

"Dom!" Jess said, delighted. "As if you ever need to beg my forgiveness. What brings you here?"

"You, of course," Dom said, a slight hint of reproof in his tone.

Her cheeks flushed slightly, "I didn't think you would be able to leave the monastery so easily, I thought the new monks had to stay close."

"Jess, I took my vows nearly four years ago. I am long past the stage of being a 'new monk.'"

She sighed as she drew him to an armchair by the fireplace. "Was it really that long ago?"

"You know it was."

"It doesn't feel like it."

It still hurt like it had happened days ago, not years.

"I still remember the day we first met you know," Jessica said.

"Me too," Dom said. "What was it you said, 'I hope my horse won't lose a shoe until autumn, if that is the quality of the work done here.'"

"And I know you were about to roast me with words until you realised that I was the princess," she retorted.

Dom put on a pompous voice. "Then I said, 'Never fear, my lady, I am but the lowly apprentice, my work is not good enough even for a rocking horse and I would not be trusted near any horse you brought in.'"

Jessica chuckled and then sighed. "You really were a terrible blacksmith."

"You giving me that job in the library was definitely the best thing that could have happened to me that summer," Dom said.

He'd been indispensable as a librarian that year, especially when researching dragonlore, but Jessica had come to appreciate more than just his work. Her brother and parents had been aware of her growing feelings for Dom and they had all hoped her love would be returned. Sadly, through reading all of the books in her library, Dom had found another calling.

"My princess," he had called out to her as he bounced into the room one morning, picking her up and twirling about in a circle with her. "I have finally seen the light."

Jessica's heart beat even faster and she licked her lips and asked, "What light might that be, my scholar?"

"I have been accepted to be a Monk at Oakville, I told them of my work in your libraries and they showed me their collection. They have more books than all of your libraries combined. I could spend my whole life reading and still leaves pages unturned! Once I have finished my induction to the order, I will be working with Brother Sage, in the library. Isn't that amazing?"

He hadn't known he was shattering her heart.

"Have I ever told you that I'm sorry?" he asked, seeing the former pain echoed in her face.

"You know you have," she smiled ruefully. "More times than you ever had too. It wasn't your fault."

"Okay, I won't say it again," Dom joked. "So, what brought you to Ivywood?"

"My personal safety," she groaned. "My parents and brother have travelled to Aramalia and I have been sent a safe distance from the border."

"Why didn't they leave you at Dragonhome? Surely you

were safe there."

She gave a sketchy explanation of how she had initially left Dragonhome and was in Aquilegia when the rest of her family had left.

"I see. So now you are here, cooling your heels until they return and you can go back to work."

"Yes and I am already bored. I'm not expecting them back for at least two weeks. It's only been three days and I'm already bored," she knew she was whining and hated herself for it. Still, she hated it when her position as princess got in the way of her role as emissary.

"Well," Dom said, a sneaky smile on his face. "we can't have a bored princess can we?"

Jessica locked eyes with him, a mischievous gleam appearing. "What are you plotting?"

"Would you like to see some magic?"

Chapter Forty-two
JESSICA

"What do you mean?" Jessica asked.

"Well, you know I've been reading through the books in the library at the monastery?" Dom asked.

She nodded.

"I recently reached the books regarding the magic used in a certain necklace that I know always used to interest you."

"The locating spell?" she asked, enthralled.

"None other. I brought the book." She reached out eagerly, but he held back. "Would you like to know the really interesting part?"

She looked at him with exasperation, a facial expression he knew well.

"The locking down of the magic to a specific person and an object is an extra part of the spell. Anyone can use the magic to find anyone they want!" he said last bit excitedly. "I proved it tonight."

"How did you prove it, pray tell?"

"The news of your arrival in Ivywood hasn't actually reached the monastery yet, I scried for you." He smiled proudly.

"Right then, smart man. Show me."

He preened as he pulled, a handful of small vials and a small mixing bowl from his bag.

"I'll need a map," he said.

She beckoned him over to her desk and spread out a map

of the Realm. He put his little bowl next to it and starting mixing. A drop of one oil, three drops of another and a little drop of water. The mixture became a little bit foamy when he whisked it together.

"Okay," he said, excitedly. "Who do you want to find?"

"My mother," Jessica said, without hesitation.

"Great, it works best when you are looking for someone you know."

He leant over the bowl and dipped in a glass rod, picking up a little drop of the liquid on the end. He started muttering in a mixture of guttural tones and singing notes, as he waved hands across the corners of the map. After a minute, he dropped the spot of oil on the map at Ivywood. He continued his chant and with each note the bead of water and oil rolled, slowly at first and then picking up pace as it rolled east, straight off the edge of the map.

They watched, enthralled, as it kept rolling, moving the last few millimetres slowly until it stopped in the middle of one of the letters Jessica had been writing before Dom arrived.

"That's amazing," Jessica said.

"We probably should have used a bigger map though." Dom mused.

"Come one," Jessica cried, dragging Dom from the study. "We can look through the maps in father's study, he should have one that stretches past the mountains."

She tugged him down the corridors and he tried to keep his mixing bowl steady.

"Slow down," he said, laughing. "We don't want to waste any of this."

They found the study in darkness and Jessica cursed. She left Dom in the entry while she went to fetch a taper to light the lamps. Dom shivered at the cold air in the study. The room felt abandoned.

"Never mind the fire," Jess said as she entered, feeling

the cold herself. "We won't be in here for very long."

She moved over to a box that held a series of tubes and studied each closely before exclaiming that she had found the right one. She noticed that Dom had stayed in the doorway.

"Come on. Why are you hanging around in the doorway?"

"I feel like I'm intruding."

"Don't be silly, he's miles away. He'll never know."

He walked over to the desk as she was spreading out the map. The king's desk was clear in his absence and nothing had to be swept aside, unlike on Jessica's desk.

"There. Start again?"

He obliged, repeating the job of murmuring, muttering and dropping the oil.

This time, the oil drop was still on the map when it stopped rolling, positioning itself just inside Aramalian lands.

"That is so cool," Jessica announced. "If only we had known this when Daniel went missing. Although we did overcome that with Jessica's necklace. Could you try Daniel now?"

Dom agreed and they watched as the bead of water travelled towards Aramalia, slowing down as it passed the spot where Queen Astrid had been marked, but it didn't stop. They watched as it slowed right down, but kept moving, millimetre-by-millimetre, towards Terisha.

Jessica knitted her brow. "That isn't where he should be."

"What do you mean?"

"According to the plan, he was meant to travel to Terisha last night, then head back to the mountains. If anything, he should be heading to Terisha from the south, not travelling along the coast."

"Maybe their plans changed while they were on the

move?"

"Hmm," Jessica didn't sound convinced. "Do you think you would be able to find my father?"

Dom scratched his head. "I don't know, it worked easily with your mother and brother, but I have spent a lot of time with them and know them well. I never spent much time with your father. He always preferred to read my notes rather than meet with me."

"Try?" Jessica implored.

"Of course," he agreed, kindly.

He chanted again, but when he put the drop of oil on the map, it didn't move. He chanted more insistently, but it still didn't move. He mopped up the drop, stirred the oil afresh and started again, but the result was the same.

The oil drop did not move.

"Sorry," Dom said. "It looks like I can't track him."

"Can I try?"

"Sure."

Dom started talking her through the process, referring back to the book and helping her get the tone and sounds right.

"It's a guttural 'Hgh' followed by a high 'aah.' "

It took almost an hour and Jessica was regretting that she hadn't lit the fire when she was finally ready to try it.

"Try with your mother first, then we can tell if it's working."

Jessica muddled her way through the chant, pronouncing all the strange words slowly, moving her hands across the map more deliberately. Finally, she dropped the bead of water and oil on the map and they watched as it slowly rolled across the parchment. It didn't pick up pace as it had for Dom and she had to chant for a longer time, so her voice was quite raspy when the little droplet reached the same spot it had for Dom.

"Aha!" she cheered huskily, before taking a sip from a

cold cup of tea.

"Excellent," Dom beamed at her.

"Does that mean anyone could do this?" Jessica asked incredulously.

"I don't think anyone could, but we certainly shouldn't let it be known publicly. Can you imagine if suspicious wives were able to track their wayward husbands?"

They laughed at the idea.

"Do you want to take a break now?"

"No," Jessica said, her buoyancy disappearing as she remembered the real reason she wanted to learn to use the magic. "I want to find Father."

She told herself that the little bead would happily roll across the map to where they had shown her mother was, but there a little pit of worry lingered in her stomach.

"Okay," Dom said, gently dabbing the little ball of liquid from the map.

Jessica started the spell over again, thinking of her father, repeating his name in her mind as she chanted. When she reached the point where the oil should move, it stayed obstinately still. She chanted stronger and faster, almost stumbling over the strange sounds, but still the drop did not move.

Eventually she gave up. "What does it mean?"

"I don't know."

He picked up the book and began leafing through, concern and worry on his face.

"There is a section on when the magic doesn't locate, but there are only two reasons. That you don't know the person you are trying to find well enough, which can't be the case for you, or the person is..." He hesitated.

Jessica felt herself flush and her heart started to race in her chest. "Or the person is what?"

"Dead."

"But that couldn't be," Jessica said, although even she

felt that her words lacked conviction.

"Of course not," Dom soothed. "There must be some other reason."

Jessica picked up the book and leafed through it herself, but there was only one section devoted to the location chant and a small paragraph explaining where the spell could go wrong.

"It's late," Jessica said, handing the book back to him. "You should go."

"Are you sure?" Dom asked.

"Yes," her answer was cold, all of her excitement from using the spell washed away.

"I'm sorry," Dom said. "I always seem to cause you pain. Good night, Your Highness."

Jessica looked out the darkened window as Dom quietly left the room and watched the front courtyard as a strip of light flashed out when the door was opened to allow the monk to leave. He pulled the hood of a thick cloak over his head as he started to walk, then turned and looked upwards, as if he sensed her gaze. They locked eyes for a second, before the man heard a boy approach with his horse.

Jessica watched them for a few seconds more, seeing them pick up pace on the road, then turned purposefully and walked back through the manor to her rooms. She was being pushed by barely contained nervous energy and was worried and afraid. She quickly changed from her dress and petticoats to her preferred clothing: tight trousers, a puff-sleeved shirt and a fitted vest.

She strapped her dagger to her thigh, a short sword to her waist and threw a cloak over her shoulders. She went to her study to collect some maps and poured the remainder of Dom's mixture into a separate little vial. He had left the book as well so she grabbed that before heading off through the manor in search of the butler.

"I am leaving here to stay at the monastery for a few days, please hold off any engagements until my return." She didn't give the stunned man a chance to answer before she turned and left the room again.

Distrust of her stomach caused her to rush from his presence, it was fluttering desperately and she was worried that instead of spilling words, she would spill some of her dinner if she stayed for too long.

Jessica made her way out of the servant's door and headed across the yard. She walked past the stables, through a small gate to the fields beyond and kept moving at a steady pace towards a small hillock a short way away.

She climbed a short way up then traced her way around to the entrance of a cave. A deep rumbling and warm breeze came from the entrance and Jessica walked a short distance in before calling out, tentatively.

"Serix." She steeled herself, the called more confidently, "Serix. I need your help."

The dragon rumbled from within the shallow cave.

"What is it, Madam Emissary?"

"I need you to take me to Terisha to find my family."

To be continued in

Water off a Dragon's Back

Coming out in 2025.